The Betel Nut Tree Mystery

Ovidia Yu

CONSTABLE • LONDON

CONSTABLE

First published in Great Britain in 2018 by Constable

13 5 7 9 10 8 6 4 2

Copyright © Ovidia Yu, 2018

The moral right of the author has been asserted.

*All characters and events in this publication, other than
those clearly in the public domain, are fictitious
and any resemblance to real persons,
living or dead, is purely coincidental.*

A CIP catalogue record for this book
is available from the British Library.

ISBN: 978-1-47212-522-4

Typeset in Contenu by SX Composing DTP, Rayleigh, Essex
Printed and bound in Great Britain by CPI Group (UK), Croydon CR0 4YY

Papers used by Constable are from well-managed forests
and other responsible sources.

Constable
An imprint of
Little, Brown Book Group
Carmelite House
50 Victoria Embankment
London EC4Y 0DZ

An Hachette UK Company
www.hachette.co.uk

www.littlebrown.co.uk

This book is dedicated with love and gratitude to the memory of Reverend Yap Kim Hao (1929–2017)

Rain Storm

———◆———

What we came to think of as the betel nut affair began in the middle of a tropical thunderstorm in December 1936. In Singapore, chewing betel was both a blessing (more stimulating than coffee) and a curse (scarlet spit stains in public areas) but mostly taken for granted.

And Miss Chen Su Lin might be Chief Inspector Le Froy's secretarial assistant, and cultural liaison at Singapore's new Detective and Intelligence Unit, but I had spent most of the day mopping floors, like a servant girl or spinster aunt. The Detective Shack, as we called it, was in a modern brick building with two floors, but rain blew in under the doors and around badly fitted windows.

If the rain continued, the afternoon's high tide would bring more flooding. Chief Inspector Le Froy was shut in his office with his papers, but the rest of the case files had been carried upstairs to the little room where I slept during the week. The zinc roof up there was leaking and they were stacked, with my clothes, on the narrow bed, everything covered with a tarpaulin.

I like the stormy rains of the monsoon season. Once when I was five years old I hid under my grandmother's bed during a storm and flash flood. The family panicked as swirling waters swept past with fallen trees and dead animals and I was nowhere to be found. Later Ah Ma told me, 'Thunder is the sound of Lei Gong, the Dragon God of Thunder, punishing bad people. If you have done nothing wrong, you have nothing to be scared of. He punishes only bad people.'

Since then I've felt thunderstorms were on my side. And if the rain slashing down ruined the wedding rehearsal up the road at the Farquhar Hotel, I wouldn't be sorry . . .

I gasped and spilled the slop pail when the door of the Detective Shack crashed open, letting in a sheet of rain and Sergeant Ferdinand de Souza, second in command to Le Froy. He was a huge man, as muscled as a wild boar, and he was covered with what appeared to be blood – a lot of it. Behind him, the slighter figure of Constable Kwok Kan Seng looked no better. Their rain-slicked faces were streaked and smeared, their khaki uniforms soaked in the thick red-brown liquid. I couldn't tell where or how badly they were injured.

'Sit!' I shouted. 'Don't move more than you have to. You should have gone straight to the hospital!' I would go for Dr Shankar or Dr Leask, after I'd examined any open wounds. I hauled the first-aid box from under my desk, knocking over the snowy Christmas tree de Souza had made from brush bristles and Lux soap flakes, and sending the matchboxes he had painstakingly painted and filled with sweets skidding over the wet floor. I cursed my dratted limp as I stumble-ran towards them. Childhood polio had left me with one leg shorter than the other but I can move when I have to.

'We're all right, Su Lin. Don't fuss,' de Souza growled. He looked furious but didn't seem to be in pain. He picked up the matchbox crib that had landed by his feet and straightened the tiny ornament with gentle pudgy fingers.

I pushed the miserable Constable Kwok backwards onto a chair and grabbed his hands. His fingernails were a healthy pink under the dirt and his pulse was strong . . . and there was something strange about the texture of the blood on his arms.

'Who is hurt, then?' I demanded. 'How many? Where? At the wedding rehearsal?'

'*Alamak*. Nobody, *lah*.' Constable Kwok said. He was on the verge of tears.

'De Souza. Show me your hands.'

I was just the office assistant but de Souza didn't argue. He held out his enormous hands to me, turning them palm up, then down. His fingers were steady and, apart from the terrible stains on his skin and uniform, he showed no signs of injury.

The pounding in my throat eased slightly. Neither man was hurt.

When I had taken the job at the Detective Shack everyone – Uncle Chen, the ladies at the Mission Centre and my friend Parshanti's mother – warned me of the dangers of working with men I was neither related nor married to, but these men had accepted me and we had become a team.

'What happened?' I demanded, then jumped as the wind snapped a window hook out of the wall and the wooden frame slammed open, letting in a fresh sheet of rain.

De Souza pulled it shut and looped his lanyard around the stub to fasten it. 'Nothing happened. Don't say anything. Just forget it. We must get changed before the chief sees.'

Years on the sidelines of my grandmother's businesses had equipped me to distinguish between what was privately acknowledged and what could be made public. I made the decision. 'Go to the back and change. Then pass your uniforms to me and I will soak them in salt water.' That would get the blood out. Or give me a chance to find out what the substance was, if not blood. I sniffed my fingers. The smell was familiar but I couldn't place it.

We were too late.

'What happened?' Chief Inspector Thomas Le Froy came out of his office and saw his men. 'Su Lin, get Dr Shankar!'

Constable Kwok jumped to his feet, almost knocking over his chair.

'No, sir!' I caught and steadied it. 'Sir, they say they aren't hurt.'

De Souza said, 'No, *lah*. No need doctor! Don't tell anybody! *Aiyoh*!' The door burst open behind him, sending him stumbling forward.

Parshanti Shankar tumbled in, along with a gust of rain pellets. She pushed the door shut and leaned against it, panting, as she struggled to close her wet umbrella. She seemed to be having trouble breathing. I reached for my first-aid box again, concerned, then saw she was laughing.

'You should have been there, Su!' Parshanti said to me. 'It was such a hilarious joke! It was so funny! You can't be angry, Ferdie.' This was to Sergeant de Souza. 'It was just a joke. You all take yourselves too seriously when you're in uniform. They wanted to get some flash photographs, that's all. They're trying out the camera for the wedding. Come on. Be a sport. Kan Seng, you're all right, aren't you?'

Constable Kwok didn't look at her.

'He's not hurt,' I said. 'That's not his blood.'

'Of course it isn't!' Parshanti started to laugh again, 'That's not blood at all. It's betel juice!'

'What happened at the wedding rehearsal?' Le Froy asked. 'Are you two all right?'

'Yes, sir.' Constable Kwok nodded but kept his head down, biting his lip.

'De Souza. What happened?'

'Sir. We were on duty outside the ballroom as directed. Then somebody shouted that the groom was injured so we rushed in. He was lying there with blood all over him. But it wasn't blood. When I bent down to check his pulse he spat betel juice at me. He had a mouthful. Then all the others joined in, pouring betel juice over us.'

'They were laughing and saying things about driving out demons and evil spirits,' Constable Kwok said. 'My grandma chews betel, but that's to calm her stomach, nothing to do with evil spirits.'

Parshanti was laughing. 'Sorry, but it was so funny! It was just a joke – a betel bomb, that's what they call it. Fashionable people are always playing jokes in the West.'

'Did they send you to apologize?' Le Froy asked.

'No. I just thought—'

'Off-duty it would be a joke. But we were in uniform,' de Souza said.

'Go to your quarters and change,' Le Froy said, 'then get back to the rehearsal.'

The men exchanged glances, clearly unwilling.

'We are providing official surveillance for that rehearsal and the wedding,' Le Froy reminded them.

'They only want us there to *sabo* us,' Constable Kwok said miserably. 'There is no risk to anybody.'

'It's an assignment.'

Governor McPherson, who was new to the post, had come in person to the Detective Shack last week to request the unit provide security for the Glossop-Covington festivities. Could he have been in on the practical joke?

'Let me know when you're ready. I'll come back with you.' Le Froy said.

'No need, sir,' Constable Kwok said. 'If they bomb just us, it's a joke. But if it's you—'

'Whether me or you, it's the khaki,' Le Froy said, referring to the khaki shirt and shorts of the police uniform. 'I'll come back with you when you're ready. The khaki keeps people safe, whether they appreciate it or not. We will observe from outside the hotel.'

They saluted him, then went to change, looking more like battle-scarred nursery-school teachers than victims. Le Froy nodded coldly to Parshanti and closed his office door.

'It was just a joke,' Parshanti said defensively. 'It was funny. You should have been there!'

I had wanted to be part of the surveillance team, but Le Froy had refused. Had he expected this? Or something worse of Governor McPherson?

Abdications of Responsibility

◆——

Gregory McPherson, Singapore's new governor, had been in office for almost three months when he had turned up at the Detective Shack.

He was not tall for an *ang moh*, standing just over five feet eight. His short grey hair and military posture suggested army connections, and his dark brown tan indicated previous postings in India or Africa. A slight pot belly suggested a love of good food. He was said to be a down-to-earth man who didn't stand on ceremony. I believed that – he'd arrived without an escort other than the driver he'd left outside.

But the governor's request was unexpected: 'I want you and your men to make sure the Glossop-Covington wedding on Christmas Eve goes smoothly. The bride-to-be has received threats. Not surprising, given all the mutterings against married American women going after our titled boys. And you and your men should be at the rehearsal too, to get an idea of the situation.'

'Surely this comes under police jurisdiction rather than the Detective Unit,' Le Froy said.

The British Empire was still reeling from the king's abdication and the Detective Unit had been created to defuse unrest before it escalated. If you believed the wireless reports, lawless anarchy was just around the corner.

'If the former king and Mrs Simpson came to Singapore, the Detective Unit would be responsible for their safety. Here you have an upper-class Englishman with an American wife-to-be. Consider it an exercise.'

My time in Government House had taught me not to trust people just because they were British and in authority. Still, I liked our new governor. I had caught glimpses of his wife in town, flanked by their two young sons. The boys seemed respectful and respectable, which is always a good sign. I learned from helping at the Mission Centre that difficult children often have difficult parents.

'I've heard about you, Le Froy, and I respect you,' Governor McPherson said, 'but this is a personal request from the groom, Victor Glossop. I gather from Victor that you and his father, Sir Roderick Glossop, are old friends.'

'You're an old friend of Sir Roderick's yourself, Governor?'

'Never met the fellow,' Governor McPherson said genially. 'Advantage of being out of England so much. I'd rather deal with natives in the colonies than those back home. Young Glossop only came to us because my wife is some distant relation of his mother. And, of course, she took to Mrs Covington's child. You know how women are.'

'Child?'

'The bride's little boy is here with her.'

Le Froy raised one eyebrow. A sign he was balancing his thoughts. 'A long voyage out for a child. Where is his father?'

'Dead.'

'So there's no "Mr Simpson" in the picture?'

'Nothing of the sort. But the lady has received threatening letters. It's the damned press, linking them to the abdication and upsetting royalists.'

'The press?'

'It's in the *Weekend World*,' I said helpfully. Parshanti had been going on about it. According to Pip's Squeaks, a column in the paper, Victor Glossop had proposed to Mrs Nicole Covington on board the RMS *Queen Victoria* on the evening of King Edward's abdication. Victor had gone down on one knee in the dance hall and declared that, like the king, he was in love with his 'American missus', whereupon the band had launched into 'The Way You Look Tonight' to cheers and applause and calls of 'Kiss the bride!'

'So romantic!' Parshanti had gushed.

I would have preferred a more private proposal myself so I could say, 'Let me think about it', then check on the man and his family. And, yes, I know my attitude is one more reason why no one is ever likely to go down on his knee for me.

But I was excited too. This was my big chance. My dream was to be a journalist with stories in international papers like the *Saturday Evening Post* and the *Weekend World*. So far, my pieces had been dismissed as well written but 'not of interest' to their readers.

Well, Victor Glossop was clearly of interest to their readers. He came from an old English family and was known for wild parties, daring pranks and being seen with the Mitford sisters at Hitler's Nuremberg rallies. Nicole Covington was a young, rich and beautiful American widow, which meant that, though Mrs Simpson was neither young nor beautiful, Nicole could be lumped with her for being American. Hence the threats.

If I could attend their wedding party at the Farquhar Hotel, I could write it up for the international papers. I might even be able to get photographs of the ceremony . . . 'I can help,' I offered. 'You can't send a man to watch Mrs Covington and her little boy.' I was being forward. But I often served as female chaperone when the police had to interview women without their relatives present.

'And you would be . . .?' Governor McPherson looked pleased.

'Chen Su Lin. I am the cultural liaison. I do translations.' I also managed the office logistics and accounts better than any of the men could, though they never admitted it.

'No, Su Lin.' Just like that, Le Froy had crushed my dream as he would a cockroach.

'But, sir, I have to! I mean, you need a woman there in case— I just want to help, sir!'

'You have work to do.' Le Froy had said. 'De Souza and Pillay will go.'

I had been furious enough to serve Le Froy lukewarm coffee on the morning of the rehearsal. Now I wondered if he had suspected something. Had the Glossops really been worried for their son's safety or had Victor Glossop and his friends come up with that idea for other reasons?

Le Froy hadn't answered when the governor asked if he was a friend of Sir Roderick. Did that mean they had not been friends?

I wondered even more about Victor Glossop. There was definitely a story there.

Parshanti

———◆———

Two days later it was still raining. The storm was over but
plump drops were falling, their steady drumming on the roof
almost musical.

I had pulled my desk and typewriter away from the wall where
the paint was showing damp patches. It was worse across the road
where brown water pooled in the construction site of the new
police headquarters. It should have been completed at least a year
ago but it looked like there would be more delays.

Parshanti had come to visit me at the station. This suited me
since it was another slow morning. Even criminals have a break
during the monsoon season. Petty crime takes second place when
the canals are full of fat fish, drowsy jungle fowl are easily caught,
and durians and mangoes are ripening on the trees.

'If you had been there, you would have seen it was just a
joke!' Parshanti was sulky because I wouldn't walk to the hotel
with her 'just to look' at the Christmas decorations. Parshanti
Shankar was my best friend but there were times when I wanted
to smack her. I yawned instead. It was the kind of weather that

sends children out in search of tadpoles and puts grown-ups to sleep.

'I'm so bored,' Parshanti said.

She tossed aside the latest *Weekend World* she had brought over from her father's shop. I picked it up and put it safely in a drawer. I had already read the latest Pip's Squeaks, but I wanted to go over it again.

'Pip' mocked moral hypocrisy, saying the domination of King Edward by Mrs Simpson perfectly reflected current relations between England and America. The column had so much high-society insider gossip from both sides of the Atlantic that I had once wondered if the playboy prince might not himself be the author. But not after I'd read Pip's claim that Mrs Simpson's control over Edward came from sexual practices she had learned in a Chinese brothel. Surely no man could write such things about the woman he loved. Even in jest.

'Couldn't you get your handsome boss to hire me too? He could start a women's department. I'm sure I could do what you do.' Parshanti poised her fingers over the typewriter on my desk. 'I could learn to do this. And I could use forty-five dollars a month. Dash it, I could use the seventy cents a day I'd get working in a factory! What are you supposed to be doing now?'

'I was going upstairs to check if the rainwater buckets need emptying. Do you want to do that?'

'I'd have to get a suit made if I come to work here. My mother has a Simplicity pattern for a slim-cut skirt that would suit me perfectly. Won't you ask the chief inspector for me? Please? We'd be colleagues. I could have a desk next to yours and it would be like being back in school.'

'I'll ask him once you learn to type,' I offered. 'You can use the typewriter pad I drew up. And if you want to study shorthand, I'll give you the title of the book I used. The Mission Centre has two copies.'

Parshanti made a face at me. 'I've had more than enough of studying, thank you.'

Parshanti was in what I called her 'society' mode, with any sense she had buried under a thick layer of silliness. She thought it was fashionable to flirt. I didn't see the point. Though I had to admit it won over men – even police officers who should know better.

Dr Shankar, Parshanti's tall dark Indian father, and Mrs Shankar, her short plump Scottish mother, had somehow produced between them a Mata Hari. Parshanti was tall and slim, with honey-coloured skin, huge long-lashed eyes and thick curly hair usually pulled back into a thick plait but brushed loose over her shoulders for social occasions. Like wedding rehearsals, apparently.

The way men looked at Parshanti made me feel even shorter and more handicapped than I was. Sometimes, so that I could go on being best friends with her, I had to remind myself that she couldn't type or take shorthand and envied my 'real job'.

'Why were you at the wedding rehearsal?'

'I was there for Mam. She's making the bride's wedding gown and going-away dress and they asked her to check none of the decorations would clash.'

Mrs Shankar was a skilled seamstress popular with fashionable *ang moh* women. She could copy anything in the fashion magazines her husband brought in. Dr Rajan Shankar was an

Edinburgh-trained doctor and surgeon, but Westerners in Singapore did not trust an Indian doctor and locals did not trust Western medicine so Dr Shankar operated a pharmacy that sold magazines and Kodak film, and developed photographs in a darkroom that was also Mrs Shankar's sewing room. Mrs Shankar's dresses were worn to all the top social events in Singapore, though being married to an Indian meant she was never invited to any.

'Shanti, you hate sewing!'

'No difference. Mam has no time to change anything but it got me in. You should have come with me! We could have told them you're a dressmaker's assistant's assistant. It was full of people who don't know them. Su, it's going to be the event of the year, the most interesting thing that's ever happened here! The hotel ballroom is enormous – they've put coloured streamers on a whole wall of fans and a row of Christmas trees in the corridor!

'And it wasn't even really a rehearsal,' Parshanti looked dreamy, 'more like a party. I didn't see the bride but she wouldn't be in her dress anyway. Mam's still working on it. We tried the food for the reception and it was super top-notch! When I get married I want my reception to be at the Farquhar.'

Parshanti might have found it fun but I didn't see the point of a party unless I could write about it.

To be honest, there wasn't much point to most of my life right then. Until last year, staying at school long enough to get my General Cambridge Certificate had been my main goal. The ladies who ran the school at the Mission Centre talked about the GCC as if it were the Holy Grail. But when you get your grail home and find nothing changes, don't you wonder if it's really holy?

Parshanti and I had been among the first five girls in Singapore to take the General Cambridge exam. But what good had it done us? I knew I wanted to do more with my life than fetch coffee and transcribe wireless communications. And Parshanti only wanted to get married.

Parshanti's parents were willing to pay the fees for her to attend a teacher-training course. They even said that if Parshanti or her brother wanted to go to university they would find the money somehow, but she wasn't interested.

Sometimes I was so jealous of Parshanti, with her brilliant father and her loud, cheerful and occasionally foul-mouthed mother – but, to be honest, I was jealous of most people with parents.

After my parents had died, fortune-tellers advised my grandmother to send me far away or put me down a well. Otherwise the bad luck I carried as an orphan and polio victim would infect the rest of the Chen family. Instead, she enrolled me in the mission school to see if the Christian God could counteract my inherited bad luck. That was how I became the first member of my family to go to English school.

I knew how lucky I was. I knew I was only alive because Ah Ma had broken traditional rules, which made it easier for me to bend and break rules myself. Please don't get me wrong, I like rules. Rules make life easier. The problem is, everyone follows different ones, sometimes without even being aware of it.

What I really wanted was to be a lady journalist like Henrietta Stackpole, who is by far the most interesting character in *The Portrait of a Lady* by Henry James. That the woman who lent it to me turned out to be a murderess didn't change anything. I still liked the book. I still wanted to be a journalist.

His Final Trick

———◆———

'I say, I saw Nicole Covington yesterday evening. With a group of friends. I recognized one of them at the party – the rehearsal.'

Parshanti's deliberately casual voice drew my attention. I looked sharply at her. She picked up one of my pencils and drew a circle in my notebook. Then she surrounded it with petals and turned it into a daisy. All without meeting my eyes.

Parshanti was the kind of girl who shrieked when she saw seagull droppings on a railing or a cat grab a rat off a sack of rice. She had been raving about Nicole Covington and Victor Glossop ever since their wedding announcement. If she was that calm about meeting Nicole Covington it was because she was hiding even greater excitement about something much bigger.

I looked around the office. Sergeant Pillay was standing in the doorway looking out at the rain with a cigarette and Sergeant de Souza was engrossed in the newspaper. I leaned in to her and asked, 'What is it?'

Parshanti's eyes were shining. I recognized the look: she was in love. Again.

'Who is it?' I amended my question with a sinking feeling. 'This time.'

Parshanti's mixed race and her unconventional parents meant both locals and foreigners found her unsuitable for their precious sons. But that didn't stop her falling in love regularly.

'Keeping the plate warm', in her canny Scots mother's words. Mrs Shankar had found true love in the brilliant Indian medical student boarding in her parents' house in Edinburgh. She seemed confident that, in time, Parshanti would do similar.

I found this naive. Yes, Dr and Mrs Shankar were probably the happiest married couple I knew. Once when visiting Parshanti I'd seen them waltzing in their tiny living room to music from the gramophone. But how often do you get so lucky? Thanks to my grandmother's interest (and interference) in extended Chen family marriage arrangements and negotiations, I knew what a complicated business marriage was.

'I don't know what you're talking about. They were getting out of a car in front of the Farquhar Hotel. I recognized Nicole Covington at once, of course – she's even more beautiful in real life than in the magazines,' Parshanti said. 'So slim and smart and elegant – and her hair! I wish Mam would let me bob mine! Nicole was wearing a red dress and red shoes and she had a white scarf with black polka dots on her head. And the most fabulous sunglasses.'

'You stood there and stared at her? Why was she wearing sunglasses in the rainy season?'

'Nicole Covington is famous, silly,' Parshanti said. 'Celebrities have to wear sunglasses so they won't be recognized and have people staring at them.' She rolled her eyes.

I thought wearing sunglasses without sun sounded like a very good way of attracting attention. 'You recognized her,' I pointed out. 'And I'm sure you stared.'

Parshanti waved that away. 'I pay attention to what's going on in the world. I recognize famous figures.'

'That's not true. You only read fashion and lifestyle pieces in the papers.'

'Anyway, one of the young men stayed behind to pay the cabbie while Nicole and the others went into the hotel. I was just standing there, out of the way. And then he turned to me and said, "Can I buy you a drink, pretty lady?"'

'Parshanti! He must have thought you were a—'

'No! Don't be absurd! He was totally respectful. Hadn't he seen me at the rehearsal party, he asked, and was I staying at the hotel? I was so taken aback I couldn't answer. I know! Stupid, stupid, stupid girl!' She rapped herself lightly on the side of her head. 'But he gave me his card and said, "Another time, perhaps." Oh, Su Lin, he has the loveliest smile. And such a sophisticated name card!'

I had a bad feeling about this. 'What's his name?'

'Suzy-Poozy, you have bad feelings about everything! I'm not going to tell you if you're just going to warn me to stay away from him.'

'It's not safe, Parshanti. You saw the kind of things those people get up to.'

'I don't see why you're being so stuffy. Even the boys agree it was a joke. Right, boys?'

Le Froy and the other men had returned from the hotel without further incident. I soaked the betel-stained uniforms in a tub of carbolic soap under the zinc sheets behind the station, cutting up and adding several kaffir limes to the solution. Their acid helped release the stains from the khaki. No lasting harm had been done. But I knew we would not be so easily taken in again.

Which might have been why, when word came that Victor Glossop had been found dead at the hotel, I thought it was another trick.

A young and very wet boy burst into the Detective Shack. He was a message runner. 'Urgent! Very urgent and very important, sirs! You must send many policemen immediately. To the Farquhar Hotel. To Mr Victor Glossop's room. You must send Inspector Le Froy and many men. Right away.'

'Find a constable on patrol or go to the callbox,' Sergeant de Souza said. 'This is the Detective Unit.'

Neither Sergeant Pillay nor Sergeant de Souza moved. A summons from a hotel was always 'urgent' and 'important' but usually had to do with rich tourists losing their wallets, being cheated by rickshaw-pullers or demanding a police escort to go sightseeing.

'I'll telephone HQ and ask them to send a constable round,' Sergeant Pillay said. 'Go back and say somebody will come soon.'

'Sir, you must all come now! Urgent!'

'Someone will come soon. What are you waiting for? You want me to *hantam* you?'

But the messenger stood his ground. He was young and skinny and clearly terrified but not of the policeman pretending to aim his baton at him.

I felt sorry for him and went over to the doorway where he was standing in a growing puddle of water. 'What happened at the hotel?'

'There is a body. A dead body.'

'A man? A woman?' Sergeant de Souza was on his feet now.

'Why didn't you say so right away?' Sergeant Pillay was already pulling on his raincoat. 'I'm on the way.'

'A man,' the messenger boy said. He was shivering. '*Ang moh* man. I saw. Inside the room. All covered in red blood. He looked like a monster!'

De Souza shook his head slowly. I saw him thinking he wasn't going to be caught a second time by the same trick.

'Wait, Pillay. Pull yourself together, boy. What exactly did they tell you to say? And where was the body found?'

'I saw it myself, sir. I was called in to take a message. It was in one of the small outside rooms. The room is registered to Victor Glossop. Inside a dead man is covered in red blood!'

The detectives exchanged looks.

'It's another trick,' de Souza said. 'You weren't there that day. You don't know what those men get up to.'

'We can't take the chance. I will go to secure the scene,' Sergeant Pillay said. 'De Souza, get HQ to send the constables over. Girl, find Le Froy and tell him.'

'Please!' Parshanti grabbed my arm. 'The man I met, his name is Kenneth Mulliner. Please find out if he's all right. Just let me know it's not him!'

Le Froy

———◆———

C hief Inspector Le Froy had not come into the office that morning. Recently he had been absorbed in some big secret project. He seldom shared his suspicions until he had proof. It was not that Le Froy didn't trust the team – although Sergeant Pillay had once accidentally leaked information on an upcoming raid to a woman who asked why he couldn't spend the evening with her – but that he observed and analysed better on his own.

I suspected he had spent the night undercover in some opium parlour or gambling den. He always purged his system the morning after such immersions.

Most *ang mohs* in senior government positions lived in large, luxurious black and white 'colonial' bungalows outside the city centre. Le Froy lived in town on a side street lined with local residences and noisy hawkers.

Number 4 Street 51 was off the main road the Detective Shack stood on and it usually took me ten minutes to get there. Today I made it in seven but arrived panting and sweating so I stopped to catch my breath.

From the outside, Le Froy's narrow-fronted house with its bright yellow terracotta tiles looked just like its neighbours. Inside was a different story.

'Sir? It's Su Lin. Good morning, sir.' I rapped on the door.

'What do you want?'

'There's been a death, sir. At the Farquhar Hotel.'

'Ah.'

I waited. When no steps approached, I unlocked the front doors and pushed through the ornate *pintu pagar*, the wooden half-doors. Le Froy had given me the key last year, when he made me his housekeeper: Uncle Chen had tried to persuade me, somewhat forcefully, to marry one of his employees, 'Because a woman needs protection. And Chou Ning needs someone to take care of his old mother and five children.'

My uncle meant well, but he was always pig-headed when trying to do good. Come to think of it, I hadn't seen Uncle Chen for a couple of weeks now. Had he given up on marrying me off? I should have been glad, but strangely I was a little disappointed.

Anyway, when Le Froy had given me a job at the Detective Unit, I'd suggested that keeping his spare key at the office might be a good idea. 'You're the chief inspector. What if someone breaks in in the night and attacks you?'

'Then I would be dead.'

'What if they only beat you up and cut off your hands?'

'Then I would be half dead. Without hands.'

But he had agreed.

I shook my umbrella and stood it in the tin bucket by the door. In local homes, the reception hall is a showplace of the most expensive and uncomfortable teak furniture, the household altar and ancestral portraits. Le Froy's hall was crammed with books and bizarre objects. One such object, stretched out between a pile of rolled-up maps and a stack of specimen boxes, was my boss.

I could tell Le Froy had got home not long before. He slept little but intensely, having trained his system to adapt to his all-night reconnaissance sessions. For him, gathering and processing information didn't stop with work. He took a scientific approach and each new fact had to be found a place within an existing theory. When new data didn't fit, the master plan would be adjusted. To him facts counted more than theory, and theories and rules existed to organize knowledge and information, and generate improvements. Which didn't always make him popular with the other expat colonials, who longed for the good old days and things 'back home'. In fact, Le Froy seldom spoke of England and had not gone on home leave since he had taken up his posting.

I resented rules I didn't see the point of. But instead of ignoring them, I found ways to work around them. The British men who created our laws didn't understand us locals any more than they did their own women.

But observing Le Froy taught me there were different kinds of laws: those of nature and science that are man's way of understanding the world, and those created by men in power designed to keep themselves in power. Chief Inspector Thomas Le Froy should have embodied the second set of laws but he didn't.

The other colonials would have liked Le Froy better if he had taken a local wife and gone drinking and gambling with the other men. He looked like a combination of all the heroes played by Rudolph Valentino, Douglas Fairbanks and John Barrymore but he had turned down all the ladies who had tried to catch his attention (no, I wasn't one of them).

That morning, Le Froy was still wearing the cheap, shabby clothes he had gone out in. He reeked of sweat and tobacco, and must have passed for a Eurasian or Indian sailor. I hated to disturb him, but this might be important.

'Can I make you some coffee, sir?'

'Good idea. Strong.'

'Yes, sir.'

His eyes stayed shut as I stepped carefully over him. I knew my way around the kitchen, which was in the open courtyard at the back of the house. He allowed me to move freely within his home only because he saw me as a subordinate colleague rather than as a 'lady'. Le Froy avoided the ladies.

I found and rinsed out the kettle and a coffee cup. There had always been more servants than family members in Chen Mansion where I grew up, and I smiled to think how humiliated my relations would be to see me making coffee for an *ang moh*. 'As though we cannot afford to pay somebody to marry you!' Uncle Chen would say.

I pulled my thoughts back to the present as Le Froy said, 'An accident?'

I heard him moving around, bumping into something, and took the bottle of Nyalgesic out of the cupboard. 'I don't know, sir. The hotel sent a runner.'

'Who's dead?'

'The runner didn't know. But he said it was an *ang moh* man

24

"covered in red blood". He saw the dead man himself and said he looked like a monster. But, sir, the room is registered to Victor Glossop.'

A snort came from Le Froy: he must have remembered the trick the wedding party had played on his men.

As I filled the metal kettle with rainwater from the ceramic dragon pot in the open kitchen yard and lit the charcoal fire, I heard Le Froy shuffling through some papers – his notes from last night, very likely – then making his way upstairs.

The kettle was boiling. Just in time to complete the waking-up process. I spooned coffee grounds into Le Froy's stainless-steel *kopi* pot. He drank cheap local coffee, made from beans wok-fried with lard and sugar, then coarsely ground with cloves. Once you got used to this fragrant, potent brew, the pure expensive European coffee had no kick.

I poured hot water into the ground beans and stirred, enjoying the heady fragrance. It would take four or five minutes to reach the strength Le Froy preferred.

'That woman the Glossop pup is marrying, Nicole Covington. Who is she? What's she done?'

Given Le Froy's intricate knowledge of poisons, languages and legalities, it was always surprising (and pleasant) to find gaps in his knowledge. Even if I only knew who Mrs Covington was thanks to Pip's Squeaks and Parshanti.

'She's very rich and goes to parties. Her husband died and left her even richer.' Parshanti would know more. I should have paid closer attention to her. If the Cambridge exams had tested us on fashion and celebrities instead of English, geography and mathematics, Parshanti would have beaten my score hands down.

'And she's getting married again. To another man with a very rich father,' I added.

I packed sugar into the bottom of the coffee sock and poured the thick black mixture of coffee grounds and water into it. I didn't have the skill to *tarek* it, like the professional coffee-makers, but I poured the brew carefully between pot and mug a few times to cool and froth it, then added it to the condensed milk I had already put into the mug. I also shook out a blue shirt from the stack of laundry the washerwoman had left by the kitchen door.

Le Froy's papers were stacked on the kitchen counter. I glanced at them, but didn't disturb the order they were in. They were mostly notes and reports on covert Japanese military action in the Chinese provinces of Hebei, Shandong and Shanxi. They were setting up puppet governments after the invasion of Manchuria. He couldn't have these papers in the office because the official stand of the colonial administration was not to get involved with Japanese militarism.

Japan had defiantly resigned from the League of Nations after being censured for attacking Shanghai. But the League had done nothing, while forbidding the Chinese to deploy their own troops in their own cities. The Anti-Japanese Volunteer Army, formed by some Chinese to defend their homes, was condemned as a terror organization.

In fact, anyone in the Crown Colonies who tried to speak against the Japanese invasion could be arrested for treason. The authorities were more concerned about appearances than the ongoing carnage in China.

Officially, at least, Le Froy had to support that. And I understood. My grandmother was angry but she also understood.

Despite the terrible stories coming out of China, she had forbidden Uncle Chen to join the Communists in raising funds to support the Anti-Japanese Volunteer Army. Ah Ma put his safety, and that of our family, first.

And Ah Ma was still good to the Japanese tradesmen. Uncle Chen wanted to kill them all, but Ah Ma had said, 'The ones trying to earn a living here are not the ones raping children with bayonets.'

'Thanks.' Le Froy's voice brought me back from the horrors. He was freshly washed and shaved but still wearing the clothes he had slept in. He took the coffee and didn't speak again until he handed over his cup for a refill. 'The hotel sent someone round instead of telephoning?'

'Yes, sir. That's why I came for you, sir. Someone would have checked to make sure it wasn't a trick before sending a boy over. And the boy said he saw the dead body himself.'

Le Froy said something I couldn't make out. I turned and saw he was struggling out of his shirt. A more ladylike young woman would have screamed and fainted, or at least closed her eyes. I reached over and undid the two buttons my boss had missed, freeing him.

'Sorry, sir. What did you say?'

Le Froy's face appeared, clear of his shirt. 'Go back to the office. Tell de Souza to meet me at the hotel with a tape recorder.' He put on the clean shirt I had picked.

'I brought the tape recorder with me, sir, and my notebook.' And my shorthand skills. 'I brought my camera too, just in case.' It was the folding pocket Kodak my grandmother had bought for me to photograph her rental properties. A lady reporter like

Henrietta Stackpole would not miss a chance like this. A celebrity death was much bigger news than a celebrity wedding.

'Who's at the hotel?'

'Sergeant Pillay. Sergeant de Souza went to get the reserve corporals from HQ.'

'I saw Victor Glossop at the hotel when we went back after the betel bomb. I thought him a fool. A damned conceited young fool. I never thought there was any real danger.'

'Fools are killed too,' I said. 'And Mr Glossop didn't get any threats, only Mrs Covington.'

Besides, we had been told to watch the wedding and the wedding rehearsal, not to protect the groom. But that was following the letter of the law, which Le Froy wasn't good at doing.

'Stop talking and start the car,' he growled. Le Froy's black and green Plymouth was in front of the house as usual.

'I can't drive, sir.' We both knew I had been driving my grandmother around for years. And that I didn't have a driving licence.

'What the blazes – get the engine warmed up. Keys in the prayer bowl.'

'Yes, sir.'

The Body at the Farquhar

◆

The Farquhar was one of the oldest hotels in Singapore and by far the grandest. It loomed like a palace along South Coast Road, and had a wide driveway lined with sealing-wax palms and bougainvillaea bushes. Its clientele were mostly Caucasians and Eurasians, and ordinarily I would have stayed away. But a dead body makes any hotel irresistible.

Christmas wasn't as big a festival as Chinese New Year or Deepavali, but all the umbrellas along the driveway were trimmed with damp tinsel and the valet wore a red Santa cap. 'The valet will take your car, Chief Inspector.'

Darwin Van Dijk himself greeted us in the drizzle, showing how serious the situation was. He was the general manager of the Farquhar and far more imposing than any of the hotel's owner-investors.

'The dead body on your premises, it's a guest?' Le Froy asked, without preamble.

Instead of answering, Van Dijk looked disapprovingly at me and said, 'I will get a taxi for your companion.'

29

Companion? The man assumed I was there with Le Froy because he had spent the night with me! I felt furious and humiliated. Had I had a gun in my hand, I would have shot the general manager in his stupid, smug face.

Instead I took out my camera and shot him with that. The flash made him blink and wince. 'For the record,' I said. I held onto my camera bag and hoped I wouldn't be thrown out.

'Miss Chen is a member of my team. She will be assisting me,' Le Froy said. His tone was mild. His eyes were challenging.

Darwin Van Dijk gave a noncommittal nod. I felt better.

(Though I'm looking back on this many years later, it still gives me a little thrill to think I was once mistaken for Le Froy's lady companion!)

Van Dijk brought us to the servants' entrance, answering Le Froy's questions along the way.

'Yes, Mr Victor Glossop. It is not the suite he is registered in, but an additional private room he took.'

'In English, man. Not hotel jargon.'

'Mr Glossop was one of a party of five. They took connected suites on the second and third floors. But the gentlemen also took an additional room. A smoking room with a balcony and garden access.'

In other words, a room with a discreet entrance for private visitors.

'How long have Victor Glossop and his party been staying here? Which liner did they arrive on?'

As we walked, Le Froy was looking left and right, up at the ceiling of the dim, narrow corridors and down to the bare floorboards, throwing out questions as he went. He barely acknowledged the responses and I made sure I remembered them so I could record them.

They walked fast and I struggled a little, determined to keep up. But by the time I pushed open the door that connected the stifling service passage to the airy, plush-carpeted guest corridor, both Van Dijk and Le Froy had reached the door where Sergeant Pillay was on guard. He greeted Le Froy with relief and rose from the chair he had used to block the entrance to the room.

'Sir. It's a Caucasian male in his twenties. Not officially identified yet, but it is Victor Glossop's room. Nobody has been allowed in. I told everybody to wait for you.'

'Good.'

'Miss Chen, maybe you should wait outside.' Prakesh Pillay lowered his voice. 'It's a mess.'

I smiled my thanks and hurried through the door with my camera before anyone decided to stop me. I almost wished I hadn't when the smell hit me, making me gag.

It was dim inside the room after the modern electric lights in the corridor. The stench took me back to the sickroom in which I had last seen my dead father. It was the smell of recent death, of meat just starting to go off. And of betel. Not betel spittle but fresh betel . . . laid over faecal matter and urine.

The heavy scent of expensive perfume made things worse.

I was careful where I put my feet on the thick carpet, careful to breathe slowly and not retch. 'Imagine the substances are your own and they won't make you nauseous,' the mission-school teachers had said during Basic Nursing. As prim as they were tough, those English ladies dealt unflinchingly with conditions they were too genteel to put into words.

As my eyes adjusted I saw I was standing in a small foyer that opened into a room with a bed, two armchairs and a writing desk. To the right, there were windows, the curtains pulled shut, and to the left, cupboards. In the corner by the bed, two doors stood at right angles.

Le Froy stepped into the room and stopped, studying the scene. I did the same. A vase lay shattered on the floor about a foot from the bed, and what was on the bed explained the messenger boy's monster.

The face of the man lying there was swollen into a grotesque mask. There were blister-like swellings on his naked torso too, and it seemed someone had drawn red spots, crosses and swastikas all over him. He looked like Togog, the red-faced *wayang kulit* clown. In fact, along with the stuffy, stinking heat, that terrible room felt like one of the lowest levels of Hell.

All the magazine photographs I had seen showed Victor Glossop as fair-haired and handsome. But the bloated figure on the bed was hideous. The half-closed eyes were staring, and his swollen lips seemed to part over a giant pink maggot – oh, it was his tongue.

I had been holding my breath and now when I gasped the foetid air choked me. I thought I was going to faint or be sick.

'Vomit,' Le Froy said sharply.

'What?'

'Someone else was in the room with him. The vomit over there is a different consistency from what came out of him on the bed.'

I saw he was right. I took out my camera and unfolded it. It is always easier to study a scene through a lens. This is true literally as well as metaphorically. I switched into working mode and felt the dizziness and nausea recede.

'It looks like he is wearing lipstick, sir. And I think the marks on his body are lipstick as well.'

I looked more closely. Some of the spots looked like little red hearts.

'Make sure you get pictures of all the patterns,' was all Le Froy said. 'Especially those that look like words.'

I photographed the body on the bed from different angles. He was shirtless but wore a sarong of light and dark blue checks. He might have picked it up in the street market outside the hotel. It was not folded and tucked native style, but bunched around his hips with a leather belt.

'Shall I open the curtains, sir?' Van Dijk's voice startled me. I had forgotten he was there.

'Yes,' Le Froy said, without turning.

'Wait. Just a moment, please.' I wasn't trying to be difficult: I could see that the general manager's chilly disdain might have come from the effort of holding in his own guts.

As quickly as I could I took some photographs of the closed curtains, and was glad I did. 'Chief, look.'

There were splashes of what seemed to be blood on the fabric. But the colour was wrong. The texture was, too, for clotted blood. I leaned closer and sniffed to be certain, and heard Van Dijk gasp, in horror or disgust, and retch. There was something else on the floor just behind the hem of the curtain. I pushed the cloth aside and picked it up with my fingertips. It was an open tube of Lucky lipstick, a cheap brand I had seen sold on market stalls. But the colour was different from that used on Victor's body. I passed it to Le Froy.

'What do you think?' Le Froy asked. His eyes were bright and dispassionate.

'It's old betel juice, sir, on the curtains.' Perhaps they had practised spitting in here before pulling their rehearsal trick.

Le Froy nodded. 'And this lipstick?'

'It's a different colour from the one used to draw on his body. This is more orange than brown. But it may change on contact with skin.'

'Agreed. I want photographs. And find samples. Then get Pillay in here to turn him over.' He nodded towards the body. 'Photograph his back, his hands and feet, his ears . . . Look for anything unusual.'

I got down to work, glad I had two spare canisters of film in my bag and very glad my stomach had settled.

'Dr Leask is on his way,' Constable Kwok came in to say.

'Don't let anyone into the room till he gets here,' Le Froy said. Then, to me, 'Make sure you get photographs of the whole room. Sergeant Pillay, you have the fingerprint kit?'

'Yes, sir.' He made a face behind Le Froy's back. Taking fingerprints was a messy business and no use unless you had prints to compare them to. I was trying to sort the ones already on record in the police files, but there seemed no way to classify them. Fingerprinting was a new gimmick and no one at the Detective Shack except Le Froy really believed it could work.

'Mr Van Dijk, can you tell me what happened here? Who found Mr Glossop? When were you informed?'

Van Dijk answered, 'Housekeeping. The chambermaid knocked and called, then let herself in when there was no answer. That is standard. She saw him there on the bed and panicked. Two of the houseboys heard her screaming and rushed in.'

'Very courageous of them.'

'Gentlemen guests sometimes express excessive affection towards housekeeping staff,' Van Dijk explained, 'which can interfere with the cleaning schedule. Usually a houseboy turning up is enough to set things right. On seeing the man was dead, they came to me. I sent one to run for the police.'

'Good boys. Do you know if one of them was sick by the bed?'

'I – no. No idea.'

I wondered if Van Dijk had left his breakfast on the carpet.

Suddenly one of the inner doors swung open and a large man dressed in dark grey appeared next to me. Startled, I jerked away, bumping into Le Froy. I'm not superstitious but in that instant I thought he was the spirit-collector, come for the dead man. Sergeant Pillay touched me lightly on the arm to comfort me. Or maybe to seek comfort. His fingers were cold and trembling.

'I am Dr Taylor Covington. I demand to know what's going on here. You have no right to keep us out of a room we've paid for. I represent the Covington party.'

At that moment, if Dr Taylor Covington had said he represented the devil, I would have believed him.

Taylor Covington

———◆———

'**D**r Covington, my name is Le Froy.'

'You must be Chief Inspector Le Froy. Roderick Glossop spoke of you.' Dr Covington looked mollified. He glanced at the bed but made no move towards it. He had entered through the connecting door, not from the outside, and he kept his distance from the corpse.

'I heard what the servants are saying. I suppose there's no mistake? Victor Glossop is really dead? Nicole's Victor?'

'The dead man has not yet been formally identified,' Le Froy said. 'I must talk to Nicole Covington as soon as possible. Unfortunately, we don't have women officers on the staff, but my associate Miss Chen will assist me in the interview.'

Dr Covington took another look at me. He seemed surprised. 'You employ locals?'

'All staff are local residents, whether short- or long-term.'

'Of course.'

My role was news to me too. Fortunately, I was prepared. I always carried a notebook and pens in my bag. With my camera,

36

I could even photograph the witness. I nodded like I thought a police associate would nod.

Dr Covington was a large, heavy man with thick hair the rich orange colour of cooked yams. He was perhaps in his late fifties. The sheen of sweat on reddened skin showed he had not been out east very long, and the yellowness in his eyes indicated an overworked liver. I could tell from his manner he was used to being in charge and obeyed.

He inclined his head slightly and said, in passable Mandarin, '*Ni hao.*' I appreciated the gesture, though his Mandarin was possibly better than mine. In my grandmother's house I had learned Malay and Hokkien and picked up marketplace Cantonese, Teochew and Tamil. At school, we had learned English and a smattering of French and German, but not Mandarin.

'*Xie xie*,' I replied. 'I can speak English, sir.'

'Glad to hear that.'

I know better than to judge on first appearances and decided to try to like Dr Taylor Covington. You shouldn't dislike people just because they startle you by popping up in a room with a dead body.

Le Froy looked at the carpet and the shoes Van Dijk and Dr Covington were wearing, but I could tell he was studying Dr Covington with attention.

'Shall we move into the corridor?' Le Froy suggested. The other men agreed and I followed them.

I knew Le Froy's method of working. At the starting gate, he considered every person a suspect, then factored in motives, personality and opportunity, and adjusted the odds accordingly. He would have the hotel staff on his list too, Van Dijk included.

Le Froy's next question was addressed to the general manager. 'Your guests have rooms upstairs as well as down here? Is that routine?'

'Just the two,' Van Dijk murmured. 'By special arrangement.'

'One is for my young grandson,' Dr Covington said. 'We play games and do lessons, and down here he can work off his energy. We can get in and out without disturbing the other guests. When Victor heard about it, he got a room down here too. Nicole thought it a grand idea till they told her it was for men only. Then she kicked up such a fuss—'

He stopped abruptly. There was acute discomfort on his face. He passed a hand distractedly through his hair. 'Please forgive me. I am an old fool under stress and, God's truth, I have not felt stress like this since losing my boy, Radley. Good of you to come, Chief Inspector and Miss Chen. I appreciate it. Le Froy, you must do all you can to clear this up.'

Le Froy nodded, acknowledging his pain. 'What was the fuss about?'

'Normal for Nicole, really. She is quite, quite . . .' He shook his head but no description emerged. 'Please understand. Nicole hasn't had an easy life. She's very highly strung and, as you can imagine, this is a terrible shock to her.'

'Nicole is your daughter?'

'My daughter-in-law.' There was a twitch of impatience in his voice. As though he suspected Le Froy was making fun of him. 'She was married to my son Radley – my late son, Radley. She was engaged to marry Victor—'

'I want to talk to her as soon as possible,' Le Froy said again. 'Now.'

Le Froy once told me (after I accidentally killed someone who was trying to kill me) that immediately after a shock is both the best and the worst time to interview someone. You can learn a great deal even if you don't get a single answer out of them. I wondered if he suspected Nicole Covington of killing her husband-to-be.

'Nicole's suite is on the third floor.' Dr Covington started for the broad central stairwell, a hand on Le Froy's shoulder. 'This hotel believes in propriety with a capital P. They could have packed all of us into one of their damn suites but they insisted the bride-to-be had to bunk in on a different floor. No complaints from Nicole, though. The Farquhar put her in rooms usually reserved for visiting royalty and only VIPs get to camp there.'

I glanced at Van Dijk, who remained diplomatically impassive. 'Fortunately, December is low season for travellers, due to the monsoon winds,' he remarked, to no one in particular.

Perhaps I had judged Van Dijk too hastily. It is harder to figure out the living than the dead.

Following them up the stairs to the third floor, I noticed Taylor Covington had a slight limp. Earlier, I had seen him studying my limp and now I knew why. But he had said nothing. If you don't have to think twice about going up or down a staircase you won't understand. It's like seeing another Straits-born person in a room full of *ang mohs*: it brings the comfort of knowing someone 'like me' is present even if you don't exchange a single word. Unless you were hoping to blend in, in which case you resent him or her for reminding you of how impossible it is.

I didn't think Dr Covington was embarrassed about his limp. But maybe that was because I was extrapolating from the only other doctors I knew – Dr Leask, who was socially awkward and stammered unless he was talking about his studies in blood infections and poisons, and Dr Shankar, Parshanti's father. I have seen Dr Shankar jump off a moving bus to ask a roadside vagrant if he could reset his broken leg for free, not out of pity or charity but because he wanted to test a bone-setting frame he had developed.

'Seems to be obvious what happened in there,' Dr Covington was saying, as I finally joined them on the third-floor landing, 'going by the state of the room. Some local addicts must have broken in or been brought in by Victor. You can see they treated the place like a spittoon. Addicts are all over the island, chewing that ghastly stuff. Victor tried it and had a bad reaction.'

No.

Soldiers and sailors often got drunk on their nights out. But I was sure local betel addicts were not responsible for the murder. Men who can afford alcohol don't need *sireh*. Betel-chewing was a temporary sop for pain and hunger. Everyone knows that in the long run it causes more trouble than it cures – bad teeth and raw throats coughing up bloody phlegm for a start. Especially among the poorest, who chew the dregs discarded by others. The best thing that can be said for betel is that it costs less than rice when you are starving.

'Mrs Nicole Covington?' Le Froy prompted.

Dr Covington knocked on the door of the suite.

'Go away!' a woman shouted.

Nicole

◆

'Nicole, the police want to speak to you,' Dr Covington said.
He knocked again and pushed open the door to her suite
without waiting for an answer. Le Froy and I followed him in.

There were three people in the large sitting room. The walls
were creamy white with framed watercolours and black-lacquered
beams across the high ceiling. There was a large Agra rug on the
polished floor, and the standard lamps, wooden cabinets and
upholstered furniture looked of better quality than I had seen in
the governor's mansion.

Nicole Covington was lying on the sofa with a small plump
boy, who looked about six years old. A man sat on the upright
chair beside them. He got to his feet as we entered but stared and
said nothing. He was much younger than Dr Covington and his
deferential attitude gave me the impression he was a secretary or
assistant.

I had seen so many pictures of Nicole Covington in the
illustrated papers that it felt like meeting a movie star. She must
have been wearing the new pancake make-up Parshanti had raved

about because her face looked porcelain smooth and without pores. At first sight, I thought her the most beautiful woman I had ever seen.

Her dress was made of some soft flowing material, dark blue sprinkled with white flowers, and had a prim white lace collar. And she was wearing a necklace of pearls and blue stones that might have been sapphires or lapis lazuli. Perhaps she sensed me looking at her necklace because her hand reached up to play with it as she spoke.

'Victor's dead, isn't he? And it's all because of me.' She swung her feet gracefully to the floor and stood up. She was smaller than I'd expected, not much taller than I was. Her lips and fingernails were crimson, brighter than blood against her very fair skin. I knew she was twenty-six years old, but she might have been a teenage girl, with her dark brown hair shining in a fashionable bob.

Then she cried, 'It's my fault. I killed him, like I killed all the others! If you're really the police, you must arrest me at once!' She held her wrists together and thrust them in Le Froy's direction as she tilted her head back and wailed like a child.

I gaped.

'Please pull yourself together, Nicole.' Dr Covington looked grim.

'Is that a statement?' Le Froy asked calmly. 'Who are the others you killed?'

'It's the shock,' Dr Covington said quickly. 'She doesn't know what she's saying. It's much worse for Nicole, of course, she being a woman. You'll hear her say all kinds of things but I wouldn't set too much store by any of it until she calms down some. Come, Nicole. Sit down and stop talking rubbish!'

We stood awkwardly around the weeping woman. The quiet young man looked pained but didn't move. The dark-haired little boy was standing almost at attention by his mother's side.

'Hello,' I said to him.

'How do you do?' he said formally. 'Pleased to meet you.' He had a high, sweet voice, which was all the more striking because of the care with which he enunciated.

'Oh, you are a sweetheart!' I cried, forgetting I was an associate with the Detective Unit. The serious little boy in his pale blue sailor shirt and grey shorts was enchanting. Like a talking doll with perfect manners. 'What's your name?'

'My name is Radley Covington Junior. My father was Radley Covington. He is dead.'

'My grandson. We call him Junior,' Dr Covington said. He was smiling. A glow softened his face when he looked at the child. 'He's dark like his mother, but he's the spitting image of his father at the same age.'

Grandfather and grandson exchanged a smile. They were clearly close. This made me warm to Dr Covington even more. Asian men seldom spend time with their children and grandchildren.

Now our attention was fixed on Junior, his mother stopped wailing. She looked a little put out.

'A charming boy,' Le Froy said, studying Nicole. 'He must be a great comfort to you.'

Generally Le Froy kept his distance from society ladies and young children, finding them irrational and unpredictable. Did he suspect Nicole? How could this tiny woman have overpowered and murdered her much larger fiancé?

I looked at Nicole, trying to see what Le Froy saw.

'Don't stare at me like that, girl. Take your jealous eyes off me.'

It took me a moment to realize she was talking to me. I snapped my eyes away. Was I jealous? I wasn't normally a jealous person. If I were, I would have been jealous of everyone with two live parents and two straight legs, which would have meant being jealous all the time. But something I didn't understand made me want to stay close to Nicole and go on watching her.

There was something fascinating about Nicole Covington. I saw Le Froy felt it too. I had seen that expression on his face when he was trying to find the false bottom on a smuggler's sampan.

Nicole didn't seem to mind him looking at her.

'Victor gave this necklace to me.' Her fingers dipped into the neckline of her dress and drew out the full length. She held the threaded stones towards Le Froy between two fingers. 'We were going to get married on Christmas Eve. This was his engagement present to me. That's why he's dead too. They all die because of me. Don't you see? Victor died because he was going to marry me. I'm cursed!'

She spoke in a breathy little girl's voice with an edge of hysteria, but her head tilted upwards towards Le Froy, as though she were inviting a kiss. 'I don't know what's going to happen to me now.' Her voice rose, half wailing, half moaning prettily, as she closed her eyes and rested her beautiful face on Le Froy's shoulder.

Dr Covington snorted as I felt, rather than saw, Le Froy stiffen.

Any gentleman would have wrapped his arms around the distraught woman to comfort and protect her. Le Froy always said that, on duty, he was no gentleman. His arms remained by his sides as he asked, 'Do you have a recent photograph of Mr Victor Glossop?'

'Why would I keep a photograph of Victor?' Nicole snapped, with a flare of irritation. '*He* was following *me* around saying he was in love with me. He should have been carrying my photograph around with him, not messing with other women.'

'Dear Nicole,' Dr Covington put an arm around her and steered her away from us, 'don't upset yourself. Everything is going to be all right. Chief Inspector Le Froy needs a photograph of Victor, that's all. I'm sure Kenneth can find one somewhere. Kenneth?'

'Of course,' the quiet young man said.

So he was Parshanti's Kenneth Mulliner. He didn't look like a man who would go around seducing local girls. But, then, he didn't look like a man who would play tricks on policemen either and he had certainly been among that group. I didn't trust him. To be honest, I had decided not to trust him even before I saw him.

At least I could tell Parshanti he was still alive.

'The chief inspector wants to ask you some questions, Nicole. Then you can leave him to take care of everything.'

'Take care of what? Is he going to bring Victor back from the dead?' Nicole wrenched herself away from Dr Covington and flung herself back on the sofa. I hoped she wasn't going to wail again, but she pursed her lips sulkily. It didn't look to me like great grief.

'Is she taking any medicines?' Le Froy asked.

Dr Covington nodded vigorously. 'I gave her a light sedative, just to help her over the shock. It's been very difficult for her. Not just this but the previous year ever since— I should really get her to bed. She should rest before she strains herself.'

His voice was steady and professionally caring but I noticed that Dr Covington's shoulders had squared and his neck tensed when he was talking to Nicole or even about her. It's not surprising to be fonder of a grandchild than an in-law but I wondered at the man travelling halfway across the world with someone who made him uncomfortable.

'Nicole's not strong and—'

'Talk sense, you old fool! Strength has nothing to do with it. My fiancé is dead! I'm all alone again!' Nicole grabbed her son and folded her arms around him, 'My precious baby Raddy is all I have left in the world. My poor fatherless boy!'

'Nicole, calm down.'

'Why? What good will that do? What good will anything do? Just tell me that! Get these people away from me! Can't I have any privacy? Kenneth! Do something useful for once and get these people out of here.'

The little boy watched her with serious eyes. He did not seem upset by his mother's tears. Were there tears? Nicole's eyes had not looked red or swollen when we came in. Indeed, they were still beautifully rimmed in black, with a dusting of blue powder.

Dr Covington was exasperated but calm. 'Perhaps you could come back to speak to her tomorrow when she's calmer. In the meantime, if I can be of any help . . .'

Le Froy turned to him. 'I would appreciate your observations as a medical man, sir. If you would give me an hour of your time we could go down to the station to talk.'

'I'll bring Junior with me.' Dr Covington seemed glad to agree to this, 'We'll see if they can find us some cocoa, eh?'

'Yes, Grandpa!' The child brightened.

'No,' Nicole said. 'Raddy stays with me. I need him. My life has just been destroyed and I want my boy with me. And I told you to stop calling him Junior. He's the only Radley Covington alive on this earth right now and that's his name. And his place is here, beside his loving mama.'

Dr Covington winced and his eyes closed briefly, as though in sudden pain.

'I'll bring you some cocoa,' I promised the little boy. 'I'll see if the kitchen can send up some biscuits too. You stay here with your mother while she's upset.'

'Thank you. My mother is a black widow spider,' Junior explained in a clear, high voice. 'That's why all the men in her life keep dying.'

His loving mama slapped him. Hard.

What struck me was how the child reacted. His head snapped sideways and he fell to his knees on the carpet but picked himself up without fuss. Any other child would have cried at the unprovoked attack. Did his mother hit him so often he thought it was normal?

'I'm sorry. I didn't mean to.' Nicole looked horrified. 'I'm such a bad mother, I know I am. I'm a danger to my own child.'

Spanking may be part of discipline but taking out your bad temper on a child is bullying. That is something no child should have to live with.

I stepped forward and took Junior's hand. 'We are going downstairs for cocoa. Now.' Junior seemed willing enough.

It was only when I closed the suite doors behind us that I realized I had no idea where to go.

Promise of Cocoa

———◆———

We were standing in the corridor when the doors to the suite opened again and Kenneth Mulliner slipped out. 'It might have been an accident,' he said.

'She hit him on purpose.'

'Please don't fight.' Junior tugged at Kenneth's arm. He was clearly at ease with the man, whose accent was British rather than American. I wondered if he was Junior's tutor.

'We're not fighting, Champ.' He ruffled the boy's hair with affection.

Not a tutor, I decided. Though reserved, he didn't have that air of depressed subservience that comes with being paid to supervise the very young or the very old. Rather, he had the eyes of a dragon snake. They were pale grey-green between their dark pupils and rims. The dragon snake is the quiet younger brother of the flamboyantly auspicious dragon, not the satanic creature that Westerners fear.

'We're not even talking about the same thing. But I'll change course. Nicole did smack the boy, but she didn't mean it. She doesn't hold up well under pressure. I've seen her slap herself too. Much harder than that.'

'Sometimes Mama throws things,' Junior said. 'She broke a vase yesterday. But then she's sorry and cries. I don't like it when she cries.'

I thought of the broken vase in the dead man's room, too far away from the bed to have been kicked over in his death throes.

'I'm Kenneth Mulliner, by the way. I should get back in there before your chief inspector thinks I've run away and decides to arrest me.'

'My name is Chen Su Lin,' I said.

He grinned. I suddenly saw Kenneth Mulliner was not bad-looking, despite those strange eyes and his light brown hair. But I would still have classified him as 'inoffensive' rather than 'handsome'. Good looks require personality and poise, as well as even features. In the room, Kenneth Mulliner's attitude had suggested he was used to blending in to the background.

'I know who you are,' he said. 'Your grandmother is one of the richest women in Singapore but you're working in a police station because she doesn't believe girls should go to university.'

He saw from my expression that I wasn't exactly thrilled with what he had said. 'Oops. Sorry. That may have been confidential. Look, can we talk?'

'No.' I had nothing against the man, but I was angry with Parshanti, who must have talked about me. And she had clearly spent much more time with Kenneth Mulliner than she had let on.

'Kenneth! Where's Kenneth?' Nicole's voice came from behind the doors. 'Kenneth! Come here and get rid of these people at once. Shoot the lot of them if they try to stop you. Such insolence!'

Kenneth looked between me and the door, and I saw the decision in his snake eyes. Taking Junior's hand, he pushed the door open and we heard Nicole's high girlish voice going at full blast: 'Kenneth! I need you! Taylor's being disgusting. He wants to get Victor cut up. The poor man's already dead. Why put him through that? You're supposed to be Victor's friend – come here and make them stop it.'

'I strongly recommend an autopsy,' came Dr Covington's voice. 'I am sure his family will want to know exactly what happened to him.'

'Our medical examiner, Dr Leask, will look at the body and decide if an autopsy is necessary.' That was Le Froy's calm murmur. 'Did Mr Glossop have any underlying medical conditions?'

'His liver was probably diseased, given the amount of alcohol he took. I don't suppose I could be of any help? Haven't done an autopsy in years, but it's not something you forget.'

'Kenneth!' Nicole wailed.

'Sorry, Nicole. We're off duty and going for cocoa.' Kenneth shut the door, signalling the end of his side of the conversation. There was a shriek of womanly rage from within.

'Yours might be the next dead body,' I warned him.

Kenneth flinched – as though I had made fun of him. But before I could ask what I had said that was wrong he recovered. 'Don't I know it. But there's no need to worry. Nicole's highly strung and nervous but she wouldn't actually do anything.'

Wouldn't she? I had just seen her hit a child out of sheer bad temper.

'As I was saying, Victor's death was probably an accident. There'll be a simple explanation. A snake bite. A spider bite. This is the Far East – there must be venomous snakes and creatures in every corner. Or an allergy. Something Victor ate. He was always sampling strange native foods, chicken feet and pig intestines and live frogs. He might have eaten something that triggered an allergy that led to a heart attack. Or it could have been something he picked up on board ship. Just an accident. Right, Junior?' Junior nodded gravely.

'Do you know who was with him when he died?' I remembered the lipstick and the small puddle of vomit.

'He had no pulse and wasn't breathing,' Kenneth said. 'He was definitely dead.'

He hadn't answered my question.

'You found the body?'

Kenneth sighed.

'You should go back in there and tell Le Froy,' I said. 'He'll want to talk to you.'

'Actually, Junior did.' Kenneth nodded at the child. 'You talk to him. You're good with him.'

Junior looked serious and scared, and his cheek was red where his mother had hit him. I didn't want to send him back to her. At least, not until she'd calmed down.

'Tell me,' I said.

'Junior brought me down to Victor's playroom. That's what he called it because it's next to Junior's playroom. Junior was laughing and telling us about this grand new joke of Victor's. He tried to get his mother to bring him down to Victor's room to see, but Nicole was angry with Victor and refused. Thank God. If she had been there . . . So, anyway, I brought Junior down. The door wasn't locked and he ran into the room, shouting, 'Show us, Victor!' or something like that. He ran to Victor's body and shook him. Victor was always setting up these elaborate jokes and I thought it was one of his tricks. But when Junior touched him he got the shock of his life. He knocked over some orchids when he backed away.' Kenneth shook his head as though trying to dislodge the memory. 'I got him out of there as fast as I could.'

'The broken vase by the bed,' I remembered. 'You should have told someone, and they should have sent for the police at once.'

'I had to leave Junior with Taylor first. Couldn't drag a terrified child around cops and corpses.'

'You said I was brave,' came a subdued protest.

'Yes, you are, Champ. Braver than me. I found Taylor with Nicole and told them what had happened. By the time we got Nicole calmed down and Taylor went to see what had happened the police were already there.' He put an arm around Junior's shoulders. 'Now, I believe cocoa was promised. Shall we?'

I was torn. As an assistant, I ought to get back inside the room and tell my boss what I had just learned. Then again, wouldn't a responsible assistant be following up leads that he could not?

There was a faintly mocking air about Kenneth as he studied me studying him. As though he thought I was afraid to have cocoa with him. I didn't trust Kenneth Mulliner, but that didn't mean I was afraid of him. Had he rushed out after us because he was worried about what Junior might tell me? I determined not to leave them until I'd had a chance to chat alone with the little boy.

'Let's go,' I said firmly.

'We're coming too,' said Taylor Covington, opening the doors

to the suite and ushering Le Froy out in front of him. 'The hotel's
tea room is the best destination for cocoa.'

The young police corporal who had been unobtrusively sta-
tioned just inside the main door to the suite followed them and
took a position in the corridor.

'What happened?' I asked Le Froy. It was unlike him to leave
in the middle of interviewing a witness, and there had hardly
been time for him to ask her anything.

'Hysterics. It won't be any use trying to talk to her until she
calms down. I had to give her a sedative.' Dr Covington sounded
as if he was running the case. 'And the chief inspector thought
he may as well ask Junior some questions while his mother rests
up. Kenneth, no one's going to stop you spending all your time
with Nicole now.'

'We've been through that. I'm not going back in there.' Kenneth
gave a stiff laugh.

Dr Covington ignored him. He started down the corridor to
the main staircase with a hand on Junior's shoulder. 'Come on,
Chief Inspector, Miss Chen. Junior and I will introduce you to
the joys of the Farquhar's tea room. Our treat.'

Le Froy was watching Kenneth, so I did too. Kenneth looked
at the door, then at Dr Covington's retreating back, and went back
into Nicole's suite.

Despite what he had said earlier, he seemed glad to. And
while I was still angry with Parshanti I felt sorry for her. But just
then I was mostly nervous about eating with strangers.

Previous Deaths

◆

A short digression: of course I had eaten sandwiches before, made with sugar or Bovril on *roti*, but those sandwiches at the Farquhar were a world apart.

Thin slices of soft white bread were cut into dainty triangles and filled with salted butter and cucumber, hard-boiled eggs chopped with mayonnaise or thin slices of cold roast beef with horseradish. They were served with little dishes of mango chutney, cream cheese mixed with chopped walnuts and raisins, and what tasted like a sweet, spicy jam.

I was enchanted and found it hard to believe any human with enough to eat could want to hurt another. But, of course, it was only because of the harm done to Victor Glossop that I was in the Farquhar tea room that day.

It was a cheerful, airy space with light metalwork chairs set around tables covered with white linen. The open balcony faced the sea, which could be glimpsed between gigantic palm trees and jasmine and bougainvillaea bushes. Even the gentle flapping of the rattan screens was regular and soothing.

But I was not ready to be soothed.

'Does his mother strike him often?' I asked Dr Covington quietly, as a uniformed waiter stacked one of the chairs securely on another to give Junior enough height at the table to help himself to the hot cocoa and Digestive biscuits that appeared in front of him.

It was clear the little boy was a favourite there.

'Never strike a child in front of you maternal types, eh?' Dr Covington's face was red and fleshy, and he smelt strongly of hair pomade as he leaned towards me. I drew back automatically, then felt cross with myself.

'You say this girl works for you?'

'Miss Chen speaks English as well as I do,' Le Froy pointed out. 'Why don't you ask her?'

'But you're her employer.'

'We are both employees of Singapore's Detective and Intelligence Unit. We are colleagues.'

Dr Covington laughed loudly. 'Anyone who knows me will understand that I meant no offence. Young lady, I say what I think and ask what I don't, and I'm too old to change my ways.'

'Thank you,' I said to Dr Covington. 'No offence taken, sir.'

'Well said, young lady.' Dr Covington's face creased into a smile before he turned to Le Froy. 'We Americans are built to go ahead and fix whatever needs fixing. See a problem, sort it out, that's my motto. But you Britishers do things by the book and I don't want to offend you by making a direct proposal.'

'Proposal?'

Dr Covington turned to me. 'I know your boss brought you in to watch us. What about this? While you keep an eye on us suspects, you earn a little extra from me for keeping an eye on my grandson and his mother till this is cleared up. Nicole is nervous and highly strung, and she doesn't know anyone in this place.'

I noticed his deliberate use of the word 'suspects' and wondered if Le Froy would comment on it. He did not.

'Are you worried about your grandson?' I asked.

'Not in the least. Junior's a champion.' Dr Covington paused to wink at the boy, then lowered his voice. 'Junior has asthma attacks but, between you and me, that's all psychological and due to his mama's behaviour. It's her I'm worried about. Nicole has a short fuse. As you saw upstairs, she takes it out on the boy sometimes. I hoped travelling might distract her but it looks like her silly superstitions are following her around.'

'What's following her around?' Le Froy asked.

'Death, she says. She's lost her parents, her brother, my boy Radley, whom she was married to . . . I suppose it's enough to make any woman think she's cursed.'

'When did all these deaths take place?' Le Froy's eyes were sharp, his plate empty. I didn't refuse when Dr Covington offered me a toast square topped with Gentleman's Relish.

'Take it easy, Chief Inspector!' Dr Covington laughed. 'Don't rush off and arrest Nicole. Her parents died years ago, when she was a child. She barely remembers them. Same with the brother. She never had much of a home life. If you ask me that was a big part of the problem.'

His face sobered. 'I was against my son marrying her, to be frank. I didn't think they were ready. I wanted my Radley to get a good start on his career before he had a family, but there's no talking to a young man once a pretty face has got him hooked.

If I'd foreseen any of this I would have put my foot down and insisted they wait a year at least. And maybe my Radley would be alive today.' There was no mistaking his pain.

'What happened to your son?' Le Froy asked gently.

'Car accident. They were having a bit of a tiff, as young couples do, and ran off the road. My son died on the spot.'

'Nicole was in the car?'

'Walked away without a scratch.' The anger stayed in his eyes until he reached over to ruffle Junior's hair.

Junior had finished his biscuits and was watching the door to the kitchen. We all turned in that direction and saw a waiter appear with a shot glass of chocolate pudding. I had seen no order given, but the little boy's anticipation showed this must have been a regular habit. Clearly, the Covingtons organized things well.

'So, how about it?' Dr Covington asked me.

'No,' Le Froy said. 'She's needed in the office.'

'But, sir—'

'No.'

I was stung. This was the second time he had vetoed me doing something that was well within my capabilities. But remembering the rehearsal prank kept me quiet. For the time being. I would bring it up again once we were back in the office. I couldn't do any kind of job if Le Froy was going to pad me with cotton wool.

Dr Covington sat back and looked from Le Froy to me. Was he wondering if I were Le Froy's local mistress? Drat Van Dijk for putting the thought in my head! I sat up straight and tried to look businesslike and professional. Which was probably exactly what a local mistress would do in my position.

Le Froy seemed to consider the matter closed. 'Why did you come to Singapore? What made Glossop and your daughter-in-law decide to get married here?'

'You'll have to ask the young couple – ask Nicole, I mean. I wasn't part of that discussion. Victor's idea was for them to be married on board by the ship's captain. But Nicole took a dislike to the man and insisted on waiting till we got to shore.'

'Why did you leave America?'

'Nicole had no family left after my son died,' Dr Covington said. 'As my wife died a year before our son, and I was retired from my practice, I thought a trip around the world would help both of us to get over the loss. My grandson is too young to understand what it means to be fatherless, and I hope my presence will ameliorate that somewhat. I want to provide the guidance and protection a father would.'

'What can you tell us about Victor Glossop?'

'Oh, Victor was a great joker. He'd been playing tricks on the hotel staff since we checked in. When they first told us he was dead, I was sure it was another trick. We all thought so.'

'Junior found the body,' I told Le Froy.

'Junior thought it was one of Victor's jokes. But he was really dead. Right, Junior?' Junior nodded.

'Why didn't you tell us Junior found him?'

Dr Covington shrugged. 'Don't see what difference it makes. Anyway, he didn't do anything, so no harm done. Glossop was such a young man. So full of life. This is such a waste.'

'Why did Junior say his mother was like a black widow spider?' I asked. I doubted the child had come up with that on his own.

'Junior says the strangest things sometimes. Out of the mouths of babes, eh?'

'What's that, Grandpa?'

'Just saying you're overly fond of spiders, bugs, butterflies . . . It's an inclination his mother doesn't share.' Again, Dr Covington ran a hand over his grandson's dark curly head.

'Who told you about black widow spiders?' I asked Junior. Some adult must have planted the thought in his head.

'Spiders have eight legs,' Junior informed me, through a mouthful of chocolate pudding. 'That's how you tell they aren't insects. Insects have six legs, even butterflies and mosquitoes. Spiders are Arab nits.'

'"Arachnids",' Dr Covington corrected him. 'We may have another budding scientist in the family. And Junior is a real gentleman. He understands that his mama is going through a very difficult time and we all have to take good care of her.'

'Real gentlemen take care of ladies,' said the young gentleman, whose feet dangled a good foot above the floor. 'Ladies cry. Gentlemen don't.'

He hadn't answered my question.

'The boy's had to grow up fast. Nicole doesn't really know how to handle being a mother and doesn't have a mother to show her how it's done. My Radley would have been a great pa. He loved children. Even before Junior was born we were talking about the hunting and fishing trips the three of us would be going on. Radley always said those trips with me were the best times of his life.'

Junior watched us seriously.

'Who told you your mother was like a black widow spider?

You didn't think of that yourself, did you?' I persisted. Le Froy, sitting on my other side, leaned forward to listen.

'Kenneth,' Junior said.

'Kenneth Mulliner told you that?' All my suspicions of the man returned immediately. 'What exactly did he say?'

'Kenneth says, "So, this is where the party is!"' a voice growled suddenly in my ear.

Startled, I jumped to my feet and spun around. Kenneth Mulliner had sneaked up and put his hands on the back of my chair. He was laughing – they all were, especially Junior, who was shrieking in delight.

Chatting with Junior had made me forget the grotesque corpse. The shock of Kenneth's sudden appearance brought it abruptly back. For an awful moment my head spun and the finger sandwiches that had gone down so sweetly threatened to reappear.

'Su Lin.' That was all Le Froy said, but it steadied me.

'Kenneth! Pull up a chair. Here, sit next to Junior. He's been waiting for you.' Dr Covington shifted Junior's to make room.

'No, let me. I've got it—'

'All right?' Le Froy asked, low, as our suspects rearranged chairs around the table.

'Sir, about me watching Mrs Covington . . .' I seized my opportunity.

'I thought the reason you wanted a job was to escape a lifetime of looking after children.' At least it wasn't a firm 'no'.

Interviewing Kenneth

———◆———

'I can do this! I want to!' I whispered urgently to Le Froy, behind my napkin, as the others settled down, but he had already turned his attention to Kenneth.

'I can't stay. Nicole wants Junior.' Kenneth waved aside the waiter who appeared with tea and the offer of more sandwiches. 'Come on, Champ.'

Junior seized his cocoa mug with both hands and started gulping fast.

'Hey, slow down, sport!' Dr Covington said. 'Kenneth, you stay. Chief Inspector, you met Kenneth Mulliner upstairs. Kenneth was going to be Victor's best man. If you want to know more about Victor, he's the one to ask. I'll take the boy up to Nicole. I want to check on her, anyway.'

I noticed he told Kenneth what to do as though he were an employee. And that Kenneth didn't like it.

'Even if Victor was poisoned it was probably an accident,' Kenneth said. 'Like I already told your . . . assistant. It's the Far East. Lots of things out here to poison a man.'

'What makes you think he was poisoned?'

'That Punjabi cop says you've ordered a chemical analysis of the betel juice found on Victor. And his stomach contents. What else could you be looking for?'

'Sergeant Pillay is Tamil,' Le Froy said, with polite precision. 'His family is from Ceylon, not the Punjab.'

'That's a good one. As if it makes a difference!' Kenneth snorted, as though Le Froy had told a joke.

'It does. Punjabis are an ethnic group associated with the Punjab. Indians are people residing in India or of Indian origin. As an ethnic group, Punjabis are among the largest in the world, but while Punjabis are Indian, not all Indians are Punjabi.'

I saw Le Froy was deliberately provoking the younger man to study his reaction. Whatever Sergeant Pillay's origins, I meant to tell him off for sharing information with suspects.

'Shouldn't you be working out what happened to Victor,' Kenneth demanded, 'instead of sitting down to tea? Shouldn't you be questioning the hotel staff?'

Sergeant de Souza and the constables would already be questioning the hotel staff.

'We'll be speaking to the hotel staff too, of course,'

Le Froy's slight inflection on 'hotel' worked.

'I'm not staff. I wasn't working for Victor.'

Kenneth's quick resentment suggested this was a common mistake. But he did have the servile presence of an employee. Even I had assumed he was a secretary or tutor at first sight. 'How is Mrs Covington?' I asked.

'She's weepy at the moment, but she'll get over it.'

'When was the last time you saw Victor Glossop?'

'Back to the interrogation, is it? You can't seriously think you're going to pin this on me? Sorry, you'll have to find some other scapegoat.'

Le Froy waited, not bothering to correct him. I slid my note-book onto the table and nodded silent thanks to the waiter who cleared Dr Covington's and Junior's places.

We waited.

Kenneth rolled his eyes and sighed exaggeratedly. 'All right. Last time I saw Victor was at dinner last night. I don't know what his plans for the evening were. All I know is there *was* some plan. I wasn't a part of it.'

'What kind of plan? What did he say?'

'What he *said* was that he wasn't feeling well and was going to turn in early. I guessed he was planning something to get back at Nicole.'

'For what? Why?'

'Who knows why Victor did anything? They'd had a row earlier. I wasn't there but I know Nicole scolded him in front of the kid. Victor can never stand losing a fight. I mean he never could ... so ...' Kenneth faltered, his voice cracking.

Despite the front he was putting up, his friend's death had shaken Kenneth.

'Do you have any idea where he might have gone? Or what time he got back?' Le Froy asked.

I had already made a note to ask hotel staff for confirmation.

Kenneth shrugged. 'Who knows?' He wiped his nose on his napkin and poured himself a cup of tea. 'This is stone cold.'

'We found a business card for an establishment at Japan Street among Victor's things.'

Kenneth nodded. 'It's a bar. Run by a White Russian. As soon as we landed here, Victor was back to his old tricks. He found this bar that doubled as a brothel. There were drug orgies, and the women were free as long as you paid for the powders and the booze. At least, that's what I heard. I never saw the place. My job was to keep Nicole from suspecting anything.'

Many White Russians, left stateless after the Russian civil war, had found their way out east. Because they were considered Europeans, they got away with bending laws designed to keep us locals in our place. White Russians, rumour had it, organized drug-fuelled orgies and held satanic rituals in the nude.

Of course, these may just have been stories the Chinese and Japanese prostitutes told their customers to frighten them.

I once met a White Russian girl at the Mission Centre. Ilya was very nice and neither she nor her mother showed any inclination to take off their clothes or add drugs to their tea.

'You should talk to the guy who set up his stag night,' Kenneth said. 'They called it a wedding rehearsal but it was really Victor's stag party. Nicole was livid when she found out he'd invited local girls.'

'You were his best man. Didn't you arrange it?'

'Victor said I was useless here. No contacts, no knowhow. He connected with a local bloke, Harry Palin. Maybe they had a falling-out and Palin attacked him.'

Sweet, awkward Harry Palin? I couldn't believe it. I looked at Le Froy, who remained impassive as he asked, 'So, you sat back and let a local man take over?'

'I made the hotel arrangements,' Kenneth said. 'It was my idea to call it a rehearsal so the hotel let us have the ballroom without charging the earth. It was Victor's last week of freedom, and he was just making the most of it. No naked ladies, if that worries you. But that was only because he couldn't find any who were sporting or cheap enough. Victor turned up dressed as a native in a sarong. He was spitting that betel stuff at everybody. It was so disgusting, it was hilarious. Typical Victor.' The memory brought a wry smile to Kenneth's face and then he had to dash away tears. 'It wasn't just your men he picked on, Chief Inspector. He was spitting at everyone. Everyone was spitting at everyone else. It was just good fun.'

It didn't sound like fun for whoever did their laundry.

'You should check on that Palin chap. Victor met him in the Long Bar. I'm sure someone there will know how to find him. He and Victor almost came to blows the first time they met. Maybe he held a grudge. Palin was involved in some other murder last year, wasn't he? You can't help hearing local gossip. Maybe he got away with it that time and he's back to his old tricks now.'

I liked Harry Palin. We were friends, though I had suspected him, wrongly, of murdering two women last year. But friendship grows out of shared experiences and we had shared some truly bizarre ones.

'What was the fight about?' Le Froy prompted. 'The fights. Between Victor and Harry Palin, and between Victor and Mrs Covington.'

Another shrug. Kenneth helped himself to a thin bread and butter sandwich. 'It was the day we docked. We were walking around, working off our sea legs. Victor was pretty fed up. We had just come out of a shop and he chucked a rock at it and said, "You can't get Weber Menziken cigars anywhere on this God-forsaken island!" And Palin butted in and said, "If this is a God-forsaken island why don't you get the bloody hell out of here?"'

I recognized Harry's growling Singlish-tinted Oxford accent. Kenneth Mulliner was a gifted mimic.

'And there was this idiot girl with him.' Kenneth, warmed up now, switched back to his own voice. 'Not too hard on the eyes, I thought at first. A bit too fat to be fashionable, but I'm not fussy. Then I saw she wasn't right in the head. She was giggling and going "You said 'hell', Harry! You said 'hell', Harry!" over and over.'

Dee Dee, I thought, with a pang. Harry regularly visited his sister in town. Dee Dee was a sweet, loving child-woman. She boarded at the Mission Centre where she attended classes with seven- and eight-year-old girls, even though she was ten years older.

'What about you?' Le Froy asked. His voice was so quiet and conversational that it took Kenneth a moment to register that the question was directed at him. 'Did you fight too?'

He sneered, 'Do you think everyone is like your day labourers, getting into drunken fights?'

'On the contrary,' Le Froy said. 'Manual labourers are among the best disciplined of men. Those who work with their bodies have little choice as any weakness is immediately obvious.'

'While those who work with their damaged minds can carry on for years?'

Le Froy smiled and waited, watching him. Kenneth made a show of reaching for the (now refreshed) teapot. But his hand shook and he put it down again.

'I didn't do anything. I wasn't feeling very well. It was so hot and so wet and so filthy. I didn't like Victor picking on the girl. It's just not done. Like you wouldn't kick an old dog. Though Victor would have. He was looking to scrap, to let off steam. We were glad to be back on land but in that disgusting place, with what looked like bloodstains all over the walls? The locals were chewing and spitting, for God's sake. That was what gave Victor the idea for the party. He liked getting drunk and having fun. But nobody had any reason to kill him.'

'What did Victor and Nicole fight about?' asked Le Froy.

'Nicole was being Nicole.'

'Specifically?'

'I have no idea.'

'I'll go up and try to talk to her,' I said.

'No,' Le Froy said automatically.

He was being worse than Uncle Chen. He meant well, I suppose. If I had been attacked by a crocodile, nobody would be surprised if I wanted to avoid the mangrove swamps. But I didn't.

'Yes,' I said.

'We will discuss this.' Le Froy said. 'Not now.'

Background Research

———◆———

B ack at the Detective Shack, I set out to compile and verify all the information we had on Victor Glossop, Kenneth Mulliner and the Covingtons – with Parshanti's help.

I told her that Kenneth Mulliner was alive and unhurt but nothing more. He was a suspect, after all.

Actually, Parshanti was a big help. She brought over back copies of magazines and illustrated papers that mentioned the happy couple. Most articles focused on Nicole's clothes, hair and admirers. Getting around the British news blackout on Mrs Wallis Simpson, Mrs Nicole Covington was discussed as *one of the American women* well-born Englishmen were ensnared by.

According to *Ladies' Weekly*, Mrs Nicole Covington was travelling to get over the death of her first husband. On learning that she was sailing for the Far East, Glossop had decided to join her on impulse and managed to secure one of the last berths on the RMS *Queen Victoria*.

Victor Glossop was twenty-nine years old and would have been thirty on 30 December. Apparently that was why he wanted the wedding before Christmas. He was quoted as saying, 'I want to be able to say I was first married in my twenties.'

There was nothing on record to show what his first bride-to-be had thought of that.

Photographs of the late Victor Glossop showed an elegant young man with a blasé look. He had blond hair that was slicked away from a high forehead, light-coloured eyes, and the thin moustache over his thin lips was as fair as the hair on his head. He had been slim and looked tall, though one of the photographs with him and Kenneth standing shoulder to shoulder showed Kenneth was at least half a head taller. They were laughing and scruffy in that picture and Victor was holding up a policeman's helmet.

Kenneth had said Victor was always full of ideas for jokes and pranks. Clearly Kenneth himself had been involved in the pranks.

I thought Victor Glossop looked like the kind of young man schoolgirls and servant girls were warned against. Men like him would declare undying love to you but end up marrying someone of their own class, like Nicole Covington. And even after marriage such men would continue seducing girls with lies and meaningless promises.

Victor had taken a house in London after coming down from Oxford. The *Tatler* had had him on its list of Most Eligible Bachelors for the last five or six years. People were starting to say he might be a confirmed bachelor, but since he wasn't an eldest son, the family hadn't pressured him.

Anyway, the Glossops weren't nobility, just very rich. Their money came from the distillery business. There were whispers that Sir Roderick Glossop and his brother-in-law, Colonel Oswald

Mosley-Partington, were encouraging talk of war because distilling fuel for war machines would make them even richer.

The name Colonel Oswald Mosley-Partington rang a bell. He had been involved in the case that had led to Le Froy being exiled to Singapore, which the chief inspector never talked about.

Victor Glossop had asked Governor McPherson to help arrange things so they could marry in Singapore on Christmas Eve. As non-residents, they needed his permission to marry on the island without banns being called. The governor and his family had originally accepted an invitation to spend Christmas in Sarawak but had been obliged to cancel due to this unexpected wedding.

'So romantic and so tragic.' Parshanti sighed. 'If only he hadn't died. And if only Mrs Simpson was a widow instead of a divorcee . . . Isn't love so sad?'

I looked at her suspiciously. Parshanti came to the Detective Shack often enough and I had been too engrossed in my notes to pay much attention to her earlier. But now I saw that, instead of her usual workday dress, she was wearing a dark blue frock with a white belt and a flared hem I hadn't seen before. And gloves. Gloves? In Singapore?

I stared at them.

'I had to carry all those magazines and papers over,' Parshanti said defensively. 'I was worried about paper cuts.'

'And a new frock? On a weekday?'

'I'm just trying it out to make sure it fits. It was from a new pattern.'

But the eager way she looked around the Detective Shack told me she hoped to run into Kenneth Mulliner again. Being questioned as a murder suspect, perhaps. What can you say to a friend who is almost as smart as you most of the time but dumb enough to fall in love with a murder suspect?

Parshanti peeled off her gloves and tucked them into her mother's calfskin handbag. Yes, she was carrying her mother's good bag instead of her usual woven straw basket.

'Are we sure Nicole Covington is a widow, not a divorcee or a polygamist?' Le Froy came out of his office.

'Yes, sir. Her husband was killed in a car accident just after their son was born. It was less than a year after they were married.'

'Still no news from the hotel?'

'No, sir.'

Nicole Covington remained too traumatized for an interview, but Dr Covington had promised to let Le Froy know as soon as she was ready to talk. Le Froy had returned to the hotel that morning intending to interview her regardless. To no avail. We were surprised. Few witnesses could fend him off.

'What happened?' I asked.

'She started undressing,' Le Froy said. 'Don't have to put that in the official report. Just the working record. So the men know what to expect. She announced she would show she had nothing to hide and proceeded to remove items of clothing. Dr Covington stopped her, gave her some soothing powders and sent Mr Mulliner in to calm her down.'

'She might have been hiding something,' Sergeant de Souza said. 'You should have let her finish.' He looked as if he wished he had been there.

'American women have such a flair for the dramatic,' Sergeant

Pillay said. 'I can see why men find them attractive. If I were the king, I wouldn't have abdicated. I would have kept that American woman as my concubine and gone on being king.'

'He's not just a king. He's a man in love. Giving up his throne for her is the most romantic thing anyone could do.' Parshanti sighed.

Sergeant Pillay looked jealous, but Parshanti did not notice. When you are beautiful like her, you can ignore how men look because, chances are, it's you they are looking at.

'Mrs Simpson is too old for him,' Sergeant Pillay said sourly. 'The king should first marry a young woman who can give him sons. That's his duty. Then once he has a son to become the next king, he can marry his Mrs Simpson. That's what I would do. And I would arrest and execute all the newspaper people and ministers who say I can't. That's what the secret service is for, right?'

Le Froy went back into his office with a snort. But he didn't contradict Pillay.

I was sure Nicole Covington was hiding something, but not under her clothes. Undressing in front of strange men was a stunt to distract. De Souza hadn't even been there and he still had a glazed look in his eyes so it clearly worked.

Nicole Covington struck me as a cross between Wallis Simpson, Scarlett O'Hara and the Whore of Babylon. Flirting with men was her way of broadcasting her femininity, like the *tok-tok mee* seller rattles his wooden clappers to announce that fresh-cooked noodles are available. And we still didn't know what she and Victor Glossop had fought about on the day he died.

Could Nicole have killed her fiancé because he wanted to call off their wedding? Or . . .

'What if Nicole found out that Victor was having an affair?' She looked like a woman whose jealousy was in the Hell Hath No Fury category.

'Here?' Parshanti said dismissively. 'Who with?'

'Someone who followed him out here or someone he had just met . . .' Neither seemed likely, given how he had followed her onto the ship to make his dramatic proposal. 'What if Victor found out that Nicole was seeing someone else?'

'Again, who?'

'Kenneth Mulliner?' I suggested.

'I'll leave the magazines with you.' Abruptly, Parshanti got up and left.

I'd thought we were going to lunch together, but guessed she was going home to change out of her new dress since there was no one in the office worth getting it dirty for.

I thought about Nicole Covington. She had slapped her son for calling her a black widow. But 'black widow' doesn't really apply to a woman who's lost only one husband. And I still didn't believe a child Junior's age, no matter how interested in bugs, would know the term or apply it to his mother. Junior must have heard someone using it. Had that someone also planted suspicions in Victor's mind?

It had to have been Kenneth or Dr Covington – unless, of course, it had been Victor himself.

But it was no use speculating before I'd had the chance to talk to Junior again. I returned to the magazines. The gossipy specu-lations and advertisements for teeth whiteners and scented hand creams made me feel as if I had eaten too much coconut ice. I don't know how people read these things for fun. But then I found an old article that made me knock on Le Froy's door.

'Sir, here's a Pip's Squeaks piece that claims Radley Covington married Nicole Robert because he suspected her of being interested in someone else.'

'Name?'

'No name given. He's referred to here as' – I read from the magazine – '"a Jewish university professor up in an ivory tower who writes cutting pieces warning of the rise of fascism in the slums below". I could ask Nicole . . .'

'Get hold of the writer and find out what other information he has.'

'No one knows who the writer is, sir. "Pip's Squeaks" is written by an anonymous source. Even the papers claim they don't know his real identity. He writes about American and British high society from the inside, so he has to keep his cover.'

'Did this "Pip" discuss Glossop's upcoming marriage?'

'No. Only the proposal.'

Le Froy started to say something about wiring the papers, but just then I saw something out of the window that made me leap out of my chair and push past Sergeant Pillay, who had just come in with tea.

'Stomach?' Sergeant Pillay asked sympathetically. 'You want charcoal tablets?'

'No.'

Parshanti had not gone home to change her dress after all.

'I think you should take a harder look at Kenneth Mulliner,' I called, as I headed out. 'I don't trust that man!'

Trusting Kenneth Mulliner

The rain had stopped but it was not yet hot. Small birds were squabbling for bugs in the roadside weeds while larger ones scrabbled around the buildings for discarded food or, oddly, cigarette ends. Singapore had just had a bath and felt pleasantly new and fresh.

What was less pleasant was seeing Parshanti and Kenneth together further up the road. I hadn't been mistaken. I hurried back into the Detective Shack. Three surprised faces turned in my direction. 'I'm going for an early lunch.' I grabbed the umbrella that served as a walking stick as well as protection from people and weather. Sergeant de Souza started to say his mother had prepared her special *lontong* for everyone in the office to share, but I waved and left.

I wasn't really following Parshanti. I meant to keep my distance as long as they stayed in public. But Kenneth noticed me and stopped. Parshanti didn't look pleased. Well, that made two of us. At least she had taken off those silly gloves.

'Hello, there! Where are you going in such a hurry, Su Lin?'

If Parshanti's wearing a going-out frock instead of a work dress in the middle of a weekday hadn't warned me, her suddenly high social voice would have.

'Shouldn't you be at work?' The eyes she narrowed at me warned me not to say anything that might make her look bad in front of Kenneth.

He stubbed out his cigarette (on someone's pristine white-painted window ledge!). 'Parshanti was just telling me that you and Harry Palin are friends. She didn't realize you see him as a suspect in the murder case.'

'Everyone is a suspect. Even you, Mr Mulliner.'

Parshanti gasped and hit my arm – much harder than a sweet, flirtatious young lady should. 'Su Lin! You can't say things like that to a friend!'

'It's practically libel,' Kenneth said lightly. 'In America, you could be strung up for saying things like that to a white man.' But he said it in a way that suggested he was teasing rather than threatening me. He swept off his sun hat and made me a mock bow. 'But I don't mind. Kenneth Mulliner, murder suspect, at your service.'

They both laughed and I saw my mistake. Now they had shared (what they thought was) a joke, Parshanti felt even more comfortable with him.

I remembered what the Dale Carnegie book in the Mission Centre said about winning trust. 'You must feel terrible about what happened to your friend. Is Mrs Covington any better? Do you know if her friend who writes the Pip's Squeaks articles has been in touch with her?'

'Pip's Squeaks?' Kenneth raised an eyebrow. 'What makes you say that?'

'Do you know it? I have no idea how much of what he writes is true, but "Pip" is very entertaining!'

'I think you can rely on pretty much everything you read in Pip's Squeaks. Seems to be a matter of honour with that chap.'

'I wonder how he knows so many famous people.' Parshanti got back into the conversation. She only read Pip's Squeaks for the people Pip mentioned, not caring about his clever observations or the way he manipulated language.

'He might write about you one day and make you famous, Miss Shankar.'

'Oh, if only, Mr Mulliner.' Parshanti giggled. She might fancy herself sophisticated, but the truth was, she didn't have any more experience with young men than I did. Her mixed race (evident in the golden skin that a new blue frock showed up so well) frightened off most serious admirers. Mrs Shankar frightened off the rest.

'Call me Kenneth. Can I call you Patricia?'

Parshanti looked embarrassed. I realized she must have assumed he remembered her as well as she remembered him. She recovered quickly, 'My name is Parshanti, but you can call me Shanti for short.' A tendril of hair escaped her plait and she was winding it around her finger with her head tilted. It was a familiar gesture that filled me with dread. Sometimes I think the presence of an attractive man cuts off the blood supply to her brain and makes her stupid. And I could see she found Kenneth Mulliner attractive. The sharp dread you feel when a dog with big teeth fixes its eyes on you assailed me.

'Shanti. Shall I or shan't I, Shanti?'

Parshanti giggled again. Then there was an awkward pause. If

I had had the least bit of tact, I would have left them alone to get to know each other better. But I have always valued facts over tact.

'Come on.' I tried to get Parshanti away. 'Let's go to the fishball noodle stall. I'm hungry.'

'What's the hurry? It's too early for your lunch break, isn't it? You always say you can't just leave work when you feel like it.'

'Why don't you go and question your friend Harry Palin over lunch, if you've nothing better to do?' Kenneth suggested.

'Is it true the police suspect Harry Palin? Su Lin, you can't believe that! Poor Harry! You know he'd never hurt anybody.'

Once I got the chance I was going to have a serious talk with Parshanti: she had to learn not to talk to suspects about suspects.

'We will be interviewing everyone who knew the dead man,' I said. 'Especially Mrs Covington, when she feels up to talking. I thought Dr Covington was Nicole's father at first. Don't you find it strange they're travelling together when they don't seem to get along well?'

'Su Lin! You can't say things like that!' Parshanti hissed.

'Anyone can see Dr Covington doesn't get along with his daughter-in-law.'

'They were living together in America,' Kenneth said, 'and travelling together is just an extension of that. Nicole must find the old man useful. He spends more time with Junior than she does. And Taylor is a very rich man, of course. Our Nicole hates being alone and likes rich men. She'll keep Taylor around until she finds the next. It should have been Victor, but now poor little Nicole will have to start again with someone else.'

I had theorized that Kenneth was secretly in love with Nicole, based on his letting her boss him around. Most women wouldn't have dared till after they were safely married. But now he sounded as if he didn't even like her. Of course, he might just be a very good actor, which meant I shouldn't trust what he was saying now.

Or it might be a front the two of them had cooked up together, which would raise Kenneth Mulliner to the top of my suspect list, along with his possible lady love.

'And what about Dr Covington?' I asked. 'Why does he put up with her? Why doesn't he settle somewhere with his grandson?'

Parshanti flared, 'If Nicole Covington was travelling with her mother-in-law instead of her father-in-law, everyone would be singing her praises. Like Ruth and Naomi in the Bible. *Entreat me not to leave thee, or to return from following after thee: for whither thou goest, I will go; and where thou lodgest, I will lodge: thy people shall be my people, and thy God my God.* Stop being so judgemental, Chen Su Lin!'

I was taken aback. I hadn't thought Parshanti paid any attention during our Bible-study classes. *I* hadn't. After all, Bible study (though compulsory) had not been a subject in the Cambridge exams.

Kenneth was also stunned. He stared for a moment, then threw back his head and laughed so hard he had to wipe tears from his eyes and snot from his nose. 'I never thought to travel halfway around the world to have Bible passages quoted to me by an Oriental!' He offered his arm to Parshanti. 'Mademoiselle, walk with me back to the Farquhar. We'll have lunch there, and perhaps I can persuade you to tell your friend I am innocent.'

Parshanti glanced at me to see if I appreciated the honour she was being offered. I shook my head urgently. Parshanti took Kenneth's arm and they turned in the direction of the hotel.

'Mr Mulliner,' I said, 'were you waiting to see Chief Inspector Le Froy about something? You were lurking outside the office.'

'What's that? Oh, no, not lurking. I decided to take a walk. See something of the town. Glad I did.' He patted Parshanti's hand.

'And why do you continue spending time with Nicole, Mr Mulliner?'

'Because of your chief inspector,' Kenneth called back, without turning. I suppose he didn't think it necessary when walking away from an Oriental. Lucky for him I wasn't petty enough to mind. 'If he's keeping me on this damned island I might as well make the most of my time here.'

Parshanti's glance over her shoulder was a mix of excitement and pleading. *Look who I'm with!* And *Please don't spoil this for me!*

I should tell her parents: that would be the smart thing to do. But they would be so furious with her and she would be furious with me. And I had no proof – yet – to justify putting Kenneth Mulliner at the top of my list of murder suspects.

They clearly didn't want me around. So, of course, I followed them.

Kaeseven

———◆———

'Excuse me, miss.'
    I jerked my face out of the bougainvillaea hedge (ouch!) and saw a tall, thin figure behind me. I thought it was a suspicious hotel employee. I was on the street side of the bushes flanking the lawn patio of the Farquhar's tea room, peering through thorny branches to keep an eye on Parshanti and Kenneth at their table.

As long as my friend was in sight I knew she wasn't being murdered by my top murder suspect. Though, of course, we didn't yet know how Victor Glossop had been killed. If he had been poisoned, there was nothing to stop Kenneth Mulliner slipping something into Parshanti's soup even as I watched.

I knew I couldn't say that to the hotel staff. If challenged, I planned to tell them I was Parshanti's servant girl and had been told to wait outside for her. As it turned out, I didn't have to lie.

'Miss Chen! I thought that was you.'

The white uniform was unfamiliar, but I remembered the voice and grinning teeth.

'Cookie!' I exclaimed (quietly) in delight. 'What are you doing here? I thought you went back to India after – after the trial and everything,' He had been in charge of the kitchen at Government House when Harry Palin's father had been acting governor.

'Kaeseven at your service, Miss Chen.' Cookie – sorry, Kaeseven – looked as glad to see me as I was him. 'I am no longer employed as a domestic cook. Now I am number-two chef here in the Farquhar Hotel.'

'I am so glad.' And I was, but not only to see an old friend. It might be very useful to have someone I trusted working at the Farquhar.

'You must come and see my kitchen. I want to feed you again, Miss Chen.'

Oh, how I wanted to. Watching people eat always makes me hungry. My stomach was growling, and I was so thirsty I could hardly think of anything else. But I was there on a job, even if self-appointed. 'I can't right now. Sorry. Oh, Kaeseven, do you think you can you bring me some water?'

Kaeseven pushed his face into the shrubbery as I had been doing. 'Your friend and her companion will be here for some time more. They ordered dessert and coffee to follow their meal. You can come back here to watch when I send out their dessert. Come, Miss Chen. Does the inspector know that Mr Victor and Miss Nicole had a big fight the day he died? And that later the same night Miss Nicole had a big fight with Mr Kenneth?'

He knew me well, dangling the information like bait.

'We heard Victor and Nicole had a fight but we don't know what about.'

'Come,' said Kaeseven. 'Eat first, then talk.'

Kaeseven settled me at a table in the open-air space behind the kitchen. It was where vegetables were prepared and there were trays of water chestnuts and mung bean sprouts awaiting attention. I started topping and tailing the sprouts as I watched the goings-on in the room. I was surprised things were not busier during lunch hour.

'Dinner service is much busier than lunch. Most of the guests prefer to eat out at midday,' Kaeseven explained, when he came back. He looked approvingly at my efforts and took over as I greedily drained the glass of sour plum juice and started to eat the simple dish of yellow rice and curried vegetables he had fixed.

'We get a few locals coming in for business lunches. When they are working they never notice what they eat, so it is a good time for the younger cooks to practise.'

Even if the diners did not notice, I saw all the dishes were brought out to him for vetting before they were taken into the dining room. Kaeseven was still the exacting 'Cookie' I had known in the governor's mansion. I was glad his cooking had got him a hotel job.

'Those people, there is a small boy with them. Nice boy, but he steals things.'

'Junior? What things?'

'Small things. Like a little dog that's burying things to dig up later. No point reporting, but if you find my *makkhana phirni* upstairs, bring it down for me. It is my own, not belonging to the hotel.'

'Just now you said Nicole fought with Victor Glossop the night he died. And then with Kenneth Mulliner. Do you know what either of those fights were about?' I spoke with a mouth full of aubergine, sweet potato and cauliflower deliciously seasoned with coriander, cumin, turmeric and who knew what else?

'Miss Nicole wants to go to Mr Victor's party. He says it is just for . . . bachelors.' There would have been professional female companions for the bachelors. Perhaps that was what Nicole had been upset about.

'Miss Nicole wants parties with dancing and cocktail drinks.'

'How do you know that?'

Kaeseven shrugged. 'Sometimes, when people shout at each other, you cannot help knowing. And then Miss Nicole came to the kitchen and shouted at me, the number-two chef.'

'What?' This startled me enough to stop eating. 'Nicole shouted at you? Why?'

'She asked me to make a big cake for the party. Big enough that she can hide inside and jump out. She said in America all the best hotels without fail provide big cakes for women to jump out of.'

'What did you say?'

'I told her that for such cakes she must order in advance. Special equipment is needed. You cannot tell me in the afternoon that tonight you want a big cake to jump out of.'

'What did she say?'

Kaeseven signalled and a serving boy put two cups of aromatic mint tea on the table.

'Miss Nicole said she will complain about me to the manager. She will tell the manager I was rude to her. She said she is going to tell everybody that my kitchen is dirty and full of rats. And that night she didn't eat dinner in the restaurant. None of them did.'

He looked sad. No matter how ridiculous, a white woman's word carried more weight than the truth in Singapore. Nicole's wild accusations might cost Kaeseven his job at the hotel.

'Don't worry. Nicole has other things to think about now than jumping out of cakes. Cookie— Kaeseven, Le Froy will want to know this. If I type out what you told me, will you sign it and answer any questions he has?'

'You read it to me first and I sign it. But I don't like to answer questions. I am a chef, not a spy. The things white people ask for. Women jumping out of cakes, I ask you . . .' A dreamy look glazed Kaeseven's eyes. 'It would have to be a big cake. And there must be something underneath for structural support . . . a bamboo framework maybe. On a rolling tray. I could use marzipan over gingerbread over a frame . . .'

I could almost see the cake forming in his head. But just then the serving boy returned. 'Sir? The table you asked me to watch? They are ready for dessert.'

———◆———

Back at my vantage point, I saw Kaeseven had been true to his word. The desserts had not yet been served. But now Parshanti and Kenneth were standing by their table and Kenneth was talking urgently to Nicole Covington, who had just appeared.

Whatever he said seemed to satisfy her. She waved Parshanti away without looking at her, sat down – on Parshanti's seat – and looked at the dessert the serving boy hesitantly placed in front of her.

Parshanti said something to Kenneth, who answered briefly. He didn't look at her either. His whole attention was on Nicole as he moved to sit on the chair beside her rather than across the table.

Parshanti hesitated, then fled the restaurant. She would be upset but, more importantly, she was safe and I had been right. Kenneth Mulliner was in love with Nicole Covington. What I had just seen weighed in favour of my theory that they had planned the murder of her fiancé together.

Of course I couldn't tell Parshanti I had followed her. Once she was safe, I was annoyed with myself for being alarmed. There was no reason why a modern young woman should not lunch at the Farquhar Hotel with a modern young man.

But until Nicole had turned up at their table, Parshanti and Kenneth had seemed so comfortable and happy together. Shouldn't I want my friend to be happy?

That gave me more reason to prove Kenneth Mulliner was a murderer. It would show I wasn't trying to destroy my friend's potential happiness, just saving her life.

Facts and Fancies

◆

Back at the Detective Shack, I compiled Kaeseven's information. On the night of Victor's death, Nicole had stayed in her suite with a headache. Taylor had kept Junior with him, their dinner sent to Junior's downstairs playroom.

Typing always calms me. I find the steady clicks more soothing than any mantra, and I found myself regretting I had not been nicer to Kenneth Mulliner. Or, at least, not shown my suspicion so openly. Guilty or not, he had known Victor Glossop better than anyone else there. A casual conversation might have drawn nuggets of information from him that wouldn't come up in an official interview.

My grandmother always said it is important to know our enemies. The mission-school ladies had told us to love our enemies. I thought Parshanti was carrying that too far but it might be helpful if I asked her what she and Kenneth had talked about.

It was hugely frustrating not knowing what had killed Victor Glossop. Neither his medical records nor the autopsy results had been delivered yet. If it turned out that the man had died of a chronic heart condition, all the excitement would be over and life would resume its dull, rainy routine.

I hoped there would be more information in the photographs I had taken in Victor Glossop's room. Sometimes the focus of a camera lens highlights things you miss amid the distractions of real life. But although Dr Shankar had started developing them immediately (pulling down the blinds in Mrs Shankar's sewing room), it took time: photograph development depended on silver halides, not quicksilver halides, as he liked to joke.

Until we had facts, there was little we could do aside from collecting background information. It is hard to question suspects when you don't know for sure that a murder has been committed.

I looked up as I heard Sergeant Pillay say, 'Pass them to Miss Chen.' I smiled at Corporal Wong as he came to my desk with last night's records from HQ. All police incidents that might relate to gangs, drugs, prostitutes or spies were copied to the Detective Unit.

I liked Corporal Wong. As one of the youngest officers at HQ, he was always getting stuck with the night shift. Luckily, he seemed to be holding up well, though I know he was teased by the other men because his mother and grandmother took turns to bring a cooked supper to him at the night desk.

'How were things at HQ last night?'

'Nothing much. Disturbance at O'Reilly's Bar. Some men got into a fight but don't want to talk about it. The owner wants the police to make them pay for the damage. An imported mirror was broken. Very expensive, he says.'

O'Reilly's was a foreign-owned bar, frequented mainly by

foreign sailors on shore leave. A local owner would never have put a mirror in a pub where it would attract demons and spirits. And a local owner would have used his own connections – my uncle Chen, most likely – to settle things rather than call the police.

'And a woman found dead at Yap Pun Kai. Looks like a self-kill.' Corporal Wong lowered his voice and used the Cantonese term for suicide.

Yap Pun Kai, literally Japan Street, was Trengganu Street, which ran along the massive old betel-nut plantations and housed most of Singapore's Japanese brothels. Le Froy was convinced it was also full of Japanese spies, but the Home Office in London refused to see Japan as a threat.

'Karayuki-san?' That translates as 'women who have gone overseas' and refers to Japanese sex workers from famine-struck farming regions in their country. The Japanese consul general in Singapore had banned Japanese brothels almost ten years ago, but Japan's women were still its third-largest foreign-currency earner, after silk and coal. Those women fuelled the Japanese economy with sex.

'Looks like it. No sign of violence. She was alone in her room and two of her house sisters found her. She had drawn erotic love pictures all over herself, as though planning to meet a client, but she didn't go out last night and no one visited her.'

That surprised me. Japanese women with families to support seldom committed suicide. But maybe she was sick, or maybe the parent or child she had been working to support had died, leaving her without reason to work or live.

'I checked for signs of assault but there was nothing.' Corporal

Wong didn't quite manage to hide a yawn. 'I think there were bugs in her room. She was all swollen.'

'Thank you, Meng. Get some rest.'

'I hope to work in the Detective Unit one day. If your boss needs help here, can you mention my name?'

'Of course.'

Why couldn't Parshanti fall in love with a nice, safe young man like Corporal Wong? My brain answered my own question even as my mind asked it: Wong's very Cantonese family wouldn't approve of her. The Wongs wouldn't even have approved of a Malay Straits-born girl like me.

Not to mention that nice, safe young Corporal Wong Meng Kong was dull.

'Miss Chen?' Corporal Wong alerted me from the open doorway. Once he saw he had my attention he pointed, then slipped out and disappeared.

Looking beyond him I saw a man getting out of the large official car parked in front of the Detective Shack.

The rains had stopped but the unpaved road in front of the office was still muddy. All of us who had been outside were muddied up to the ankles at least. But the man standing in the doorway of the Detective Shack was spotless. Governor McPherson was back.

'Good morning. Is Chief Inspector Le Froy here? I'm afraid we don't have an appointment.'

'Please come in, Your Excellency. I will get him for you at once.'

Le Froy was not in the office. In fact, a quick look around told me I was alone in the office. De Souza had gone to relieve Constable Kwok who had spent the night at the Farquhar. I hoped

Sergeant Pillay had seen the governor's car and gone for Le Froy without telling me, but I doubted it. Prakesh had been disappearing more and more often recently. I suspected he had found himself a girlfriend. But this was not the time to think about it. As soon as I'd got the governor a chair and a drink I would run out to fetch Le Froy myself.

'Please take a seat, Your Excellency— Oh! Good morning, madam.'

The governor stood aside to let his wife enter before him. Mrs Viola Jane McPherson was small and round, like her husband. I hadn't heard anything about her other than that the Government House cooks and servants liked her.

According to Kaeseven's sources, as soon as she arrived Mrs McPherson had delighted her new staff by saying, 'Aside from pigs' intestines and frogs' legs you can surprise us!' when discussing the Government House menus. She even allowed local *kueh*s and almond jellies alongside the Victoria sponge on her tea table.

'Good morning.' Mrs McPherson seemed surprised to see me. I hoped she wasn't one of those ladies who didn't approve of women in the workplace.

I gestured towards the wooden stools that were all we had for visitors. It seemed wrong for the governor and his wife to sit on them, as though they were locals being questioned. Perhaps I could pull out the chair behind Le Froy's desk. But for Mrs McPherson?

'If you want to talk to Chief Inspector Le Froy, he can come to see you at Government House.'

'Didn't want to bother the man. He must have his hands full. Unofficial visit, this.'

'Would you like a cup of tea?' I could set the kettle to boil before I went for Le Froy.

They both declined. Mrs McPherson settled herself on a stool with a smile and tugged her bemused-looking husband onto another next to hers. 'I love these wooden stools,' she said. 'Traditional furniture made the traditional way. That's what I call authentic culture.'

'Governor McPherson,' Le Froy said, coming in. I released a huge breath of relief. Sergeant Pillay winked at me as he slipped in behind him. He was still breathing hard. He must have run all the way to find Le Froy. And had they run back? Le Froy didn't seem out of breath but, then, he never did.

Governor and Mrs McPherson

◆

'**G**ood morning, Your Excellency. I'm sorry to keep you waiting. Good morning, Mrs McPherson. How can I help you?'

'The Glossop boy,' Governor McPherson said, suddenly all business. 'Victor Glossop. Found dead in his hotel room. Should have sent me your results. What do you have?'

'The Glossops are family friends,' Mrs McPherson said. 'Or, rather, family acquaintances.'

'My condolences,' Le Froy said. He went behind his desk but did not sit. 'We communicated the news to Sir Roderick Glossop only yesterday.'

'Sir Roderick wired,' Governor McPherson said. 'And Colonel Mosley-Partington. Godfather to the dead boy, you know. Wanted to come over. Put him off. By the time he gets out . . . no. Not in this climate. Pointless. Told him we would do all we could. As for our own son.'

I discreetly recorded the governor's words in my notebook. The governor and his wife might have come in search of information but, as friends of the Glossops, they were a valuable source of information.

'Victor Glossop was like a son to you?' Le Froy asked.

'Great heavens, no!' Mrs McPherson exclaimed. 'No, no, no. Our boys are not going to grow up into Victor Glossops, not if I have any hand in the raising of them.'

'Viola Jane—'

Little Mrs McPherson laid a plump hand on the governor's arm, hushing him.

'Gregory, if he's to do his job, the chief inspector needs to know everything we can tell him about Victor Glossop. So you just sit yourself down and be discreet while your irresponsible wife tells all.'

'Bit of a bounder, that boy,' the governor said. He obviously supported his wife's opinion, though he could not bring himself to speak ill of the dead. 'Boys will be boys.'

Mrs McPherson patted his hand. I liked the new governor's wife more and more. Singapore was a business investment for our colonial masters, and profits counted for more than people when major decisions were made. But how those decisions were administered on a personal level made a huge difference.

Le Froy moved out from behind his desk and leaned against it, facing the governor's wife. 'Mrs McPherson?'

'You would think Victor Glossop was a good catch, wouldn't you? A second son born after five girls. Of course you can't control these things, though goodness knows why not. A woman can read Marie Stopes even if she's not allowed to talk about her.'

'Viola Jane—'

'I'm sorry, Gregory. It just makes me so angry, smart women

acting helpless and ending up useless. Anyway, as I was saying, the Glossops have a healthy elder son so this second boy came as a bonus. Their first, David, is such a nice, dull boy. Never gave a moment's trouble and married an earl's daughter. But even the best families sometimes produce children who are a little difficult, especially when there are so many of them. It must be a little like governing Russia, trying to feed and educate the masses.'

In her forthrightness, Mrs McPherson reminded me of Parshanti's Scottish mother. Seeming to feel my eyes on her, she glanced in my direction and gave me a sudden sweet smile.

'Of course, this is all confidential,' the governor said. But I noticed he did not seem uncomfortable at letting his wife talk. So, he was less concerned with how he looked than with getting things done. And he didn't mind a woman taking charge of the doing. 'Thought knowing more about the boy might help you. Victor might not have looked much, but he was joint heir to the Glossop family distillery. The Glossops established themselves with cheap alcohol but money made by one generation can be lost by the next. Word has it things are a bit rocky for them right now.

'Times are hard all round,' he went on, 'but the Glossop factory equipment is all ready to switch to distilling fuel for war machines. A war would make the Glossops rich again. Richer. It would have been a good time for a young man like Victor to get into the family business. But he wasn't interested in work. No sense of discipline. Got himself sent down from Oxford.'

His wife elaborated: 'No matter where they sent him, Victor gravitated towards the very worst crowd. He had a real talent for that. They can't have been sorry when he decided to get out of

England. "He's coming your way. Give him something to do to keep him out of trouble," his father wired Gregory. As if that boy did anything other than get into trouble!'

Mrs McPherson turned to me. 'When Victor visited us in London he made Ellie cry. Ellie was my daily girl. I asked her to help Mrs Covington and her son when they stayed with us,' she explained to me. 'Ellie wouldn't tell me what happened to her but she wouldn't come back to work till after they'd left.'

'Nicole Covington was staying with you in London?' Le Froy asked. 'I didn't know that. How do you know Mrs Covington?'

'Don't know her. Victor turned up with them. No warning,' Governor McPherson said flatly. 'Bad form. But what's one to do? You can't send a young woman to a hotel alone, even if she's American. Viola Jane sorted it all out. Blankets, bathtubs, everything. You are a blessing, my dear.'

Mrs McPherson's smile showed the pleasure this gave her. But she didn't allow herself to be distracted. 'Victor was staying in his family's London house. But it wouldn't have been correct for Nicole to go there. No engagement had been thought of then. It would have been a scandal. The papers are so terrible, these days. Victor said he needed a place to put up some friends of his. I was expecting a couple of Oxford boys and instead I got Americans!'

'Was Dr Taylor Covington staying with you too?' I asked, so caught up in her recital that I spoke without thinking. 'And Kenneth Mulliner?'

The governor looked surprised, as though he had forgotten I was there. But his wife nodded, as friendly as if we were having a good chat over stringing beans. 'Oh, yes. Dr Covington came to us. Pleasant enough, for an American. Mr Mulliner stayed with

Victor, but came to visit. Victor introduced him as the son of his father's vicar. At first I didn't trust him. I have nothing against the young man, but as a friend of Victor's . . .'

'I thought Victor was polite enough,' Governor McPherson said.

'Oh, to you and me the boy was all sweetness and light. Well, of course he was. He asked you for money, didn't he? Just to tide him over until his father's came through?'

Her husband's noncommittal laugh confirmed this.

'In fact, at the time I thought it was Mr Mulliner who was interested in Mrs Covington. He reminded me of an old Boxer we used to have.' She turned to her husband. 'Remember Lord Fartescue? How he used to follow you around drooling? That's how that vicar's son—'

'Mulliner. Kenneth Mulliner.'

'That's right. That's what Mulliner looked like. His eyes following Mrs Covington around every time she moved.'

Kenneth Mulliner had been following Nicole? That cemented what I had seen at the hotel. I wanted to jump up and down in excitement and dash out to question him. 'We should talk to Kenneth Mulliner!' I cried.

'I think the governor has something else to say,' Le Froy observed.

'Hmm. Well. Yes. That's the thing. Colonel Mosley-Partington sent another wire this morning,' the governor said.

I could tell we were coming to the real reason the McPhersons had turned up at our temporary shack without warning. 'He says the autopsy will most likely show the boy died of natural causes. That that would be best all round.'

'Dr Leask and Dr Shankar are testing for a range of poisons,' Le Froy said. 'Chemical tests that take time to show results.'

'Mrs Glossop and Mrs Mosley-Partington are cousins,' Mrs McPherson put in, 'Daphne Mosley-Partington was a de Havilland before her marriage. Not sisters, though they hated each other like sisters.' She looked to her husband, as though she was nudging him to continue.

The governor's eyes landed on the former king's portrait on the wall. 'What a waste. Waste of a good frame too.'

Mrs McPherson stepped in: 'The colonel says you must not be allowed to use Victor's death to trump up your new Detective Unit. He told us he has issued a statement saying Victor died of an eastern fever and the Colonial Office will tolerate no further attempts to harass the grieving family.'

I jumped to my feet. 'He didn't die of a fever! He was fine earlier that evening. All ready to go out to party—'

Mrs McPherson held up a plump hand. 'That's the official stand, dear. We can't say anything to upset the men now, with the economy doing so badly. But Lilian Glossop sent me a personal message, saying her mother wants to know what really happened to Victor.'

'And there's some other information here that may help you find out.' Governor McPherson passed a plain brown envelope to Le Froy. 'You can trust it. You don't need to know where it comes from. But for now, as far as we are concerned, the boy officially died of an eastern fever.'

Lipstick and Pigtails

◆

The plain brown envelope contained a private investigator's research into Mrs Nicole Covington. It seemed to have been commissioned by Victor's family and put together in a hurry. I had already seen most of the information in newspaper articles and Pip's Squeaks. The only thing new was the name Eric Schumer, an old flame of Nicole's.

'Is he a Jewish university professor in an ivory tower?' I wondered. 'Could Eric Schumer be trying to get Nicole back?'

'Eric Schumer is dead.' Le Froy passed me the next page of the report.

It added weight to Nicole's black-widow image, but didn't increase our pool of suspects. And officially there was now no case. Until the autopsy report came back, maybe even after that, Victor Glossop had died of some unnamed fever. There was also no information on the woman who might have been with Victor that night, although a ten-dollar reward had been offered to her for coming forward.

◆

When I collected my crime-scene photographs from Dr Shankar, Sergeant de Souza (with some embarrassment) said the betel and lipstick patterns on Victor's body resembled the erotic designs with which some of the Japanese prostitutes adorned themselves. 'Not as professionally done, of course. Looks like he drew them himself.'

'Yes.' Le Froy was studying the prints intently. Dr Shankar had magnified them, so you could see the individual dots that made up each photograph. 'He was right-handed and clearly drew them on himself. But someone else painted his back.'

The patterns there were crude outlines but clearly done by a more experienced hand.

'De Souza, you say the Karayuki-san paint these patterns on themselves?'

'On themselves and their partners, sir. They are known for drawing erotic pictures on their skin before sex. To be licked off, I believe. Sometimes men picked up drunk have lipstick traces left on them.'

Le Froy seized a pencil and scribbled questions he wanted passed to Mrs McPherson or wired to London.

———◆———

Later I typed them out with three carbons because his handwriting was a schoolteacher's nightmare. I could only decipher it because I had learned to follow his thought processes. When his brain was fermenting wildly, he might forget his questions before the answers came.

But I'd been surprised when he slipped out of the office soon after without giving any further instructions. His mind was clearly on something else, his secret project. But what was it?

'I wish the boss would send me to interview Mrs Covington,' Sergeant Pillay said. 'I'm sure I could get her to talk. You have to know how to talk to women.'

Sergeant Pillay fancied himself a ladies' man and we still had not managed to get a statement from Nicole Covington. Le Froy had gone to see her at the Farquhar again. When he asked why she had not mentioned the fight between her and Victor, she became hysterically upset and refused to say more. After that, to our (my, at least) surprise, Le Froy had let her alone. I hoped her womanly wiles hadn't won him over.

'She wasn't at the stag party,' Sergeant de Souza went on. 'She can't know anything about what killed him if you think he was given poison that evening. And what poison takes two days to act? Anyway, I don't care if she poisoned him or not. And I'm sure she didn't. I just wish I could interview her. I want to ask her for a photograph.'

I was irritated by how stupid men could be. Even the men who were supposed to be detectives wouldn't take a female suspect seriously if they thought she was good-looking. The Farquhar Hotel was not pleased that Victor's death had been officially ascribed to malaria or yellow fever, possibly both. The Colonial Office was so afraid of those diseases that it advised travellers to avoid Singapore.

With the boss out of the office, I slipped away to look for Parshanti. Never mind interviewing Nicole Covington, I hadn't even managed to have a good talk with my old friend since I'd followed her with Kenneth Mulliner.

I had tried to get Parshanti alone several times, not only to tell her she was better off without him (which even she must realize by now!) but because I wanted to find out exactly what he had said. The lies people come up with can tell you a lot about them.

But Parshanti was suddenly too busy to meet me.

'It's important,' I pleaded, when I finally found her helping with the hemming in her mother's workroom behind the pharmacy. 'I have to talk to you.'

'You can talk in front of Mam. She'll keep whatever you say secret, won't you, Mam?'

'What's that, dearie?' Mrs Shankar paused the treadle on her Singer sewing machine. It was super-speedy and much faster than hand sewing, but so noisy. She had a lot of work to catch up on since she had been shut out of her sewing room when her husband had commandeered it to develop our prints.

'Has Su Lin found a young man?' She smiled at me sweetly and seemed to think my glare at her daughter confirmed this.

Mrs Shankar might be much more liberal than my family, but I didn't want to tell her that her daughter might have fallen in love with a murderer. Much as I distrusted Kenneth Mulliner, I couldn't betray Parshanti in that warm, busy workroom.

So, I went back to the Detective Shack. I had run out of typing and filing and was wiping down the backs and undersides of the desks when I saw, standing in the doorway, Dr Taylor Covington with Junior. It gave me a blip of pleasure to see grandfather and grandson together. Le Froy had returned and stood looking at them with a preoccupied expression.

'Dr Covington,' I said.

'Wanted a word with you. I hope we're not interrupting

anything,' Dr Covington said politely. He must have thought Le Froy was not busy and could be interrupted.

But Le Froy, his mind spinning complicated connections, looked impatiently at them. 'What do you want? The autopsy results aren't out yet. We'll let you know.'

'If Victor Glossop died of fever, why are we still being kept here?'

'Germs. Possibility of spreading infection. As a doctor you must understand.'

'You know very well—' Dr Covington stopped.

'Why don't you come and sit down?' I pulled a stool forward. 'I'm going to make tea,' I said. 'Would you like some orange squash, Junior?'

The child nodded, without releasing his grandfather's hand.

'He's crazy about orange squash,' Dr Covington said, 'aren't you, Junior? And I would appreciate coffee over tea, if there's any available. But don't put yourself to any trouble on my account.'

Le Froy also preferred coffee.

I wondered if American fathers spent more time with their children than Asian or British fathers. In fact, Junior seemed more comfortable with his father than with his mother . . . Startled, I caught myself. I had forgotten that Taylor was Radley's grand-father, not his father.

This was even more unusual. In my experience, grandmothers and unmarried aunts helped with children, not grandfathers. I had few memories of my own grandfathers, apart from being pushed towards them to offer my respects at Lunar New Year and at family weddings.

I returned with coffee, orange squash and a plate of Huntley & Palmer's biscuits. We had been given a huge tin by a trader after Le Froy had traced how his imported cigarettes were disappearing.

'Cookies!' Junior cried. 'Grandpa, may I?'

'Ask the pretty lady.'

'She's no lady. You said she's a pig's tail, not a lady.'

Taylor Covington made a little gesture that any adult would have recognized as 'not now'. Junior interpreted it as 'Repeat that more loudly, please,' and obliged with a little hop of pleasure as he looked up at his grandfather. 'Pig's tail. You said she's a pig's tail.'

Le Froy was looking at the doctor with interest now.

'I probably said she has a pigtail,' he explained genially to Le Froy. 'Like so many Orientals, you know. Men and women all with their pigtails.' He tugged gently at the hair at the base of Junior's head, making him squeal in laughing protest. 'Do you want a pigtail?'

I didn't have a pigtail. My hair was plaited and coiled around my head as usual. I wasn't offended by Junior. It was Taylor Covington taking the trouble to explain himself to Le Froy that made me think he had used the term as an insult. And I wondered what else Junior might have picked up from his grandfather. The black-widow-spider comment, for example.

'How is Mrs Covington?' I asked.

'That's why we're here, actually. Nicole wants to leave.' He was clearly glad of the change in subject. 'She heard on the grapevine that you've been questioning a local pilot. If you've got your man, there's no point in keeping us hanging on, eh?'

Harry Palin had indeed been taken in for questioning at Police Headquarters. But he had been released that morning without charge after the Colonial Office had decreed Glossop's death was due to fever.

'After what happened, you can imagine this place has unpleasant associations for her. She's eager to move on. I thought that, once you've given us the okay, we'd stop by the Cunard Line offices on the way back to the hotel so that I can book our passage. We thought of going on to Australia, given it's just a hop and a skip away from here.' He stopped as though waiting for Le Froy to comment.

Le Froy nodded. He didn't tell Dr Covington we knew that he and Kenneth Mulliner had already tried to book passage for their party out of Singapore and been refused till the police gave permission. 'We should be getting the autopsy results soon.'

'You've been saying that for days! Surely it makes no difference where we are when you get them. Nicole's impatient to be gone. She's not used to Singapore's climate and it's getting to her. No matter what caused Glossop's death, there's no reason to keep us here. And if it wasn't an accident, why, I'm sure you can sort it out without us. We're not vindictive folks. We'll leave it to your justice system. Look, man to man, how much is it going to cost me to speed up this business?'

Was the man openly offering to bribe Le Froy? I waited for Le Froy to tell him off or take him down.

'What do you think of the rise of Aryan supremacy and German nationalism in Europe?' Le Froy asked.

Dr Covington

◆

'I beg your pardon?' Dr Covington looked as taken aback as I felt.

'You took your daughter-in-law to watch Mr Hitler speak at a rally in Germany. That was where she met Victor Glossop, wasn't it?' That had also come out of Governor McPherson's envelope. I couldn't see how it was relevant but it was interesting to observe Dr Covington's reaction.

He nodded. 'We're not political. A lot of influential Americans think Herr Hitler's got something we can learn from and I thought we could see for ourselves. Yes, we met Victor Glossop there. There were a lot of British aristocrats around. I thought it would be a bit of a change for the poor girl, that's all.'

'Why did you tell us they met in London? Which was it?' Le Froy's voice was calm and conversational but he didn't smile when Dr Covington tried to laugh it off.

Le Froy always said there were two kinds of liar: those who lie for a purpose and those who lie out of habit. He said those in the second category were more dangerous because they so manipulate the truth that they fool even themselves. I could see he was trying to figure out which category Dr Covington belonged in.

'Is that the big question that's made you see us all as suspects? Well, let me explain things to you. They met first in Germany, then again in London. When you travel the world, you're thrown together with all sorts of people. And if they're civilized and English-speaking in a sea of damned foreigners, you become the closest of friends within ten minutes of meeting. But once you're back on home soil it's over. Nicole and I ran into Victor and Kenneth in Germany and we shared an English translator at those rallies. He told her to look him up if she got to London and she did. That's where they were officially introduced, if you like. Satisfied?'

'How did Mrs Covington enjoy the Hitler rallies?'

'Nicole's not intellectual.' Dr Covington shook his head. 'She goes in more for society than social improvements. She wasn't much interested until she met that young man. She perked right up on meeting him. She was taking an interest in life, fussing about clothes and talking about getting married again. I couldn't stop her heading for England once Victor left, although I'd planned for us to do a tour of the Alps. When they got engaged, I thought at least some good had come of it. And then this happened. The woman has bad luck with men. I can't explain it, but you can't deny it.'

Dr Covington saying 'bad luck with men' made me feel sorry for Nicole. I knew only too well that having people decide you're 'bad luck' makes your luck bad. I had been labelled 'bad luck' after polio and my parents' death. But it was to counter this that my grandmother had sent me to an English school, which had turned out to be a huge stroke of good luck for me. I felt sorry for Nicole Covington and wondered if she had been allowed to go to school.

The teachers at the mission school scoffed at the idea of 'luck'. 'There's only God, no such thing as luck!' I remember Miss Johnson saying. But if not for my childhood polio, I would never have gone to school. There is definitely an element of luck in our lives. Or you might call it an element of chance that you can't control, no matter how hard you work. It's never certain whether, in the long term, something will turn out bad or good.

'Losing her husband doesn't mean Nicole has bad luck with men,' I said. 'Her husband was your son. Losing him doesn't mean you have bad luck with children.'

Le Froy looked curiously at me. Then even more curiously at Dr Covington, to see how he would take it. For a moment the older man stiffened. He paled, and it was as though his brain was having difficulty processing what I'd said. His son's death was obviously still raw and painful. I was about to apologize (and never bring it up again) when he let out a great roar of laughter.

'You've got a brain on you, girl. I like that. That's a good point you made.' He reached over and squeezed my shoulder approvingly with a huge hand, and Junior grinned at me. 'I lost my Radley, that's true. He was my only son, my pride and joy and my hope for the future. And Junior here lost his only father. But we're making it up to each other. We're a good team, aren't we, Junior?'

'Yes, Grandpa,' the child said. 'We're the Covingtons!' His serious sweetness made us all smile.

'But my son and Victor weren't the only men Nicole has lost.' Dr Covington lowered his voice: 'You must have read or at least heard about the most famous book in America, *Gone With the Wind*?'

I'd heard of it, and nodded. Again, Dr Covington looked approving. 'It's all about the civil war in America. Well, our family roots are in Clayton County, Georgia, where the most important parts of the book are set. And, like Miss Scarlett O'Hara in the book, our Miss Nicole is every inch a Southern belle. That means she's almost as pretty as she makes people think she is.'

'I read *Uncle Tom's Cabin*,' I said. At school there had been a copy in the cupboard that served as a library.

Dr Covington snorted. 'Don't waste your time. That book started the war that crippled the South. Anyway, after what happened to my Radley, Nicole just couldn't settle down. She was talking about wanting to get away from everything. I thought it might be a good idea. And I had some business to take care of. So I took a house in New York for half a year. But we hadn't been in the city more than a couple of weeks when Nicole met someone new.'

'What was his name?' Le Froy glanced in my direction and I reached for my ever-ready notebook.

'Eric Schumer. A very pleasant young man but not at all the sort I would have thought Nicole would be attracted to.'

Eric Schumer! I turned to a new page in my notebook and underlined the name.

'Why wouldn't she?' Le Froy asked casually.

'Nicole's always had admirers, of course. That's not surprising. I suppose I thought she would want to take some time to get over Radley. To be with her boy. And young Mr Schumer – well, back home Nicole would never even have come across someone like him to say "Good day" to, let alone be thinking about getting married again.'

'Was she thinking of marrying him? What happened?'

Before answering Le Froy's question, Dr Covington glanced at Junior. The boy was fully occupied, colouring pictures in an old newspaper with the crayons Sergeant de Souza had produced. Satisfied, he continued, his voice even lower. 'I was informed by my banker that a Mr Schumer had made enquiries as to Nicole's accounts. He even enquired into my affairs. That was how it came to my attention. Old Harrison's son called me to verify that I had agreed to the investigation and I told him I had done no such thing. I knew nothing of it. Naturally I ordered everything stopped. I asked Nicole if she knew anything about it and she said Eric had asked if she knew how much Radley had left her to live on and she'd told him she had no idea. Apparently he'd taken that as licence to dig into our affairs. Good thing I've been dealing with Old Harrison for years. His son knows I wouldn't stand for some stranger snooping around my accounts.'

'Why not just tell Nicole how much money she has?'

Dr Covington took a deep breath. 'I didn't want her to know Radley hadn't left her much. He was young, you understand. Just starting out. He was barely finding his feet in business when he died. But Nicole has nothing to worry about. I'll make certain she's well looked after and has everything a young woman could want for a good life. She is the mother of my grandson, after all. Everything I have will go to Junior eventually. Radley was my only son. Who else would I leave it all to?'

'What if Nicole marries again?' Le Froy asked quietly.

'Whom she marries is entirely up to her. There's no changing that girl's mind once she's made it up. But no matter what Nicole does, Junior will always be my grandson,' Dr Covington said firmly. 'My only grandson. Nothing can ever change that now. I can't expect you to understand but the one focus of my life now is to do right by the boy. I only hope I stay alive and vital enough to see him grow up to be a man his poor father would have been proud of.'

I felt tears in my eyes. 'My grandmother brought me up after my parents died,' I said. I knew Ah Ma felt just as responsible for me as Dr Covington did for his grandson, although she would sooner have swallowed chicken droppings than make such a sentimental speech. 'I owe her everything. She says that grand-parents are as deeply invested as parents, but with more experience.'

Dr Covington nodded. 'I'm doing it as much for my son as my grandson. Junior is a bright boy. Nicole doesn't seem to understand he has lost as much as she has. More, in fact. She may find herself another husband. Junior has lost his only father for ever.'

Le Froy didn't seem affected. 'I gather Schumer changed his mind about Nicole after learning she depends on you for money?'

Dr Covington shook his head. 'I told Nicole he had been nosing into her affairs and she went and had a regular set-to with him. That's a Southern belle for you. Can't walk two steps in the sun to throw a ball with her little boy, but she'll brawl in the street in front of strangers. I wasn't there but, from what I heard, Nicole confronted Schumer over dinner. There was a scene in the restaurant, then on the street outside, and eventually she stormed off. No one can say what happened next. Nicole says she doesn't remember.' Again, he looked in Junior's direction. 'Eric Schumer was killed in a car accident that night.'

I stopped scribbling. 'Did he kill himself because of Nicole?' I couldn't help asking. Suicide was an offence against God, according to the mission ladies, and against your ancestors, according to my grandmother. I thought the worst thing about suicide was that you were giving up on life before you were forced to.

'The police don't think he killed himself,' Dr Covington said, 'Anyway, that's when I decided it was time to get Nicole out of America for a bit. I'd always wanted to visit good old England and do the grand European tour. Nicole had never been out of America, and it would be an educational experience for Junior. So, I booked us a passage on the Cunard Line. That was how we ended up in Germany. The rally was just a bit of fun.'

Radley Covington, Eric Schumer, Victor Glossop. I wrote in my notebook. *Three dead men who were involved with Nicole Covington.*

'You can't think Nicole had anything to do with any of those deaths,' Dr Covington added quickly. 'They were all accidents. Given the number of men interested in her, it's not all that surprising.'

'One accident, perhaps,' Le Froy said. 'With your son, that's two "accidents". And Victor Glossop makes a third.'

'You do think Victor's death was an accident, then?' Dr Covington said, so quickly that I saw he wanted to know very much how the investigation was going. 'Victor Glossop led a very sheltered existence until he came out east. He may not have been aware of some underlying condition, some fatal allergy . . .' He reminded me of Kenneth.

'I'm sure Dr Leask will appreciate any suggestions you can make. Is Mrs Covington feeling better? I still need to speak to her,' Le Froy said.

'You know how women are. When they feel they're not looking their best they don't want to be seen by anyone. Especially not by any man.'

'Would she let me come and talk to her?' I asked. 'If I come to keep Junior company, it wouldn't really count as her seeing anybody.' I wasn't pushing myself forward. This was only what Dr Covington had suggested that first day.

'No,' said Le Froy, automatically.

'Come by the hotel tomorrow,' said Dr Covington, 'after breakfast.'

'Eight thirty a.m.?'

'If you want to talk to Nicole, noon would be a better bet.'

Harry Palin

———◆———

T here were times I would never cross Le Froy.

And then there were the other times.

After the Covingtons had left, Le Froy said, 'I'm sending Sergeant Pillay to the hotel with you.'

'That would leave Sergeant de Souza on duty here without back-up. What if there's an emergency?'

'HQ can loan us a corporal.'

I didn't think Sergeant Pillay would be much help with Nicole, but 'If you do, will you ask for Corporal Wong Meng?'

'Is he good?'

'No. Not yet. But he wants to be a detective.'

He shook his head in a gesture that incorporated recognition and resignation. I could identify it because I had seen that look on my grandmother's face. I was doing what they would have done, not what they wanted me to do.

There was just one person I wanted to talk to before I was done for the day. His interview was one of those noted as completed in the day's report from HQ. There was no urgency, but if my plan was successful I would be spending the next few days at the Farquhar Hotel with Nicole.

I didn't wait for the trolley bus because there would still be a long walk after that. Singapore might have the largest trolley-bus system in the world, but trolleys only ran where Europeans wanted to go. I was lucky to find a mosquito bus heading west to Chua Chu Kang Village and Kampong Belimbing. It wasn't full and the driver agreed to take me to Tengah, charging me only for the distance between his last stop and the air base.

Still, it was evening by the time I banged on the door of Harry Palin's quarters in the small *kampong* that had formed around the Tengah air base.

'Nobody here. Go away!'

I took that as an invitation. In any case the door was ajar, with the loop of the hook latch torn out of the wall.

'Oh, it's you. The chaps are off on night training. I got the evening off.' Harry, sitting in his undershirt and shorts on a bunk bed with its sheet pulled half off, was unshaven and seemed not to have slept for some time. The room looked even worse than he did.

'I heard you were in for questioning. How did it go? They took you to Headquarters?'

Harry nodded. 'Was there all day, all night and all day. Just got out. Being a murder suspect gets boring quite quickly. They even came and trashed my office and quarters here, looking for what I used to poison Victor Glossop. And if you're here to ask, no, I didn't. But I'll confess to anything you want if you get me tea and something to eat.'

'What?'

'They're holding my wallet and "effects" till they get the paperwork saying I'm in the clear.'

Oh, those stupid young corporals at Police Headquarters!

'Sit.' I went to the window to call down an order for fishball noodles to the bored looking *tok tok* noodle man across the road. 'Soupy or dry?'

'Dry. I'll have to owe you for it. And I need a drink.'

'I'll take it out of petty cash.' I was carrying it with me. It was what I bought our office lunches with and this was part of an investigation ... sort of. 'Coffee?'

'Chrysanthemum tea, if there is any. With ginseng powder. My throat's so sore.'

I put money into the roped basket tied to the window and waited for the man to load it with change and food. Harry had become more local than the locals.

'I hear you've been going to see Dee Dee.' Harry's temper sweetened as the noodles disappeared inside him. He used chopsticks like a native.

'Not as much as I'd like.'

'She told me you're very busy working, but you took her to do her Christmas shopping.'

'Oh, yes.' I smiled. 'We got you one sock each so please be surprised that they match. It was her idea.'

'Thanks for spending time with her, Su.'

'I like her,' I said honestly. Once you accepted Harry's sister's condition, she was the sweetest seven-year-old anyone could know.

'I thought I'd got past all this villain-outsider, prime-suspect stuff. But once something goes wrong, I'm the first person the bobbies haul in for questioning. I thought Le Froy trusted me.'

'Le Froy wouldn't have recommended you to the RAF if he didn't trust you. And you know they had to question you because you were drinking buddies with Victor Glossop and got the girls and drink for his stag party.'

Harry moaned and ran his fingers through his hair. 'No girls, no booze. I've told your people so till my throat is raw. I wouldn't know where to start looking. Victor wanted betel juice. He said Nicole wouldn't leave the hotel because she was terrified someone would spit it at her and she'd catch some terrible disease. Victor wanted to dress up as a native and spit on her. Crazy guy. Stupid idea. But I figured, if she's marrying the man, better she finds out what he's like before the wedding rather than when it's too late. There was nothing wrong with the betel quids I got Victor. I made sure of that. Unless he had an allergy or something. Some of the other guys chewed them too. I showed them how. They thought it a hoot. The minty tingle, spit like bloody orange juice.'

'You packed the *makan sireh* yourself or bought them ready-made?'

'That's the kind of thing those bozos should have been asking me but didn't. All they did was keep going at me about the girls who said I approached them. Me! Hah! Never thought I'd be glad that—' He shook his head and popped a fishball into his mouth. I was glad I'd paid for extra fishballs as well as extra chilli.

'I bought the quids off a street-seller. The boy said his grand-mother prepared them, traditional style. He probably packed them himself, using roadside clay. But what's a little dirt, right? We're all made of dirt and to dirt we'll return.'

'Dust, not dirt, if you're quoting Genesis or Ecclesiastes.'

'Same thing.' Harry had stopped eating.

'When was that?'

'Two days before he died. When they were planning the stag night. So even if he was poisoned by something in the betel juice, it wouldn't have been the batch I got him. Those guys acted like I tried to kill him. I would never have given Victor anything that would hurt him.'

'How well did you know Victor Glossop?' I asked suspiciously. Harry was as prone to unlikely impossible crushes as Parshanti.

'Not well at all. We had a few drinks together. That sly friend of his was always around, spying on him for Nicole. Made it impossible to talk. Say, do you people know what really killed him? I mean, could it have been his heart or a spider bite or something?'

'We don't know yet.'

'You'll tell me when you find out, won't you?'

I didn't know if I would.

I liked Harry Palin. And I trusted him more than any other *ang moh* I knew, excepting only Le Froy and Parshanti's mother. But Harry could be impulsive and reckless.

'Actually, I met Nicole first, you know.'

'What?' I hadn't known he'd met her at all. 'Where? At a bar?'

'Oh, no. She came around to the air base with that friend of Victor's.'

'Kenneth?'

'Kenneth the good-looking snob, yes. She was looking for someone to fly them out of Singapore.'

'Where to?'

'Anywhere. Just out of here. Nicole said she was sick of being here and, after the trip out, didn't want to be trapped on board ship again. Said she wanted to try flying. But I told her we didn't take commercial passengers.' Harry grinned wryly, 'That offended her. I didn't realize, when she was being so nice to me, that I was meant to fall in love with her and bend the rules for her. I said I was sorry I hadn't noticed she was flirting and that made her even madder.'

I could imagine. I almost felt sorry for Nicole, trying to make an impression on handsome, oblivious Harry.

'She went off and told Victor I'd assaulted her. Insulted or assaulted, he wasn't clear which. But he said Nicole had sent him to teach me a lesson.'

'What did he – you didn't—'

'No way. Victor thought it was a huge joke. Said if I'd been a native he would have whipped me to death, but if I could fix him up with women for his stag do we'd call it even. I pointed him to Yap Pun Kai – Japan Street – because the Japanese working women want the money and it's doing them a favour. I mean, if they want to earn it . . .'

I ignored Harry's awkwardness. I was thinking about Nicole, seeing her differently. Nicole had told the police she had not gone beyond the hotel grounds but it seemed she had been as far as the Tengah air base – with Kenneth Mulliner for company.

'Kenneth told us you and Victor got into a fight on the street.'

'Kenneth's a good liar.'

I remembered the dead Japanese prostitute found in Japan Street. 'Do you know where Victor went in Japan Street?'

'No. I don't know anyone there. I just gave him directions.'

'Did you tell the police all this?'

'I tried to. But they only wanted me to answer the questions on their list. This wasn't on their list. Did Nicole set them on me? Did she tell them I killed Victor?'

'I can't say.' I really couldn't.

'That woman is a witch,' Harry said. 'If someone killed Victor, she's the one I'd put my money on. Only . . .'

'Only?' I asked.

'Only why didn't she wait till after they'd got married to kill him?'

That reminded me of Junior's words. 'Harry, what do you know about black widow spiders?'

'I don't know anything about spiders except to stay away from them. Why?'

'Nothing.' I turned and looked around the room. I had straightened what I could while he ate. The bed was made, the drawers closed and the clothes folded in the cupboard. 'I must get back to town before the buses stop running.'

'I'll run you back on the bike.'

'No. You need to go to bed, Harry. Thanks.'

But at street level a yellow-top taxi cab was stopped in front of the building. Its front door was open and the driver, a dark Chinese man I didn't recognize, was cutting his toenails. He put away his knife and stood up when he saw us.

Harry stepped forward and pushed me behind him, his weary misery instantly gone. 'We didn't call a taxi. Who are you? What do you want?'

The driver looked at me. 'I am here to drive Big Boss Chen's daughter,' he said in Malay.

'Big Boss Chen is dead. You won't get any ransom money

from him,' Harry answered, also in Malay. The driver looked at him with more respect.

'Small Boss Chen told me to bring his brother's daughter home.'

'Small Boss Chen' was Uncle Chen. My late father had been 'Big Boss Chen'.

'Home where?' I asked.

'Back to the detective station in town. And to bring you and your *ang moh* boss to Chen Mansion to pay your respects to Chen Tai tomorrow afternoon.'

'I will have to ask my boss first.'

'Is your family spying on you?' Harry was shaking his head in disbelief.

'It's all right. He'll take me to the Detective Shack. Good night.' I was used to my grandmother's ways. And I was glad of the ride back into town.

I was also glad to have seen Harry. And to learn the beautiful Nicole had been trying to sneak out of Singapore with Kenneth. I felt sure she was involved in her fiancé's death and thought she was going to get away with murder . . .

Poisoned

◆

When I came down from my room the next morning, Le Froy was already in his office sitting over a contraption full of wires that hadn't been there yesterday. He must have collected it himself from the post office.

'Close the door,' was all he said, when I looked in. I would find another time to broach the visit to Chen Tai.

◆

'Su Lin?' Parshanti's father was in the doorway, looking excited. Dr Shankar, normally so careful, had tracked in mud from last night's rain.

'Good morning, Su Lin. I'm here to see the chief inspector.'

'He's not had his coffee yet,' I warned. Dr Shankar was one of the kindest, gentlest men I knew, and no match for Le Froy before his morning coffee, especially as the chief inspector might not have slept the night before.

'He'll want to hear this. Andrew asked me to double-check his test results. I ran them twice, just to make sure.'

Dr Andrew Leask, the official medical examiner, was a young man who trusted and depended on the older and far more experienced Dr Shankar.

'He couldn't come himself this morning. You know how it is with maggots. Once you begin you have to go on till you get them all. But when I confirmed his results we both thought Le Froy should see them right away.'

'What would I want right away?' Le Froy's voice came from his room. 'What maggots? Get in here!'

I followed Dr Shankar into Le Froy's office.

'Dr Leask is removing maggots from a woman's leg,' Dr Shankar explained. 'She is a rubber-tapper with five children and no husband and she needs both her legs so he is doing his best to save it. But he said you ought to see this without delay.'

Le Froy took the piece of paper that Dr Shankar held out to him.

'I offered to take over the maggot extraction, but Andrew's eyesight is far better than mine. His hands are steadier.' Like a proud mentor, Dr Shankar praised Dr Leask's skills every chance he got. 'And I am not overly fond of maggots.'

'What is it?' I asked, looking between the two men. Neither answered.

Le Froy blinked several times, a sign that he was rapidly assessing something.

'Can you talk me through the ramifications?' he asked Dr Shankar. Then, without waiting for a reply, 'Take Su Lin's chair. Su Lin, help him.'

'Sorry to discombobulate you, Su Lin.' Dr Shankar's eyes were shining in excitement.

'Should I take notes?'

Le Froy waved a hand in a vague gesture but I could see he was barely aware of my presence. 'Coffee. Get us coffee. And dough fritters.'

As I left I heard him say, 'So there is no doubt Victor Glossop was murdered.'

———◆———

Coming back with coffee, I met Sergeant Pillay on his way out. 'Where are you going, Prakesh?'

'Boss told me to go to the hotel and tell those people he wants to see them all at the office. As soon as possible. Mulliner, Covington and that beautiful woman.'

'They may not agree to come,' I said, thinking of Nicole Covington.

'He said to tell them they will be given Victor Glossop's official autopsy results.'

———◆———

According to Dr Shankar's and Dr Leask's test results, Victor Glossop had been poisoned with something that had made him bleed, much like snake venom. But though traces were discovered in his mouth and on his tongue, it had not been detected in his gullet or stomach. And the swelling of his face, arms and chest suggested that he had been exposed to a far higher dose than one snake could deliver.

The powdered concoctions put down to kill rats would have the same effect.

Even if all the previous deaths in Nicole Covington's life had been accidents and bad luck, Victor Glossop had been murdered and there was no getting away from it.

'Victor was wearing lipstick,' I said. 'Not just on his mouth. The hearts on his face and arms looked like they were drawn on with it. Some were in places he couldn't have reached for himself. Can you find out who drew them on him?'

'It must have been Nicole,' Le Froy said. 'Unless Victor Glossop had other female companions.'

'Other companions,' Dr Shankar pointed out. 'Not necessarily female.'

———◆———

I would have to send word to my grandmother that I would not be visiting her, I thought, as we waited. Ah Ma did not like using telephones and rickshaw messengers so I usually communicated with Chen Mansion through Uncle Chen. He went to the Katong house regularly, though he now lived above his shop in town. But I had seen little of him for some weeks now. His wife, Shen Shen, told me there had been a big fight between him and Ah Ma. Uncle Chen had wanted money from Ah Ma to support the anti-Japanese troops in China, and Ah Ma had refused. Uncle Chen and Shen Shen had not been back since to the big house for dinner.

Uncle Chen was Ah Ma's only surviving son, as well as the main supervisor of the Chen family business dealings, so this was serious. 'Your uncle is very angry with your grandmother. I am afraid he will go to China to fight. Your grandmother will blame me for influencing him,' Shen Shen had worried. 'If he comes back alive, she will use it to get him to take another wife.'

Given that everyone knew Uncle Chen had got his pig-headedness from Chen Tai, it was unlikely she could blame Shen Shen for anything he did. But Shen Shen had already lost two babies and my grandmother was a practical woman.

I was just thinking I was lucky not to be in Shen Shen's position when Le Froy brought up the subject of my family. 'That reminds me, Su Lin. I told your grandmother I had to see her about something and she said we could go over this afternoon.'

'Why do you want to see her?' That explained Ah Ma's message last night. Le Froy might have asked for a meeting but, to save face, she had to be the one who summoned us. I stared at him. What could he have to say to my grandmother?

'I think our visitors are here,' Le Froy said.

Confrontations

———◆———

'If you are not going to arrest us, you have no right to keep us here!' Nicole Covington's voice rang out over the noise of the street even before the engine of their taxi cab stopped.

Our visitors had arrived.

I scuttle-limped out to greet them. And then I stopped and stared.

When I had seen her at the hotel, Nicole Covington had, of course, been in turmoil. No matter how many beaux a woman has had, it must still be a shock to have one suddenly drop dead.

Today I barely recognized the woman striding past me into the Detective Shack. She was totally different. She was a photograph in one of Parshanti's magazines come to life.

Nicole Covington paused and posed like a fashion model with one hand on a tilted hip. Taylor Covington and Kenneth Mulliner stood on either side and slightly behind her, like courtiers with their queen or savage priests at a human sacrifice.

I sensed Kenneth was there reluctantly but didn't know what gave me that impression. Nicole was so much the centre of attention that it was difficult to look at anyone else. She was like an actress at the climax of a movie, but without a musical score I couldn't tell if it was a moment of suspense or threat.

Nicole's wide-shouldered white jacket was almost masculine in its cut, but the bright yellow dress beneath was soft with a girlish flared skirt. Her soft turban hat and shoes were orange.

She reminded me of the beautiful painted statues outside the new Sri Vadapathira Kaliamman Temple in that I couldn't tell whether I was looking at a warrior goddess or a beautiful demon. Nicole Covington might have been either as she stood there.

Le Froy, in his street uniform of khaki shirt and shorts, looked as if he was trying to work out whether or not the strange dog in a chicken run was rabid.

'Please come. Please come and sit down,' Sergeant Pillay said.

I hurried forward too. 'Let me get you a drink. Would you prefer tea or something cold?'

Nicole, statue like, kept her eyes on Le Froy and her mouth shut. It was Dr Covington who nodded thanks to Prakesh, and said, 'We're fine,' to me.

'Well, we're here,' Nicole finally said. 'What do you want?'

'Please. Have a seat,' Le Froy invited.

Nicole and the doctor sat, but Kenneth remained standing by Nicole's chair.

'We have the results of the autopsy.' Le Froy said. 'Victor Glossop was poisoned.'

'No!' Dr Covington sounded amazed. 'I thought— Are you sure? I would swear that – but, no, I never—'

Kenneth said nothing. He looked as if he was going to be sick.

'We are trying to determine the source of the poison,' Le Froy continued. 'In the meantime, we have more questions.'

'Men die,' Nicole said coldly. 'They do stupid things and they die. If Victor was poisoned, it was probably something he ate off the street. I warned him a hundred times that he was going to poison himself. Now it's settled there's no infection, I want to leave. I'm sick of your island. Does the governor know about this? Governor McPherson and his wife are very good friends of ours and they won't like it.'

Le Froy looked calmly at her. 'Mrs Covington. You had a disagreement with Victor Glossop the day he died. What was that about?'

'This has been a very difficult time for me,' Nicole said. Suddenly there was a tremor in her voice and tears in her eyes. 'Please try to understand. I thought I was finally getting another chance. I believed Victor loved me. And he betrayed me.' Nicole stood and held out a hand pleadingly towards Le Froy. He put a handkerchief into it. 'Thank you,' she said. Then she seemed to wilt against him like a bean sprout going soft.

Le Froy held her by the shoulders, steadying and lifting her off him at the same time. Kenneth grabbed a stool, shoved it behind Nicole's knees, and Le Froy eased her onto it.

Kenneth said, 'Look, Inspector, it doesn't make sense for Nicole to have been involved. If she'd wanted to kill Victor she would have waited till after the wedding.'

That wasn't what Nicole wanted to hear and she smacked away the hand Kenneth put on her shoulder.

'Victor Glossop was poisoned,' Le Froy repeated. 'Strychnine and brucine were detected in his body. Dr Shankar will explain the test results, if you like.'

Dr Shankar bowed slightly.

'You let that man cut Victor up? He probably planted the poisons to try to extort money from us!'

The expression on Dr Shankar's face made me want to slap Nicole Covington.

'Calm down, Nicole,' Dr Covington said. 'Hush yourself and calm down.' He didn't seem shocked. As a doctor, he might even have suspected it.

'You're just a stupid old man,' Nicole said. 'If Radley was around he would horse-whip that man for looking at me that way. Nobody's watching out for me now.' She burst into tears and threw herself into Le Froy's arms. This time he didn't dodge in time and he caught her automatically.

Le Froy pushed her carefully back onto her stool and unwound her arms. She might have been a giant squid – valuable, but slippery with slime.

I saw her glance flicker to me. I tried to arrange my features into the expression I saw on Parshanti's face when she talked about Kenneth. It worked.

'Lend me your girl,' Nicole said.

Le Froy stared at her blankly. Dr Covington and Kenneth looked alarmed.

'Nicole, I already arranged—' Taylor Covington began.

But Nicole continued over him: 'Can't you see how upset I am? I'm traumatized.' She turned to Le Froy. 'If you're making me stay here I need someone to help me. The hotel staff are lazy and stupid. Lend me your girl. She looks clean and she understands

English.' She raised her chin so that her thickly lashed eyes almost closed as they remained fixed on Le Froy. 'Don't worry. I'll send her back to your bed at night so you're not inconvenienced.' Le Froy's stare provoked a shrill of delighted laughter. 'I am only joking! Relax, Mr Bobby. But I do need someone clean and honest. Besides, your girl likes me. Don't you, Miss Butterfly?'

'Yes, I do. Yes, I'll do it,' I said quickly.

'Her name is not Butterfly.' Le Froy said. 'And she is not a servant. Su Lin, may I have a word?'

We stepped outside. I spoke quickly before Le Froy could: 'You already agreed with Dr Covington that I could go to the hotel to watch her. If she thinks it's her idea it'll be even better.'

'You are here as an office assistant, not an undercover agent. And that woman is mad.'

'I want to do this, sir. Mrs Covington asked for me and I think I can get her to talk to me.'

'On the condition that you inform your grandmother and get her approval,' he held up a finger to forestall my protest, 'when we call on her this afternoon.'

'But she'll never agree! She doesn't like me staying *here*, even with someone on duty all night in HQ opposite.' Ah Ma had wanted me to stay with Uncle Chen, but that would have meant sleeping in the kitchen and I had fought for my little upstairs room. The room I was afraid of losing now.

'So, what's the verdict?' Kenneth had appeared in the doorway, 'Nicole wants to know.'

'Paperwork has to go through Headquarters first,' Le Froy said, sounding like a bored administrator.

'You said Victor was poisoned.' Kenneth licked lips that were dry and cracking. 'He didn't suffer, did he? Was it something he ate?'

'No point thinking about that,' Le Froy said, not unkindly. 'The worst is over for your friend.'

Should I have been surprised that he was more sympathetic to the dead man's friend than to the woman Victor Glossop had been going to marry?

Chen Mansion

◆

I had worried that my grandmother wanted to scold me for going out alone at night or that she had another marriage arrangement for me. If Le Froy had requested this meeting it was a different matter altogether, but he wouldn't tell me why.

Chen Mansion was in the east of Singapore, almost an hour's drive away in Katong. My grandmother received us in her shabby day room. This was a high compliment and, even in my stressed state, I hoped Le Froy appreciated it.

Ah Ma didn't care how her living quarters looked. She always maintained that only poor people worried about appearing rich. Her bedroom, where I had slept for years, was still cluttered with the same old furniture I had grown up with.

The only previous time Le Froy had visited Chen Mansion, Ah Ma had received him in the formal visitor's room. That was much grander, for 'outsiders' or non-family members. The furniture there was formal and imposing, carved teak inlaid with mother of pearl. Photo portraits of my grandfather and father glared from behind the ornate chair where Chen Tai saw people who came to ask favours. At least things were better than they had been ten years ago. In the worst days of the Depression, people in America were jumping out of skyscrapers because of losing all their money. Ah Ma had said that, since we didn't have skyscrapers in Singapore, we had to help each other.

Ah Ma's day room was comfortable and homely. It smelt of fresh jasmine and fragrant old sandalwood. This was where the mahjong tables were set up for all-night sessions during new year and funerals, and where the private family altars were kept.

As I always did, I bowed three times at the altar where the photos of my dead parents stood, along with a pair of baby shoes representing my brother who had lived less than two weeks. I don't know if the dead see us. Paying respects was my way of remembering I had once had parents. There was a cup of tea in front of my parents' picture, another in front of the baby shoes. I lit two joss sticks.

'This is a beautiful room,' Le Froy said to Ah Ma in Malay. 'I am honoured to be invited in here.'

It was the right thing to say. My grandmother smiled at him.

'Why did you agree to see us? What do you want to tell him?' I could not be comfortable until I knew what was going on.

'So unfilial. Why so long never come and see me?' Ah Ma never got to the point immediately. 'This *ang moh mata*,' she pointed at Le Froy, 'is he good to you?'

This was routine and not an innocent question. Ah Ma knew Le Froy understood the Hokkien-Malay patois she spoke and I knew she didn't worry about Le Froy treating me badly. Her spies would have told her if he made me miss a lunch break, let alone bullied me. No, Ah Ma was only making sure that Le Froy had not managed to win over my loyalty.

'He is a good boss and a good teacher,' I said, returning to the script.

Ah Ma turned to Le Froy who sat quietly listening. 'Is my useless granddaughter giving you a lot of trouble?' she asked, in Malay.

'Su Lin is a great help to us. You have brought her up well. There is not much trouble above ground, these days. That is why I am glad you agreed to see me. I have been wanting to ask your advice on things that are going on under the ground.'

Ah Ma watched him and waited. I saw she was pleased that Le Froy was coming directly to the point, but she was not going to help him.

'The tongs, triads, clans are all quiet. What are you worried about?'

'That is what worries me.'

'I don't know what you mean.'

'You know everything that goes on here. The Chen family is powerful because when the small fry don't get along the Chens keep the peace.' Le Froy had realized this early on. Working with the Chens, he had been effective at bringing down levels of petty street crime in Singapore. While ignoring what they did outside Singapore.

'You know the colonial authorities have ordered us to arrest anyone supporting China in the conflict against Japan.'

'Do you know what the Japanese are doing to people in China now?' Ah Ma demanded.

'The British fear the Communists more than the Japanese. Japan is also a monarchy and is not likely to disrupt social order. Britain and the British Empire will stay neutral in this conflict.'

'They are butchering farmers' livestock and children with the same weapons.'

'China can look after itself. Your son can be arrested and charged for treason if he is caught.'

'My son has done nothing except throw money into the sea. Even you British cow-eaters cannot call that treason,' Ah Ma said stubbornly.

'Once he is arrested for treason, it is out of my hands,' Le Froy said.

'Ah Ma, Japan can't win,' I said. 'China is so much bigger. With so many more people. Besides, Germany is helping China. Germany is sending China money for food and weapons.' Back in those days I still believed what I read in the newspapers. 'Besides, Singapore is an unconquerable fortress. Britain's "Gibraltar of the East". The British will defend us.'

They both ignored me.

'Over five million people have died of famine in west China. There are no more weeds left on the ground to eat. The people have eaten them all, like starving pigs scavenging. We are not safe here. Once they have China, the Japanese will continue down south. No one can stop them. In the end, Germany will side with the Japanese. Two races that believe they are gods above everyone else. That is a real threat,' said Ah Ma. 'We Chinese are like ants. Too many of us to feel superior, so we just work.'

'The Japanese are already here,' Le Froy said, in a low voice. I suspected the secret report he was working on for the Colonial Office had to do with Japanese spies infiltrating Singapore. 'I have touched their hands.'

Le Froy believed you could tell a day worker by the roughness of his hands. Spies were from the intellectual class. Their brains were trained to deceive, but their bodies were not shaped by a lifetime of work.

'I have touched their hands also,' my grandmother agreed.

Confused, I looked between them blankly. 'Then why isn't someone doing something? Why aren't you telling people?'

'What is the point?' Ah Ma said. 'Why tell people about a real threat when you cannot do anything about it? That is just stirring up trouble. Our ancestors came here to get away from a bunch of greedy warlords fighting each other. Now there is nowhere else to run. What is the use of telling people who won't listen?'

'Chen Tai, I want you to listen now. Your son should not go to a meeting tomorrow night at the Keng Soo Clan Association,' Le Froy said. 'It would be even better if there is no meeting tomorrow night. But make sure your son stays at home tomorrow night.'

Ah Ma sat quietly for a long moment. It was the first time I had seen my grandmother look vulnerable. And I knew Le Froy had made himself vulnerable too. If I repeated what I had just heard, he would be the one charged with treason.

Finally, my grandmother spoke: 'If my irresponsible grand-daughter insists on working for strangers, she should learn a proper skill. There is a hairdresser in town willing to take her on as an apprentice.'

'Ah Ma! I don't want to be a hairdresser!'

'He has a good business, doesn't owe money and his wife died last year without children. And he has studied Chinese medicine and acupuncture. He can also teach her Japanese. These things may save her life one day.' The same reason she gave for sending me to the mission school to learn English.

'Japanese? Ah Ma!'

'Oshima Yukimoto?' Le Froy asked.

'Tell me what bad things you know about that daikon-head,' my grandmother commanded. When Le Froy shook his head, indicating he had nothing bad to say, she continued: 'The choice is between learning Japanese and working for white people. You will never be accepted by white people. But if you can speak Japanese you will be safer.'

'I have a job,' I said. 'I like it. I want to help the police solve a murder. Ah Ma, I am going to the Farquhar Hotel to guard the *ang moh* woman whose fiancé just died.' 'Guard' and 'watch' are close enough in meaning. Ah Ma nodded. I was surprised she did not object.

'I will do all I can to keep Su Lin safe,' Le Froy said.

'I know,' Ah Ma said. 'But I want to make sure that you understand what your responsibility is.'

For one awful moment, I thought my grandmother was asking Le Froy to marry me.

'Ah Ma! You can't say such things! They don't see things the same way!'

Again, neither seemed to hear me. I felt as though I was shouting under water.

Le Froy had not run away. And he still spoke with the friendly respect he reserved for my grandmother. 'Please explain to me,'

'You will be her *sifu*. If a master takes on an apprentice, the apprentice becomes part of the master's family. I am asking you to take Su Lin into your family, as her *sifu*.'

'*Sifu*' might be translated as 'master' or 'teacher'. But it was a term with many more connotations. You wouldn't learn

138

dressmaking or carpentry from a *sifu*. But if you entered religious orders or were studying the martial arts, 'Sifu' was how you would address your head monk or instructor. In Chinese and Japanese history, this was very often the same person. And the connotations were really closer to 'master-father' than 'teacher'. In the old traditions, an apprentice was like a disciple, willing to kill for – or die for – his or her master.

There was usually a formal discipleship ritual. Uncle Chen had taken on several apprentice-disciples in his shadow businesses, though he and Shen Shen ran their little sundries shop alone. They had been starving waifs who had since grown into skilled fighters and remained silently devoted to my uncle.

Such a relationship with a family of local black-marketeers could hardly be something a government detective wanted, I thought. And I saw a flicker of something – not quite, but almost, alarm – in Le Froy's eyes before he bowed his head to Ah Ma again. 'I am honoured to be asked.'

'And your answer?' Chen Tai had not kept her position by being tactful. 'You don't think my granddaughter is worthy?'

'This is a serious responsibility, not to be taken on lightly,' Le Froy said. 'I will think about it.'

Ah Ma said, 'People don't change. If you can say yes or no in ten, twenty years' time, you can say yes or no now.'

'People change,' Le Froy said. 'People change all the time. Or we would all be savages living in mud huts instead of in houses like this.' He looked around, drawing our eyes with him. 'I know you didn't want your granddaughter to work for me. Can you tell me what changed your mind?'

'What is happening in China now will happen in Singapore

if the Japanese are not stopped. If Su Lin is under your protection . . .'

Le Froy nodded. 'I will do everything I can to keep her safe.'

'Train her to keep herself safe. And another thing. There's a new *ang moh* man asking questions in town.' Ah Ma raised her hand as she spoke and the doors to the main hall were closed from the outside. 'This man went to your uncle's shop, Su Lin, and asked if he put you in the police to warn him of police checks. He also accused your uncle of passing the police information on his rivals.'

'Uncle Chen told you that?'

'No,' my grandmother said. 'Your useless uncle tells me nothing, these days. My friend happened to be passing by and told me.'

The rift between Chen Tai and Small Boss Chen was more serious than I 'd known. And Ah Ma was spying on my uncle.

Spies

———◆———

'It must have been Victor Glossop,' I said. 'If he was going around town with questions and blackmail, someone must have decided to get rid of him.'

If he had still been alive, I would have given Mr Glossop a good slap for sneaking about. But someone had done worse. I only hoped Uncle Chen hadn't had Victor killed.

And if he had, I hoped we wouldn't be able to prove it.

'What did Small Boss Chen say to him?' Le Froy asked.

'My son said, "No speak English." The man also asked other people about protection money. How much they pay the police to stay away. He asked if Su Lin is our payment to you for favours or your hostage.'

Le Froy nodded 'Do you know if this *ang moh* man was from England or America? Or Australia?'

'How would I know? *Ang moh*s all look the same, what!' My grandmother's face was bland and innocent.

'Can you make sure your son is not at the meeting tomorrow night?'

Ah Ma shrugged expansively, waving her hands as though shooing the words away, like geese. 'What can I do? My only son never comes to see me now. He is angry with me. Well, I am angry with him!'

This was new. Despite huge family fights over the years, this was the first time I had known Ah Ma to mention one to an outsider.

'I am sorry to hear that,' Le Froy said politely.

Ah Ma went further: 'My daughter-in-law is worried that my son is having an affair with a flower of the night.'

'Of course he isn't,' I said. If Uncle Chen wanted to have an affair with a prostitute he knew how to cover his tracks so that Shen Shen would never find out.

'He has been taking money and Shen Shen thinks he wants to take a second wife. I don't know what he is doing with the money.'

It was a plausible justification for missing money, and established my grandmother's ignorance in the matter.

That done, Ah Ma fixed her eyes on Le Froy. 'Is my son working for you? Spying for you against his own people?'

'No.'

'I didn't think so, but you understand I have to ask. People close to the ground, like you and me, we know trouble is coming. We are hiding like rats and cockroaches. The king is too far away in England to know what is happening here. I am an old woman and even my son keeps secrets from me. If anything happens to me, I want you to look after my granddaughter.'

'I will do my best, Chen Tai.'

'Your source of information must have made a mistake,' Ah

Ma said. 'There will be no meeting tomorrow night at the Keng Soo Clan Association.'

'I am sorry for my mistake, Chen Tai.'

Ah Ma smiled. It was a small smile, but genuine. I saw how much she trusted and respected my *ang moh* boss. Trusted him more than her own people to keep me safe.

All this time, when I'd thought I was striking out for myself by insisting on staying at school and working with the Detective Unit, had I been following my grandmother's plan? This raised other questions. I knew I had not been planted to pass police information to my grandmother, but in the Detective Shack I had heard stories about the underside of the Chen family businesses.

'Ah Ma, do you take protection money?'

Ah Ma opened her mouth, rolled her eyes and wailed, 'How can you say such things to me? My own granddaughter thinks I am a crook and a criminal! *Aiyoh*, to be accused of such things in my old age!'

I had not spent years watching Ah Ma play mahjong for nothing. Winning those games had been as much about show-manship as gambling skills.

'What terrible thing did I do to be punished like that?'

I suspected it was for Le Froy's benefit. He watched, diplomat-ically silent but without surprise. I waited.

'When you get older, you will understand how business is done. I am tired now. Thank you for coming. Su Lin, you must help me to my room.' Ah Ma brought the interview to a close.

My grandmother had a houseful of relatives and servants to help her and she never displayed any kind of weakness in front of an outsider, especially not a foreign devil like Le Froy. I suddenly saw her through a stranger's eyes. She was not just getting older – she was already old.

'Please excuse us,' I said to Le Froy, who nodded and pulled out his pipe. He would not smoke in my grandmother's presence: this was his way of telling me not to hurry.

I'd thought Ah Ma wanted to justify offering me to the Japanese man. I had quite a few things to say to her on the subject myself. But once we were in her private room with the door shut, she said, 'Your uncle Chen is angry with me. He will be angrier when he finds out there will be no meeting tomorrow night. In fact, that there will be no more meetings.'

'Uncle Chen is always angry about something.'

'Angry men do stupid things, trust the wrong people. Your chief inspector did us a great favour. But even he is not safe.'

Ah Ma's old bedchamber had not changed. The padded step stool I had once sat on to read my school books aloud to her still stood by the high bed. And the thin mattress I had slept on for so many years was still rolled up in the corner. I had assumed my grandmother made me sleep in her room in case she needed anything in the night. Now I saw it was possible she had wanted to keep me close – and safe.

'The other *ang moh*s are saying things about your chief inspector. Saying that he is a criminal. That if he did not come out here he would have been sent to prison for killing his wife.'

'What?' Yet I had been half expecting something like this.

'He is trying to warn them about the Japanese spies here,' Ah Ma went on. 'He is worried about the people here. He wants to bring in more military, more ships to protect us. His own people don't want to spend money on us so they are not happy with him. They tried to send him home, give him a promotion into retirement, but he wouldn't go. He is part of Singapore already. That is why they are trying to make trouble for him. Stupid people like to believe stupid things. I want you to go and see your uncle. Tell him I let you apprentice to the *ang moh* policeman.'

'You asked Le Froy to be my *sifu* to show people you trust him?'

Ah Ma snorted. 'If I did not trust him you would not be working for him. Any fool can see that. You should go now. Don't keep your boss waiting.'

Ah Ma gave me packages of soy-sauce braised eggs, duck and a thick slab of *char siew* to bring to Uncle Chen. She might be angry with him, but he was still her son and he and his household must be fed. 'Tell him I want to see him soon,' Ah Ma said. 'And there is a box of dried sausage and dried mushrooms for you.'

My grandmother might think she had everything worked out and settled. But Le Froy was a foreigner. And he hadn't given her an answer on my apprenticeship.

When I hurried back to where he was waiting, I didn't know for sure whether I would be leaving with him or seeing him off.

Moving On

———◆———

'I'm so sorry, sir!'

'Your grandmother is worried about you.'

'She's always worried about something.'

Le Froy went round to the driver's side of the car. I wouldn't have blamed him if he had driven off without me, but I wrestled open the passenger door and plonked myself inside. British gentleman that he was, he couldn't throw a crippled girl out of his car.

I wondered if Uncle Chen was now on his suspect list for the murder. If Victor Glossop had gone to the shop asking questions, could Uncle Chen have had him killed? I didn't have anything to do with that side of the family 'business', but I knew it existed. And if I could think it, Le Froy would be thinking it too.

But I had to deal with a more urgent matter first. Le Froy had not given my grandmother an answer. Once we were back at the Detective Shack, he might tell me to clear my desk and wish me luck in my apprenticeship, marriage (an accepted way to save on pay and board for an apprentice) and Japanese studies. 'You know what my grandmother is like. You don't have to take her seriously.'

'Anyone with any sense would take Chen Tai seriously, don't you think?' Le Froy was looking out of the window as he reversed down the driveway and I couldn't see his face.

'About business, maybe, but not about people. She's old-fashioned. She doesn't know that modern people don't take on apprentices. And you should turn the car around rather than backing down the driveway,' I couldn't help adding. That was why there was a circular driveway, after all. 'What if you run into another car coming in?'

'I didn't,' Le Froy said, with a slight grunt, as he manoeuvred the gear lever.

'But you might have done,' I said, even as the gardener's boys, who had stood on the road in front of the gates to watch for traffic, waved to us and ran to close the gates. They had been guiding him down the driveway and gleefully scrabbled for the coins he tossed them. 'You're spoiling them. They're paid to do that for visitors.'

'You are very like your grandmother, you know.' Le Froy kept his eyes on the road. 'Knowing you can't control all the big things makes you try to control the small things even more tightly. You don't like the idea of being an apprentice?'

'I – I didn't say that.' In fact, I had already come to think of myself as his apprentice. Part of me was upset that my grand-mother might somehow have sensed that.

'I wouldn't expect you to call me "Sifu", if that's what you're worried about. I think she just wanted to show she still trusts me.'

'Yes! She wants to show the public she still trusts you!' I was so relieved he got it.

'And not just the public. But a connection with a "colonial dog" like me might not be a good thing here if war breaks out. Not for you or for your family.'

'If war breaks out here? Do you really think it will?' Looking back, I still can't believe how blindly naive I was.

Le Froy stopped and we watched a bullock cart trundle slowly in front of the car. As the rich odour of healthy cow dung wafted over us, a promise of fat vegetables to come, I read impatience in his forefinger tapping the wheel. Only a fool would toot a horn at a water buffalo but Le Froy wanted to.

'What's the hurry?'

'If Victor Glossop asked Small Boss Chen questions that made him uncomfortable—'

'If Uncle Chen killed Victor Glossop, he wouldn't have warned my grandmother about him,' I said quickly. 'Mr Glossop might have asked other people questions too. I would like to find out who else he talked to, and why. I have an idea.'

Le Froy eased the car into motion.

'I suspect Victor Glossop might have been writing the Pip's Squeaks column,' I said. '"Pip" seemed to know so much about Nicole Covington and the whirlwind wedding plans that he had to be involved.'

'If he was, do you think Nicole Covington knew?'

Stepping outside my own story, I saw where Le Froy's thoughts were going. What if Nicole Covington had found out Victor had been using her to get information for his gossip articles? Or what if his nosing around had unearthed something really damning, a secret that made it worth killing him to keep it hidden? The possibility both frightened and appealed to me.

'Let me know if the damned Pipsqueak publishes anything else.'

He was wondering if the articles would die with Victor Glossop, I thought.

But he still hadn't told me what he was going to say to Ah Ma's apprenticeship proposal.

I wasn't angry with my grandmother any more. Despite all her grumbling I knew she was secretly proud of me. After all, I was her creation. When my father, her eldest and favourite son, had died, it was she who, against all advice, had refused to send me and the bad luck I carried away from the family home. Ah Ma had taught me practical arithmetic and business, taking me with her to collect rent on her properties, watching as I calculated percentages without an abacus. I suspect she was even pleased I was working in the Detective Unit. Of course, she would never tempt Fate and the gods by saying so.

'You don't have to take me as your apprentice,' I said.

'Because your grandmother has already trained you?'

'You didn't tell her I was going to work for Dr Covington at the Farquhar Hotel.'

'Because you're not.'

'But—'

'You'll be there, but as a representative of the Detective Unit.'

'I'll never find out anything if everybody knows that.'

'Let me worry about the investigation. I want you to keep an eye on Nicole Covington and the boy.'

We had to slow down to a crawl where some workers were

trying to unclog a roadside drain just outside town. The water had flooded out, pooling several inches deep on the road.

One of the workers paused and spat a glob of reddish-brown betel in the direction of the car. Le Froy swore amicably at him, and the man grinned, saluting, before turning back to his work. Ah Ma was right. Le Froy had adapted to Singapore.

'Thank you for saving Uncle Chen's life,' I said quietly.

'Only for now,' he replied grimly.

Uncle Chen

———◆———

B ack in town, Le Froy dropped me at the side road that branched off to Uncle Chen's shop. I paused on the five-foot way. Thanks to regulations instituted by Raffles, our British founder, all shophouses are fronted by a covered five-foot-wide walkway to protect pedestrians from the sun and rain. The rain had stopped and I took my time sorting out the various packages my grandmother had sent and thinking about what I was going to say. Some people claimed my uncle, Small Boss Chen, was the head of Singapore's largest black-market and loan-shark business. But I knew Uncle Chen's growling grouchiness hid a soft side, just as he had always hidden milk sweets in my pockets. And that he was terrified of his mother. If he was defying her now, things were really serious. I would tell him my grandmother wanted to see him, but wouldn't mention that I knew about his meeting or that it wouldn't be taking place.

What I really wanted to tell him was that Ah Ma needed him and his support. But I didn't know how to without making her sound weak.

I didn't think about the possibility that Le Froy had committed treason by warning Uncle Chen his meeting had been compromised. It was in character for him to follow the spirit rather than the letter of the law. I had seen him allow sergeants to warn itinerant beggars they were going clear the roads with sticks instead of just using the sticks. Where he was concerned, the point was to get the road cleared for whichever dignitary was coming by, not to hurt children.

I was still squatting over my bundles, lost in thought, when I was shocked to be addressed with a booming 'Miss Chen, isn't it? Good day!'

I saw a pair of muddy brown shoes first and struggled to my feet. Dr Covington and Junior were accompanied by Greg and Pat, the two McPherson sons. The boys chorused polite greetings, eyeing with interest the bags I was scrambling to pick up.

'Good day, Dr Covington. Hello, Greg, Pat, Junior. What are you McPhersons doing out in this weather?' The roads in town were thick with mud and dung.

'Mr Meganck isn't well,' Greg McPherson explained. 'He's in bed.'

'Their tutor is down with the Bombay stomach, Singapore version,' Dr Covington said. 'I gave the poor man something to make him feel better and decided to take the boys out for a walk. Good to get some air.'

'Mr Meganck was going to take us to the swamps to look for terns and tree swifts,' Pat McPherson explained. 'He knows all the birds. But we walked through the town and didn't see any.'

Despite the mud, the air was fresh and clean after the rain so birds and stray chickens were busy hunting down bugs dislodged from the sodden roadside weeds. I thought the boys would enjoy a walk beyond the town. The McPhersons had been in Singapore only a few months longer than Junior, and seemed as interested in snails, frogs and worms as any local children.

'Boys, always after birds,' Dr Covington said. 'Can't wait to start shooting. So where are you off to, Miss Chen?'

'I'm going to visit my uncle. That is his shop over there. He's got the best peanut brittle. Would you like some?'

'Oh, yes! May we, sir?'

'Are you sure it's the best?' Dr Covington asked, with mock sternness.

'The best you'll find on the island!' I promised solemnly. The boys' anticipation shone through their shyness.

I was not exaggerating. Shen Shen, Uncle Chen's wife, made the shop's *fah sung thong* herself. Unlike the versions sold on the roadside that were just sugar and raw peanuts, Shen Shen used sesame seeds as well as dry roasted peanuts and brushed the brittle with salted ghee as it cooled. It was rich and delicious and had comforted me while I was studying for exams. The shop always had a good supply.

'Then lead the way, Miss Chen!'

'We don't shoot birds, Miss Chen,' Pat McPherson whispered to me.

'Good,' I whispered back.

◆

Uncle Chen was alone in the front of his shop when we all trooped in.

153

'Hello, Uncle.'

'Oh, it's you. Did you eat yet? Ma wants to see you. You'd better come home for dinner tonight.' Uncle Chen delivered his usual greeting. In front of strangers, neither I nor my uncle would mention his current dispute with my grandmother.

'Good to see you again. Now your niece is here to interpret for us, I'm sure we'll get along very well indeed!' Dr Covington greeted Uncle Chen. 'So well!' He gave the impression that their visit was my idea, that I had wanted to introduce him to my uncle.

'Come in. Look around. Take your time.' I could tell Uncle Chen was not himself. He was not even pretending he didn't speak English.

I thought about Shen Shen's anxieties as I handed over Ah Ma's packages to him, but I saw no guilt in him. I assumed that men having affairs with other women would have an air of guilty secrets and care more for their own appearance than for their wives'. Uncle Chen in his singlet and sarong was as careless as ever about his looks and sounded almost gentle when he shouted to Shen Shen to bring tea because I was there with friends.

Uncle Chen might not seem guilty but something about me being there was making him uncomfortable. That was as plain to me as the hairy mole on his chin.

I remembered the *ang moh* who had come to his shop to question him and had a sudden thought. 'Did Victor Glossop tell you about my uncle's shop?' I asked Dr Covington. 'Before he died he came round here and asked my uncle a lot of questions. Did he tell you about my uncle and grandmother? What else did he tell you?'

If Victor Glossop had told Dr Covington about my uncle's shop, he might also have mentioned whatever had got him killed.

'Questions?' Dr Covington looked between my uncle and me. I could see him trying to read us and failing. 'Victor? What are you talking about?' He rapped on the counter, startling all of us. 'Has somebody been coming here and asking you questions? Miss Chen, what has your uncle been saying?'

I wondered if Dr Covington could have been sent to get information on Uncle Chen. No, that was absurd. Dr Covington wasn't from the Colonial Office. He was American, not British. The Americans feel about the British much as we 'Straits-born' feel about mainland Chinese: yes, there's history between us but we've moved on.

My family thought I understood the *ang mohs*, while *ang mohs* I met expected me to explain local ways to them. The problem was, neither group was homogeneous or easy to understand.

Still, I wanted to warn Uncle Chen not to say anything to him. So I stood there and looked stupid. Uncle Chen picked up the cue: 'You like imported cigarettes? China cigarettes, Indian cigarettes also I got,' he told Dr Covington.

Shen Shen ducked her head and started wiping the counter. She would not answer any questions.

'There's some nice stuff here. You have good overseas connections, I hear?' Dr Covington said to Uncle Chen.

'You want imported cigarettes, tobacco, whisky, all I got.' Uncle Chen said. 'The best. The cheapest.'

'And, of course, you must have a lot of dealings with China. You have close ties there?'

Uncle Chen made a noncommittal sound.

'This is not a good time to invest in China,' Dr Covington said. 'Too big, too chaotic, too unmanageable. You should let me help you invest in America. These days it's safer to keep money in America than in any banks out here. And in Germany. German technological advances are going to take us into a whole new world.'

'It can't be safe to invest in Germany now,' I said. 'They are having rallies and demonstrations. There may even be another war.'

'Germany doesn't want another war,' Dr Covington said. 'The last one was bad enough. They are only trying to bring about a new order. The German Nazi Party has many connections with wealthy Americans, like the Hearsts. They are investing in research and building factories. All these things will grow in value. Germany and America don't want another war. They are looking to improve people's lives.

'Don't forget, America was once a colony being kicked around by the British, just like your little island here. And look where we are now! The whole world looks to us for help. They want us to swear we'll be backing their side if they get themselves into another fight. But no, sir! Americans have had enough of fighting. The Brits may call themselves your lords and masters but you have to know when to tell them enough is enough.'

Uncle Chen and Shen Shen looked as blank as I felt. I don't think they were acting either. The boys didn't seem surprised. Maybe Dr Covington was one of those men who fancied himself an orator and delivered speeches every chance he got.

'Americans, Germans, not our business,' Uncle Chen said.

'I want the boys to try Shen Shen's *fah sung thong*,' I said, to change the subject.

'Good idea!' Uncle Chen said. He pulled out the square-bottomed metal biscuit tin and prised off its round lid with the back of a spoon.

As the boys looked into the tin, I saw Junior pick up two pieces and slide them into his pocket, along with the shiny metal whistle lying on the counter. Then I saw Dr Covington noted my noticing.

'Help yourselves, boys,' Dr Covington said. 'Help yourselves, take as much as you like. This is Miss Chen's family shop so it's all free for friends. Especially for the sons of the governor, am I right?'

Uncle Chen beamed and bowed, the very image of service and servility. 'Take, take. Take more,' he said. 'Take all.'

The McPherson boys were awkward. Greg McPherson pulled a coin out of his pocket and tried to offer it to my uncle, but Dr Covington took it and put it back into the boy's pocket.

Under his instructions, the boys took handfuls of the sticky sweetmeat and put it into their pockets. I winced for the state their pocket linings would be in.

'You have to be careful about trusting that boss of yours,' Dr Covington whispered to me, while the children were occupied. 'Le Froy doesn't have a very good history with women. You should ask him about that some time. Or with friends. He only makes friends with people he can make use of. And he's not very good at it. Why do you think he got posted out here? He brings bad luck to everybody around him.'

'I don't know what you mean, sir,' I said.

'Wait and see.' Dr Covington tapped the side of his nose. It was clearly meant to convey an understanding between us.

Unfortunately, I had no idea what I was supposed to understand.

Dr Covington shepherded the boys out ahead of him. Junior turned and gave us a shy goodbye wave but the McPherson boys looked like they couldn't get out of the shop fast enough.

I would have happily given them all the peanut brittle they could eat, but I would have liked to do the giving. And I would have folded it in clean brown paper, not let it pick up lint in their pockets.

'He wants to frighten us,' Uncle Chen said, when the door was shut behind them. Uncle Chen was no conversationalist but he understood far more English than he let on. 'That one is always like that. He wants to make us scared of your big-shot policeman because he is scared of him. Waste my time, only.'

'Be careful,' Shen Shen said. 'Su Lin, maybe you should stop going out to work. When big people are fighting each other, we small people are the ones to suffer.'

Or, as Ah Ma always said, whether elephants make love or war, the grass gets flattened. And we were the grass.

But we weren't the only ones suffering. An *ang moh* man was dead, murdered on our island. And the *ang moh*s were pretending that nothing had happened. If we didn't find out who had murdered Victor Glossop, we would all be haunted by his angry ghost the next time the gates of Hell were opened. Though I didn't really believe in the superstitions, I would ask the temple to put up a shrine for him at the next Hungry Ghost Festival.

'I must go to work,' I said. Uncle Chen had already gone into the back room to wash out the peanut brittle tin.

Shen Shen studied my face closely. 'You didn't sleep well last night. What is wrong?'

'Nothing. I just have a lot of work to do.'

'We've all got a lot of work to do,' Shen Shen said. But she stood there miserably instead of returning to her work. I wanted to say something comforting, but I didn't know what. Shen Shen had grown up farming pineapples on rough land between rubber plantations and was one of the most superstitious people I had met. I suspected she blamed her miscarriages on my bad-luck presence in Chen Mansion because why else would a woman choose to live in two rooms above a shop when she could live in relative luxury as Second Son's First Wife? Anything I tried to say to her might make things worse.

'Take care of yourself,' I said, falling back on customary pleasantries as I left. 'Make sure you eat enough.'

Nicole's Suite

———◆———

N icole Covington's suite at the Farquhar was grand and comfortable. There was a sitting room, a bedroom, a dressing
room and, in the bathroom, a fancy ceramic WC with a wooden
seat; a man came to empty the pan three times a day or whenever
he was summoned.

It was a very pleasant space, despite the clutter of clothes, shoes,
sweet wrappers and empty soda bottles scattered all over it.

And despite its beautiful occupant.

When I arrived just before noon that day, Nicole was still in
her dressing-gown and bleary-eyed from sleep. I saw an empty
gin bottle lying on some dirty plates and wondered if she had
been drinking the night before. She seemed to think I was late,
though we had not settled on a time for me to be there.

In fact, we had not even settled that I would be working there
or on what terms. If I hadn't been an undercover agent I would
have thrown something at her and left. And I learned something
that first day: Nicole's beauty was a performance, part of an act
she put on. When she'd come into the Detective Shack she had

been an actress playing the role of an indignant *femme fatale*. Her clothes, her make-up, her manner were all part of the act. Today in her room she was either being herself or playing a spoiled child.

'No, I don't want you to come back later, you stupid girl! It's about time you showed up. Look at the mess here! No, leave it and help me get dressed!'

Fortunately, I learned this meant helping her choose her dress for the day rather than zipping her into one. I shook out the clothes and undergarments I found draped over furniture, bundled into the closet and stuffed under the bed, and requested a box iron and an ironing board from Housekeeping. Nicole calmed down as I laid out several frocks on her double bed, lining up the matching shoes beneath.

I was amazed at how many clothes she had travelled with. And there was a collection of cigarettes and powders hidden under them.

'Put those away. Can't you see they're all wrong? And this one too. Why are you so stupid? Oh, as God is my witness I'll never wear anything but red once I get out of here.'

'Why can't you wear red here?'

'That's what that old fool Taylor says. He says if I wear red now, you local idiots will all think I'm celebrating Victor's death and believe that I killed him. And you'll drown me as a witch or something. Oh, what a bore. We weren't even married and now I have to dump half my wardrobe for him. I can't even wear my rubies. Why are backward people so stupid and superstitious? With my colouring, I look my best in red. And now I can't wear any of those dresses and gowns.'

Nicole was right. Her prettiest frocks were all in shades of pink, red and scarlet. I removed the offending garments and replaced them with a dark blue tailored dress with side pleats, a two-piece floral ensemble and two more dresses in green and brown cotton. 'I don't think anyone here will object to you wearing red, Mrs Covington. For most Singaporeans, it's an auspicious colour. And it's nobody's business but yours what you wear.'

From what I saw, Westerners were far more sensitive about the colour red. They were referred to as *ang moh*, meaning red skin, because that was the colour they turned in our sun. But as I knew from my time at the mission school, the colour red reminded them of blood (menstrual and otherwise), sin and adultery.

Come to think of it, I had never seen any of the Mission Centre ladies or schoolteachers in a red dress. But the Christmas decorations in the lobby and the corridors of the Farquhar Hotel were full of red – red holly berries on dark green leaves (made of painted cardboard), dark red knitted socks holding candy canes and bottles of rum, and little red Santa Claus dolls. They had a lot of red around for people who didn't believe it symbolized luck.

'Don't call me Mrs Covington. I'm sick of being Mrs Covington. Taylor still thinks I should be in mourning for his precious Radley. He'd like to make me wear black for the rest of my life. Like that old Queen Victoria did.'

'But he didn't try to stop you marrying Victor Glossop,' I pointed out.

'Didn't he? Well, tell me, Miss Know-It-All, am I married to Victor Glossop?' She let her words hang.

'This green dress is nice.' I held up a dark green lacy crêpe frock.

'That's not a morning dress. Good God, don't you know anything?'

Eventually she agreed to put on a blue and white sailor-suit dress and said she felt well enough to eat something.

Junior was not in Nicole's bedroom and there were no toys, books or clothes to show a child shared the space. I guessed his things would be in his grandfather's room and the playroom downstairs.

Kenneth Mulliner appeared with her 'breakfast' (though it was past lunch time). He didn't ask what I was doing there, just got straight to business. 'Nicole, you said you would decide by last night. What are you going to do with all the wine and champagne you ordered for the wedding?'

'Oh, Kenny, you are such an unmitigated bore. Just handle it, won't you? Isn't that what you're here for?'

'And what about the tons of tomato ketchup you insisted on buying? It's all just sitting in the box room and the hotel is complaining. You've put this off long enough. Just tell me what you want me to do with—'

But Nicole refused to discuss anything that didn't interest her. 'Oh, shut up, Kenny. Go and drone away at someone else. Silly-Sukey, this is disgusting. I can't eat it. Can't you get those fools in the kitchen to make me a decent omelette?'

'You said you wanted fried eggs,' I protested.

'If Nicole asks for fried eggs, it means she wants an omelette,' Kenneth said. 'Don't worry. You'll either get the hang of it or go stark raving mad. Nicki, you want some tomato ketchup with that, or are you too upset?'

Kenneth was mocking Nicole rather than me, despite his exaggerated air of concern. It seemed to me Nicole was not sorry her wedding had been cancelled. If anything, she had got over Victor's death better than Kenneth, who looked as if he had aged several years. But was this due to grief . . . or guilt? Being in love with your best friend's fiancée doesn't mean you don't feel guilty for murdering him.

'Tomato ketchup?' I asked.

'Nicole won't eat raw tomatoes – or any other vegetable, for that matter – but she's addicted to the pickled, sugared, processed product that calls itself "tomato ketchup".' Kenneth didn't hide his contempt. 'She insisted on buying up the whole stock of an American naval-supply ship, to compare the different brands. Probably paid double or triple what it was worth.'

'Maybe you can resell it,' I suggested. 'My uncle has a shop in town.'

'Bring a case up here and chuck the rest into her uncle's shop,' Nicole told Kenneth. She talked to her man friend worse than my grandmother talked to her servant girls. 'Make sure the old Chinaman doesn't swindle you. And make them send me some decent eggs.' She tipped her plate so that two fried eggs, a sausage and a slice of bacon slid onto Kenneth's shoes. He shook them off onto the carpet.

'What a waste of good food,' I couldn't help saying.

'You can eat them if you want,' Nicole told me.

Kenneth left without saying another word.

An omelette arrived fifteen minutes later.

Luck and Love

———◆———

Keeping Nicole company was like babysitting a spoiled child. I cleaned her rooms, starting with the food mess she had created, sorted out the clutter and managed to restore some semblance of order. It worked here much as it had when I'd organized the desks in the Detective Shack. Whether or not you believe in *feng shui*, a mind feels clearer when the clutter surrounding the body is tidied.

Nicole seemed to appreciate it, though the only sign she gave was not telling me to stop. She reclined on the sofa with her magazines, watching me and occasionally calling questions or instructions. But though she talked almost non-stop, I didn't learn anything useful.

'The police here are hopeless,' Nicole said. 'If Victor was poisoned it was obviously that man who gave him the hideous betel stuff. Harold. No, Harry. His name was Harry. Why don't they just arrest him? Or bring him in for questioning? I could help question him. I'm sure he'd talk to me. Oh, why didn't that idiot Victor stick to chewing spruce gum?'

'I'm sure it's more complicated than that, Mrs Covington.'

'Don't call me "Mrs Covington". If they weren't incompetent second-rate quacks it wouldn't be complicated at all!'

'I'm sure they are doing everything possible to find out what happened, Mrs – Nicole.'

I saw Nicole trying to decide if I was worth the effort of throwing a temper tantrum. I was sponging mud off her yellow skirt and she decided I was not. Le Froy was the one keeping her in Singapore till he was satisfied. She would save it for him.

'Do you know Harry Palin? He's a pilot. And he's a suspect, you know. A prime suspect. Have you heard anything about him?'

'I know who he is,' I said vaguely. I kept my eyes on the fabric but I could feel her watching me. 'I'm going to have to steam this to get it out.'

'I tried to be nice to him, but he was all strange and awkward. I could tell there was something wrong with him, but it never occurred to me he might be dangerous. I've seen it before. Men get that way when they've got it bad for you and think you're out of reach. It's worst when they're virgins, of course. Does this Harry have a girlfriend?'

'I don't know.'

'Oh, you are useless! I hate it here. I just want to go home. Except for that agonizingly long sea journey. It was so tedious. I swear I never want to set foot on board a steamer again.'

I nodded, apparently absorbed with her skirt. This seemed to convince her I wasn't interested enough in Harry Palin to be hiding anything about him. Either that or she didn't want to interrupt my ministrations to her skirt.

'You know John D. Rockefeller left over a billion dollars when he died? I should have married someone like him!'

'Wasn't he almost a hundred years old?'

'Ninety-eight. Which means we wouldn't have had to be married for long. And it would have been worth it. Just because we were a few stupid days from the ceremony those stuffy old Glossops are refusing to give me a bean!'

'I'm sorry about Victor's family. You must miss him very much.'

'Victor was a bore with his stupid tricks and jokes. I think everyone he knew would be fed up with him at some point. Doesn't the rain here ever stop?' It was drizzling outside again. A pleasant warm shower now.

Hopefully the rains would continue until February, or there would not be enough water in the reservoirs to get us through the dry season. But such things would not interest Nicole Covington.

'Would you like to walk around the hotel?' I suggested. 'Shake off the cabin fever while I'll do some cleaning in here?' It would give me a chance to have a good look through her things without her watching me. I've always had what the mission-school teachers called an 'unholy interest' in other people's things. But in this case, I was investigating, not just being a *kaypoh*, or busybody.

'What for? Nothing to see here but a bunch of dull, dull, dull people. Places like this should have warning signs. Death by boredom. Enter at your peril! And if anybody the least interesting walks in, it's like you've stirred up a hornet's nest. Someone is sure to get stung. I can't risk it. Don't you see, you stupid girl? If anyone comes here looking for me, this is where they'll come!'

Anyway, I don't like the hotel staff cleaning in here and poking through my things.'

She threw herself onto her bed dramatically but carefully, without damaging her hair or the make-up she had patted and painted onto her face after she'd had her omelette and coffee breakfast. I almost laughed. Nicole clearly believed someone – and her thoughts seemed to be directed towards Harry Palin – had killed Victor Glossop for love of her and the idea excited her more than a little.

I thought it was far more likely to be Kenneth Mulliner. I hoped he would turn up again. I wanted a chance to watch them together when he wasn't sorting out her cancelled wedding arrangements. Unfortunately he stayed away from Nicole's suite. Like everyone else. And the long afternoon dragged on into evening.

I was ready to admit I had made a mistake. There was nothing for me to learn from Nicole. I would make some excuse, say I was needed back at the Detective Shack, and stop wasting my time. I was coming up with what to say when I noticed Nicole's frenetic mood had calmed.

'You don't understand what I'm going through. Nobody understands. Nobody cares.'

I had finished refolding her clothes and was sewing a button onto one of her blouses, but something in her voice made me look at her.

It wasn't just in her voice. Nicole had sat down on the bed and drawn her knees up under her chin. Curled up like that, she looked miserable, like a child with a stomach ache after eating too many sweets. That was unlikely since all I had seen Nicole swallow that morning were a few mouthfuls of omelette and the vitamin pills she took for her health.

In my experience, children can be even more manipulative than adults. Without power or strength, they have to be. So, instead of rushing over to her with tea and comforting noises, I waited where I was. 'What do you mean, Nicole?'

She also waited, watching me. I sensed she was assessing me rather than playing with me. I had passed whatever first test she had set me.

'What is it?' I asked, more gently. I bit off the thread and tucked the blouse into a drawer, then went to sit beside her.

'My life is cursed. I'm never going to be happily married. And I know why. It's all my own stupid fault.'

I admit I was feeling sorry for Nicole. I had no business feeling sorry for a rich white woman, of course, but there was something so sad in the mountain of dresses and the bottles of lotions, the jars of creams and the flasks of perfume all designed to make her appealing. It was work for her, prettying herself up, just as you would bathe and brush a goat to fetch a better price at the market.

If Nicole had been locally born, her family or in-laws would have arranged a good second marriage for her. She was still young and had proved herself fertile. All potential husbands would be carefully vetted and all their family connections gone into before she was asked to consider them. If she had responsible brothers or brothers-in-law they would make sure her new family treated her and her child well.

Instead Nicole had to resort to meeting potential partners by chance, left to the mercy of friends who would introduce her only to men they did not think worth marrying themselves. It seemed a strange and barbaric way to arrange a business as important as a marital union.

'This will be over soon. You will meet someone else.'

'No. Even if I do, I'm never going to be happy. I don't want to talk about it. It was a stupid love charm that turned into a curse. It's ruined my whole life.' Nicole sank back limply against the pillows.

'Do you want to get a mantra from the temple?' I asked.

'What?'

'A protection mantra. Or protection beads. To cancel the effects of your curse. Or the temple medium can do a cleansing for you.'

'Don't be ridiculous. Only primitive fools like you believe in things like that.'

I had little faith in temple mediums but, then, Nicole was the one who believed she had been cursed. Surely someone who believed in curses had to believe they could be blocked. I put on my best inscrutable-Oriental face.

That seemed to work.

'Oh. You speak English so well, I keep forgetting what you are. I didn't mean your sort of curse. I meant Fate, and bad things happening to people who deserve better.'

'Like karma?' I suggested.

'No. Stop twisting my words with your stupid superstitions. I mean, look at me. All I ever wanted was to be loved. Now all the men who have ever meant anything to me are dead. Victor, Eric, Radley—'

'Eric?'

'Mind your own business. You know, I don't think you're much use as a protector. What are you going to do if somebody attacks me? I think Chief Inspector Le Froy should move into the hotel to protect me around the clock.' She moistened her lipstick with her tongue at the thought. 'You don't understand the first thing about protecting me!'

'Oh, I think Su Lin understands protection very well.'

Dr Covington came in with Junior. Kenneth followed them, closing the door after him.

'Su Lin is a member of the very powerful Chen family, aren't you, dear girl? The Chens are like the Mafia of Singapore. They probably have someone watching her all the time, so they'll be watching you too. Just don't get on her wrong side. Interesting that Le Froy, who has such a reputation for rooting out local gangs and triads, should employ her. You have to know the right people, eh?'

I felt sure he had got this information from Victor. How long had Victor been watching and spying from the sidelines before it had got him killed?

Kenneth was saying something to Junior and I felt grateful to him for distracting the child.

'Now you're all back it's time for me to go,' I said. 'I'll see you tomorrow, Mrs Covington.'

Nicole was looking at me with new interest. She pouted prettily. It was her social pout. I was beginning to recognize the signs. She wanted something and would be sweet to me as long as she thought I might get it for her.

'Don't go. Stay here with me. I'm sorry I got carried away. I'm very highly strung, you know. But don't go off in a huff, girl. Come and sit down to dinner with us. If you don't know how to use a knife and fork I'll teach you. And I've got a dress you can wear. You can't go down to dinner in that! But I can't lend you my make-up. I swear someone keeps taking my lipsticks. I lost one on the boat and another just disappeared. You should stay.'

'No, thank you.' I wanted to get out of there and was sure nothing could change my mind.

Kenneth said, 'I've invited Parshanti Shankar to join us for dinner tonight. Nicole, you met her at the restaurant the other day. She's a friend of Miss Chen's. She told me Miss Chen is working here "undercover" and I thought she might like to see her in action.'

Dinner at the Farquhar

———◆———

I stayed to dinner. I was furious with Parshanti.

She was waiting for us on one of the cushioned chairs outside the restaurant, wearing another dress I hadn't seen before – bright red, sprinkled with little white and yellow daisies. Her hair was in a single long plait pulled over one shoulder. She looked nervous but lovely as she jumped to her feet on seeing us.

'Good evening, Mrs Covington, Dr Covington . . . Mr Mulliner. Hello, Radley.' She gave me a little wave and an excited little-girl shrug.

Nicole's cool gaze slid over her. I suspected she was jealous of the red frock. Dr Covington, his hand on Junior's shoulder, said, 'Yes. Fine, fine. Everything's fine,' as though Parshanti was a member of the hotel staff.

'I thought we agreed you'd call me Kenny, Shanti.' Kenneth offered her his arm, placing his other hand over the fingers she slipped shyly around it. 'Glad you decided to risk it. I warned you, didn't I? England isn't famous for its cuisine and there are few

173

things more terrifying than an Asian cook attempting to serve British food.'

I knew his snide comments were rubbish since Kaeseven was running the kitchen. Not only was he a culinary genius but Westerners and Easterners alike raved about the Farquhar restaurant.

I suspected Kenneth Mulliner was feeling uncomfortable, even though he had set this up – to show me he knew I was there to spy on them? But was he also trying to make Nicole jealous? And worried that she might be too jealous?

Some people deal with discomfort by trying to make others feel worse. If I could help him to relax with me, I might find out if he had had any grievances against his dead friend Victor. But that was not likely to happen tonight, especially with Parshanti in the picture: there would be no chance to commiserate with him over his friend's death or Nicole's lack of warmth. Drat Parshanti!

'You shouldn't be here!' I hissed, wishing I could tell her I had seen Kenneth ditch her for Nicole in the hotel restaurant. Surely she couldn't have forgiven or forgotten that so soon.

'You look nice,' Parshanti whispered back.

To persuade me to stay to dinner, Nicole had dressed me in a silky grey shift dress of hers. It was afternoon length on her but came down almost to my ankles.

'You look so at home in a frock,' she said, 'better than those awful cotton trousers. We must get you some shoes with heels. Like normal people wear.'

Normal people? Did she see me as some kind of orang utan? But though the slippery material and occasional breeziness between my legs felt strange, the dress made me feel elegant and girlish. Almost pretty.

'You really should practise walking properly,' Nicole said. 'You look so funny when you limp and go all lop-sided. Nobody's going to ask you to dance if you walk around like that.'

'Su Lin had polio!' Parshanti burst out. 'How do you think you would walk if you'd had polio and recovered with one leg shorter than the other?'

My loyal (though silly) friend had been gazing at Nicole Covington in worship, but indignation had crushed her awe. Parshanti had learned all about American manners and British etiquette, but she was still ruled by blunt Singapore honesty. Kenneth laughed and took her arm to steer her towards the table.

'Nobody cares how I walk,' Nicole said to no one in particular. No one contradicted her. Kenneth, at whom the comment had probably been directed, had walked on ahead with Parshanti.

Nicole pursed her mouth, narrowed her eyes and followed. She had to walk beside me because Dr Covington and Junior were already at the table having a discussion with a waiter.

'Is true, sir,' the waiter was telling the boy. 'We only serve ice cream after meals have been eaten. Have you eaten your dinner?'

———◆———

Parshanti seemed happy to be seated between Kenneth and Nicole. Junior, between Nicole and Taylor Covington, had had his dinner earlier and was served a bowl of ice cream with mango chunks. This left me with Dr Covington on one side and Kenneth on the other.

That gave me the opportunity to talk to them both. I saw that though Junior managed well with his grandfather's help he watched his mother's every move. He clearly adored her. Parshanti was not much better. Her attention was on Kenneth Mulliner, and as Kenneth watched Nicole playing fretfully with the menu, Parshanti did too. As did Dr Covington, but more to make sure she ordered food as well as drink, I thought.

Nicole Covington didn't seem bothered by all this attention. She drank her wine – numbing her boredom, she told Dr Covington when he remonstrated – and couldn't decide what she wanted to eat. 'What difference does it make? It all tastes the same anyway!' I suppose constant scrutiny is the price of fame and she was used to it.

After we had ordered, Kenneth turned to Parshanti. He might have guessed Nicole meant to ignore her and monopolized her so she wouldn't notice. Either that or Kenneth thought it was good sport to entertain Parshanti while making Nicole jealous. I thought the second option more likely. Remember, I had seen how fast he had dropped Parshanti when Nicole appeared on the patio of this very restaurant.

Parshanti, giggling through a whispered conversation with Kenneth, had clearly decided not to remember it.

I felt angry with Kenneth and with Parshanti for being so silly about him. If I knew my friend (and I did) she was already dreaming of how they would live happily ever after and what she would name the cute babies fathered by that wicked, possibly murderous man.

With all this to watch, I had forgotten about Dr Covington. Now he turned to me and took it upon himself to show me how to eat soup. The ponces will tell you to spoon your soup away from you in the bowl. Doesn't make sense, does it? Forget it! You China dolls have the right idea. Just lift the bowl and slurp it all up!'

Thanks to etiquette lessons from Miss Teh at the Mission Centre – 'As our ships go out to sea, I scoop my soup away from me' – Parshanti and I knew very well how to eat soup Western-style.

'Spooning away from you, the drips end up in the bowl instead of on you,' I told him, as though he was Junior.

Dr Covington wasn't listening.

'Let me show you. You hold the bowl with one hand . . .'

Suddenly he had one arm around my shoulders and one hand cupping each of mine around my soup bowl, tossing my spoon aside. 'Lift the bowl like this. Let me show you . . .' He was crushing me, his hot chest pressing into my shoulder and back. He smelt of sweat and spice oil and old beef. The sourness of whisky was on his breath, which stank of dirty gums and rotting teeth.

I pushed against him but he squeezed his sweaty palms harder against my fingers and laughed. 'What's wrong? When in Rome, do as the Romans, eh?'

'Did you teach Radley his table manners too?'

'Radley?'

'Your son. When he was growing up.'

It was a low trick, mentioning his dead son, but it worked.

His hands froze and I jerked the soup bowl hard so that warm soup washed over his fingers and mine. He let me go with a muttered oath and settled back in his chair, wiping his hands on his napkin.

'Missed most of my Radley's childhood. Too busy making a living. Everlasting regret. Making up for it now with Junior,'

I turned back to Kaeseven's delicately curried shrimp and crabmeat soup with my spoon. I've probably eaten the best local foods and the worst of colonial pseudo-British food, and the fact-checking side of my brain told me the soup was delicious.

And wasted on me. Because I wasn't there to indulge myself. I was an undercover agent there to observe suspects and witnesses. I had to stop shaking with the shock of what had just happened.

But what *had* just happened? I couldn't believe a respectable white man had just put his hands on me. No one else at the table had noticed anything. Kenneth seemed completely absorbed in Parshanti. But the efficient way in which he was spooning soup into himself, too smoothly for someone besotted, told me he was acting.

Parshanti wasn't. With a pang, I saw she was toying with her spoon, occasionally pursing her lips to take a tiny sip. When people in love eat together for the first time, food is not what they are hungry for. Plus, I suspected she was wearing lipstick and afraid to smudge it.

Lipstick was contraband, forbidden by the mission-school teachers and Parshanti's mother. Westerners seem to think wearing lipstick and rouge will lead women towards loose morals and adultery. To locals, red means marriages and births and good-luck celebrations. A single girl wearing lipstick when out with a strange man might find it leads to all those things, but not necessarily in that order.

Some men might even see wearing lipstick as an invitation – but I was the only female at the table not wearing lipstick. I was sure I hadn't done anything Dr Covington could have seen as inviting.

Kenneth and Parshanti had their heads together and Kenneth said something the rest of us couldn't hear. Parshanti giggled, glancing at Nicole in a way that suggested Kenneth had said something about her. Nicole put down her spoon, lowered her eyelids, then struck.

'I thought I could never bear to live in America again, but Junior's got to get the right kind of education. Where else is he going to get it? It's not just about math and science. It's about learning to get along with the right kind of people. Kenneth agrees with that, don't you, Kenny?'

When Kenneth looked up, startled, Nicole continued casually, in her slightly husky little girl voice, 'Kenneth went to Oxford hoping to meet the right kind of people. People who would set him up for life. Not all white people are rich, you know. Kenneth isn't. That was why he was always hanging around Victor. Because Victor's father always paid for everything as long as Kenneth wrote his boy's papers and got him out of trouble. Maybe he hoped that after Oxford, if he kept hanging on to Victor, Victor would keep paying for everything. Who's going to pay for you now, Kenneth?'

Resentment flared in Kenneth's eyes but Nicole smiled sweetly at him and twisted a little coil of hair around her fingers.

'I can make my own way,' Kenneth said. 'I can play the markets like Eric Schumer did. But I'm not going to end up like him.'

Nicole looked startled. I saw her dart a guilty look at Dr Covington.

'You don't know what you're talking about,' Dr Covington said dismissively. 'You're being sensationalist.'

'You don't know the whole story? Nicole set her sights on Eric Schumer. He almost escaped when she met up with your Radley, but she got him back on the hook once Radley died. Next thing you know, Eric's dead too.'

This was the kind of table talk I had been waiting for! I desperately wanted to ask for details, but Parshanti, bless her soul, got in first.

'What happened to Eric?' she asked Kenneth. 'Who is he? Is he in England or America?'

Kenneth answered with his eyes still on Nicole. 'He was a good friend of Nicole's. A very, very good friend. He was killed in a car accident. Just like Radley. And now Victor's gone too. Bit messy to leave so many bodies in your wake, Nicole.'

Junior's black-widow-spider comment must have come from Kenneth, I thought. Nicole looked furious but also frightened. I saw she had chewed the lipstick off her lower lip.

A waiter removed Junior's bowl and replaced it with a cup of hot chocolate, a biscuit on the saucer.

'Tuck in, Junior,' Dr Covington said. 'Your pa had a good appetite too. You're just like him, boy.'

'Nobody thinks so except you,' Nicole said spitefully. 'If you really believed it you wouldn't have to keep saying so, would you?'

The rest of us were served beef steaks, roasted green beans, and an egg, sliced potato and cheese salad but no one at the table touched their cutlery.

I didn't particularly like beef. It still feels unnatural to eat the strong, gentle creatures that spend their lives ploughing fields, pulling bullock carts and giving us milk. But Westerners didn't think twice about it, though they are shocked by the idea of eating dog meat. But I was quite willing to try.

Only no one else was eating. My eyes met Parshanti's over the table and she looked confused. Was she wondering, as I was, whether these people gave thanks for their food after the soup course rather than before the meal? Or had Nicole's nastiness put everyone off their dinner so they would stalk away to their rooms and ring down for sandwiches later?

But what a waste of good food!

At most Asian meals, any food left on the central serving dish will be eaten by servants or put out for scavengers. But the Western custom of placing fixed portions on the plates means any uneaten food is unclean once the plate is touched and therefore wasted. I hate to see good food wasted.

'We should eat,' I said, 'or send the food back to the kitchen while it is still clean.'

Dr Covington laughed. 'You're a good girl,' he said. 'Don't worry. You'll get all the food you want.'

He put a large beefy hand over mine again. And squeezed.

What the Fork?

———◆———

Dr Covington's large, fleshy palm pressed on my hand. I tried to pull away but couldn't. His fingers curved under my palm, locking my hand to the table under his large damp one. He grinned, seeming to think it was a huge joke.

Looking wildly around the table, I saw Parshanti was oblivious (Kenneth was grinding pepper over her plate) and Nicole rolling her eyes. Did she think I was enjoying the attention? Could Dr Covington believe that? He reminded me of the gangs of off-duty servicemen who think they are doing local girls a huge favour by whistling and calling lewd compliments at them.

Well, they aren't.

I dropped the fork I was holding in my other hand, 'Excuse me,' I said, and tried to tug my hand away. 'I have to get my fork.'

Dr Covington held on. 'They'll bring you another one.'

I saw a challenge in his eyes. He knew I had dropped my fork on purpose.

I've never been good at resisting challenges. My grandmother says I don't know how to keep my head down. But why should I? Everyone else tries to keep it down for me.

I whipped the napkin off my lap and onto the floor with my free hand, then knocked over my water glass as I reached for it. 'Oh, no!'

The water splashed Kenneth as well as myself and brought the attention of everyone at the table as well as others in the room. I stood up and dabbed at my dress as two waiters hurried over and Parshanti glared at me. *Manners!* she mouthed. Well, I had something to tell her about Dr Covington's manners.

But, no. It was funny, but I wouldn't tell Parshanti or anyone else in case Uncle Chen heard and sent someone to beat up the smelly old *ang moh* with no manners.

But I had underestimated Dr Covington. It appeared that he didn't back down on challenges either.

After the waiters had done what they could and left, Dr Covington leaned across me to say something to Parshanti and Kenneth. He was looking at them and talking to them but at the same time he put one arm on the back of my chair, his hand clasping my shoulder. His other hand moved onto my lap under the tablecloth. As he talked animatedly about tides affecting travelling time, his fingers stroked my thigh through the thin, silky fabric of my borrowed dress and moved upwards, squeezing painfully. I sat, feeling terrified and stupid, and frozen in a nightmare because no one else had noticed.

Then he winked at me. That woke me up.

The waiter had brought me a new fork and I grabbed it and jabbed it with all my strength into the hand on my crotch. Dr Covington howled and jerked away. I felt the tines of the fork scraping through his flesh and forced it deep into his hand.

Thinking back to it now makes me feel angry all over again. Given half a chance, I would have plunged my steak knife into his heart, consequences be damned.

'You little—' Dr Covington roared. He used words that I cannot write down here.

There was a little blood on my dress. I jerked, startled, when someone took hold of my wrist and gently prised my fingers off the fork my trembling hand was still clutching. It was Kenneth, standing behind my chair. He placed the fork on the table. It was well within my reach. It showed he trusted me not to pick it up again and stab him.

'I'm bleeding! There's tetanus in this filthy country! I could be dying of lockjaw!' Dr Covington waved his blood-stained napkin as evidence. 'I'll have you locked up and whipped raw, you nasty little slut—'

'Did you drop your fork, Su Lin?' Nicole asked. Her clear, musical voice rose above Dr Covington's blasphemous imprecations.

'I think she dropped her fork into her lap,' Kenneth said, speaking loudly, slowly and clearly. 'How clumsy. Did you really drop your fork into your own lap, Su Lin?'

Something had changed. The two were working as a team now. And they were trying to help me.

'Yes, I dropped my fork,' I said.

Parshanti looked frightened and confused. I knew I was in trouble but hoped we could smooth it over and that they would leave her out of it.

'On my own lap,' I emphasized. 'I was clumsy.'

I knew that if there was an investigation, it would come out in Dr Covington's favour, given he was a white man. Parshanti and I would probably get into all kinds of trouble just for being at the table with white people in a public restaurant. But I was still frightened and angry enough not to care.

'I see,' Nicole said sweetly. 'Oh, Taylor. If you can't keep your hands out of other people's laps, you can't blame anyone for being clumsy! Next time I might just stub out a cigarette on you!'

She laughed. Watching Dr Covington, Kenneth joined in. So did Junior. Without understanding what had happened, the child was clearly glad people were laughing again.

'Better sit down, sir. It will slow the bleeding.' Kenneth picked up Dr Covington's chair and set it back on its legs.

'Don't fuss over me!' Like a sulky toddler, Dr Covington batted him away. He must have thought Kenneth was mocking him. The scratches were superficial. 'I'm not sitting down. It's dangerous being next to savages who don't know how to behave in a civilized manner at the table!'

'Anyway, I've finished,' Nicole said lightly. 'We ladies will retire while you men sit over your cigars. Come Parshanti, Su Lin. Taylor, do something useful for once and put Radley to bed, won't you?'

Parshanti and I followed her out of the dining room. So she did know my name, I thought, as Nicole smiled and brushed off the anxious head waiter, who wanted to know what was wrong. Why wasn't she staying for the cheeses and the dessert that the chef had prepared specially for her?

'Can we get our things from your room first?' I thought she was throwing us out of the hotel.

'Sure thing. But you're not leaving yet, sweetheart. You'll both come up to my room for a drink. I have much better wine than old Stingy Pants will pay for downstairs.'

After Dinner

◆

T hat was the point where things changed between Nicole and me.

Almost before the door of the suite closed behind us, Nicole threw herself onto her bed and rolled around, screaming with laughter. Parshanti stared at her, startled. I just stared. She had let her guard down and let us in. It appeared we had passed a test or a turning point.

'Su Lin. Come here and sit down with me.' Nicole swiped tear-streaked mascara from her cheeks. She pulled me across to the settee and tugged me down beside her. Someone had arranged a table next to it with coffee, little cakes and a decanter of some amber liquid.

'You really scored on old Taylor down there, Su Lin – scored in every sense of the word!' Nicole could pronounce my name just fine when she wanted to.

'What happened?' Parshanti demanded. 'Did you go mad?' She was a little sore at being dragged away from Kenneth in the dining room, but was glancing around Nicole's suite with hungry interest.

'Oh, the dirty old man was up to his usual tricks.' Nicole put an arm around my shoulders and squeezed lightly. She smelt of powder and flowers, with a pleasant earthy undernote. It was so natural I could not tell whether it was her or her perfume. 'Oh, you poor thing. You're still trembling! You mustn't mind the stupid old clown. He can't help himself. He's just one of those men who grab every woman they see. But you'd better stay away from him later, especially if he's had too much to drink. Taylor thinks he's God's gift to all of womankind, and that any woman who turns him down is playing coy.'

I had dismissed Nicole Covington as silly, superior and condescending. Now I saw I had stereotyped her as blindly as she had me. It's the way social and racial generalizations work. After all, if not for a murder, we would never have met. Till now, I had seen her only as a suspect. Thanks to Taylor Covington, we were connecting as females and almost as friends.

'What?' Parshanti looked shocked now. 'Taylor? Dr Covington? What happened, Su? What did he do?'

'Also, he hates not getting what he wants. Especially in public.' Nicole looked more serious. 'Taylor hates losing face. He's worse than any Oriental. It would really be much safer for you to leave and never come back. Then he can say he was just flirting a little and you misunderstood. But I wanted to talk to you first. Given what you did . . .' The memory made her laugh again. 'Oh, sweetheart, you're shaking. Don't be upset, it's just how men are. You over there,' she said to Parshanti, without looking at her, 'your friend's upset. Get her some brandy. There – on the table.'

I was not upset. I was shaking more from shock at what I had done to an *ang moh*. I expected to be taken off to jail at any moment.

Parshanti crouched in front of me without brandy. I wouldn't have known how to drink it anyway. 'Do you want me to tell your uncle? Do you want my father to come and drive you back to East Coast Road?'

'No!'

'But if you're upset . . .'

'I'm not upset. Shan, listen to me. You must not tell anyone about this. Not anybody. Not even your mother. Especially not your mother.'

Mrs Shankar was a sweet woman but she was also one of the biggest gossips I knew. 'If Uncle Chen hears about this he will kill Dr Covington. You know that.'

It would be a matter of honour. Even if Uncle Chen believed I had invited the assault by associating with *ang moh*s, he would kill the man. And then Uncle Chen and his men would be put on trial and hanged, and all the Chen family property would be seized, and Ah Ma would be out on the roadside begging for rice grains.

'Promise me you won't say anything.'

Parshanti nodded. She understood. There was no Chinese blood in her, but you can't live in Singapore for any length of time without understanding the Chinese need to save family honour.

'Who is your uncle Chen?' Nicole asked. 'Does he live in town? How old is he? Is he married?' When I did not answer, she looked to Parshanti with a theatrical shiver of fear. 'Is her uncle really that dangerous?'

'No, he is nice. He just likes to growl a lot and pretend he doesn't speak English. He's very traditional and protective. He lives over his shop in town. But the family house is in Katong, on the east coast, by the sea,' Parshanti said. 'I've been there for Chinese New Year. It's a huge, place. I think it's almost as big as this hotel.'

That was an exaggeration, of course. Chen Mansion might sit on a large property, but that included the servants' and workers' quarters, and the domestic farm that produced fruit, vegetables and eggs, chickens, ducks, geese, goats and pigs, of which there were two. It was no hotel.

'Is it really?' Nicole's eyes were suddenly sharp and calculating, though she was still smiling and being nice. 'Suzy-Q, why didn't you tell me you have a big family house in the east by the sea? I love the sea as long as I don't have to be on it. They told us this hotel was on Beach Road but there's no beach here. Just rocks and those ugly cargo docks. Why don't you invite us all over to visit you in the east? Parshanti, you should come too, of course. I love walking on the beach.'

Walking on the beach beyond Chen Mansion? The family compound stretched up to the breakwater and sometimes, at high tide, waves crashed over to soak the lawn, leaving sand and hermit crabs on the grass. Beyond, rows of wooden stakes lined the dark sand of the working beach. This was where the fishermen tied their wooden sampans and fishing nets at night. People walked on the beach to dig for clams and crabs and collect seaweed to dry for cooking, not for fun.

Thinking of the old house now made me feel homesick. I might not be allowed to do a lot of things there, but when I was at home I could take for granted that other people would not be allowed to do things to me.

'I hate staying in a hotel. It's so public and impersonal and so expensive. Taylor is always going on at me about how much money I spend. As though it's *my* fault we can't leave here! Couldn't you invite me to come stay with your family?' Nicole tilted her head to one side. 'Just say I'm a friend of yours. Say I'm sick of hotels and I'm looking for a place to stay for a while. Asian hospitality is supposed to be such a big thing, isn't it? Why don't you show me some of your famous Asian hospitality and impress me?'

Nicole reached out and grabbed my hand, swinging it like a child would. 'Please? Please? I just want to see how you people live. When I was a little girl I was always going down to the sharecroppers' huts. It used to scare my Mamie half to death, she said, because if anything happened to me they would whip her and skin her alive till she was dead. But you see? Nothing did ever happen to me. I'm fine. And I want to see how you live. Please, Su Lin?'

'I'll speak to my grandmother,' I said, crossing my fingers behind my back. 'It's her house.'

Nicole tilted her head at me. 'Look, sweetheart. I know you're really here to spy on me. Well, you should tell that stuck-up inspector of yours that you can spy on me much better if you get me away from here. I miss my old family home so much, you know. My old aunts said there was no point in keeping up such a huge house, and I was only fourteen when my parents died so I couldn't do anything about it. And Radley . . .'

Nicole lowered her voice and leaned forward, drawing Parshanti closer to listen: 'Taylor likes to play the rich big shot.

But his father was a door-to-door salesman. The Conners were dirt poor but Taylor changed his name to Covington and managed to get himself a rich wife. Radley's mother's family was in trade . . .' her voice sank even lower '. . .in ladies' sanitary products!'

Nicole shrieked with laughter. Parshanti giggled too. I didn't see why it was funny. My uncle sold ladies' sanitary products in his store, but they were expensive and you had to go to the back and ask his wife to get them out of a box. I supposed woman friends bonded by giggling over gossip the way man friends bond while smoking cigarettes over beers.

Though I didn't smoke or drink I think I would have preferred the cigarettes and beer. Now I only hoped that, with the woolly state my head was in, I would be able to remember all Nicole was saying.

'Taylor has absolutely no taste, no sense of style. You should see the lipstick the man gave me on our way out here. It had these huge coloured stones on the case. Anyone could see it was hideous, but some conman on board the ship probably told him it was the latest fashion. He got so worked up when Junior wanted to look at it. And the lipstick was a ghastly colour. Like an orange gone rotten. He kept on at me to use it till I was glad I lost it.'

'Maybe it was his wife's colour,' I suggested, 'and he wanted to see how it looked on you.'

'Not likely. Taylor's wife died when Radley was around five. That's why he won't ever talk about where the Covington money came from. And he hates it when I say the family money comes from bleeding women. But it's not like they're a real old family. Not like you and I come from.' She gave my arm a little conspiratorial squeeze and giggled.

'We should keep these rooms in the hotel so I don't have to move my trunks. Taylor can stay and keep an eye on them. Anyway, he's got nothing to do except keep an eye on Radley. He's obsessed with Radley.'

'Radley your dead husband?' Dr Covington sounded like he would be right at home with the altars to dead relations in Chen Mansion.

'Radley my live son. Looks like he's obsessed with anyone called Radley, doesn't it? Maybe I should change my little Raddy's name. You won't want Taylor in your house. He's got no real class. He can stay here in the hotel with Radley.'

I didn't like Taylor Covington, but what was 'real' class? 'My family has no class either. My forefathers came over from China as labourers,' I said, 'so going into trade was moving up for them. Anyway, we are all descended from the ancestors, whether you believe our great-great-great-grandparents were Adam and Eve or Mr Darwin's apes.' Or the formless void of the Tao, of course. But I didn't think Nicole would understand that. 'Tell me more about Dr Covington. Was he upset about you marrying another man?'

'You shouldn't read Mr Darwin,' Nicole said dismissively. 'His writing is thoroughly outdated. Nobody in America reads Mr Darwin, these days. Taylor says evolution is a hoax made up by liberals to destroy the Church and weaken Western civilization. So, when can you get me out of this dreadful hotel?'

'I have to speak to my grandmother,' I repeated.

'Oh, will you? Can you go speak to her now?'

'Not now. But I will.' I would speak to Ah Ma sooner or later, so technically I wasn't lying. But there was no way I was going to invite Nicole to Chen Mansion.

'Goody, goody, goody!' Nicole said, as though everything was already settled. Then her face slipped abruptly into boredom. 'Oh, why isn't there anything for women to do here?'

Her quick changes of mood reminded me of the old mediums who were possessed by several spirits at once. Of course they did it for money, which at least made sense.

'What do you mean "for women"?' I thought of the knitting and quilting project the mission ladies had been trying (unsuccessfully) to establish for years.

'Victor went to cock fights and wrestling matches and opium dens, and he saw all kinds of things. But I can't because ladies aren't allowed to go around unescorted out here and no one will take me anywhere.'

Parshanti and I were proof that that was untrue. But Nicole very likely didn't see us as 'ladies'.

Nicole would have made a good actress, with her quick complete changes of mood and expression. But she might have trouble remembering her lines, given she couldn't seem to remember what she was saying from one moment to the next.

'Who is Eric Schumer?' Parshanti asked.

Nicole looked at her suspiciously. But Parshanti's eyes were sympathetic and curious.

'Is he an old beau of yours? I think Kenneth's jealous.'

That hit the right spot. Nicole relaxed and smiled a little. I could have kissed Parshanti.

'Well . . .' She looked at me. I tried to match Parshanti's expression as best I could. 'What's wrong with your eyes?'

'Nothing. Please tell us about Eric Schumer.'

Eric Schumer

◆

'Eric was a friend. A dear, dear friend. But there's nothing for anyone to be jealous of. The poor man's dead.'

'Oh, no! How terrible for you! What happened?'

Nicole and Parshanti were chatting like old friends. I kept my mouth shut and listened. It was easier to listen than to talk. I tried not to think about Dr Covington bringing Junior up to say goodnight to his mother.

'It was a car accident. It was terrible. I don't remember anything that happened. Taylor says I was in shock. That's when he made us go on this dreary Old World tour. I think he wanted me away from New York City because of what happened to Eric. I think he was afraid I'd killed him.' Nicole's chin went up and she turned on me. 'Are you going to tell your darling Le Froy that?'

She knew I was. 'Did you kill him?' I asked.

Nicole glared at me automatically and started to shriek, 'How dare you—' but then she sagged and slumped backwards. 'I told you. I don't know.'

'What happened?'

194

'All I remember is us having this huge fight at the club. Eric had promised to take me dancing. I'd had a few drinks and Eric was being all stuffy and saying he was going to take me home instead. So I told him he could go home to his mama if he wanted to, but I was going dancing. I remember throwing my drink at him and then I don't remember anything more until I woke up the next morning. I got myself home all right, just not into the house. Taylor found me in the car outside the gate.'

'You drove yourself home?' I asked, more impressed than anything else. I could barely imagine driving at night even if I was full of coffee.

'I must have,' Nicole said dully. 'It's no use asking me. Taylor's asked me hundreds of times but I just can't remember. It's like there's a fog in my head covering that time. The newspapers said Eric's body was found in an alley behind the club. There were tyre tracks all over him. They said he had been hit by a car and run over several times more.'

I began to understand why Dr Covington watched over Nicole so carefully. He was afraid the mother of his precious grandson had killed a man while she was drunk. Despite what he had done to me in the restaurant, I felt sorry for him.

'It's late. We should get going,' Parshanti said, into the silence that had followed this.

'Wait! Don't leave me. I hate being alone. I can't go to sleep when I'm alone.' Nicole had another swift change of mood. 'Just help me get ready for bed, then stay with me till I fall asleep. Please?'

She was talking to Parshanti. I could see my friend would have loved to stay and even spend the night in these luxurious rooms, but her parents would be furious. Even though Dr and Mrs Shankar had liberal ideas about allowing girls to go to school and get jobs, they were strict about her not wearing make-up and staying out late. And totally against her dating anyone they hadn't first been introduced to. Dr Shankar didn't trust Eastern men and Mrs Shankar didn't trust Western ones. Between them that pretty much ruled out everyone Parshanti met.

'I'll stay,' I told Parshanti. 'Just till she falls asleep.'

I ended up spending the night at the hotel. Luckily, I had come prepared for that. But my mind was still whirling in a dizzying waltz inside my head. My impression of Nicole had changed so completely that I could barely remember why I had been so certain she was Victor's killer, why I had wanted to spy on her.

After Parshanti left, Nicole helped herself to the brandy I'd refused. But even after she'd washed down Dr Covington's sleeping powders with more – she mixed sugar and bitters into it – she stayed awake fussing and fretting most of the night. Nicole Covington had neither self-discipline nor external guidance. But now I saw her as a neglected child rather than as a calculating woman.

I settled down in a chair by her bed and listened to her grumble about Singapore's dearth of dance halls, jazz clubs and handsome young men till I must have dozed off.

The next thing I knew, Kenneth Mulliner was standing by my chair looking down on me.

'Oh!' I jumped up with a start, almost falling over.

He caught my arm, steadying me till I'd got my balance. 'You don't have to bow down to me in here,' Kenneth said, 'only in public.'

I knew he was joking – at least, I sincerely hoped he was. You never knew with those young foreigners, and Kenneth's dry manner made it difficult to tell. I suspect he wasn't always sure himself what he meant. He was the sort who waits to see your reaction so he can tell you you're wrong. I don't mind being wrong but only when it makes a difference. So I didn't respond.

'Nicole's still asleep.' This was stating the obvious. Nicole had finally dropped off and was snoring softly and regularly. I didn't want to wake her. I could see why they preferred to leave her to sleep till noon and later.

I bent to collect the book I had been reading. It had landed on the floor along with my cloth bag and spectacles. Kenneth followed me out of the room, both of us walking quietly. And I had lost my prime suspect because, having seen Nicole at close quarters, I no longer believed her capable of Victor's murder – at least, not on her own.

'I'm just looking in for a moment. You don't have to leave.' When Kenneth wasn't being deliberately supercilious he sounded like an uncertain schoolboy. 'I mean, unless there's somewhere you have to go.'

His own words made him blush and I knew he was thinking of the WC. I don't know why Westerners are so awkward around necessary functions. After all, they are perfectly comfortable eating with other people: why act so embarrassed about what happens at the other end?

'You spent all of last night in that chair? Whew! How was Nicole?'

'She's likely to spend most of the day in bed,' I told him. Last night Nicole had insisted that she felt a bout of nervous depression coming on. I thought it more likely she was drunk. And when I had helped her to the WC to relieve herself earlier that morning, her 'nervous depression' looked to me a lot like a hangover. I wasn't feeling so good myself, after a night of attending to her. My mouth was dry, my eyes gummy and sore from not enough sleep, and I was aching all over.

Dr Covington had looked in during the night. I barely stifled a scream and he looked as shocked to see me as I was to see him inside Nicole's bedroom. All the more because I had locked the door. Our encounter in the restaurant must have made him forget the arrangements he had made for me to stay with Nicole. Perhaps he thought what had happened between us would have changed my mind. Or, as Nicole had said, perhaps groping strange females was so normal to him he thought nothing of it.

He had left without saying anything.

Remembering that, I asked Kenneth, 'Do you have the key to this room too?'

'No. Nicole's door wasn't locked. I'll stay with her. You can go.'

I wouldn't be sorry to leave. I had a sore neck as well as a headache and I wanted to wash and change my clothes. But this man was dismissing me like a servant. Which I was, in a sense. But I wasn't *his* servant. And why did Kenneth Mulliner suddenly want to be alone with Nicole? My suspicion woke more slowly than the rest of me.

'Nicole doesn't want to be left alone. I'll stay with her till Parshanti comes. She should be here soon.'

Kenneth looked surprised, but said, 'Not necessary. I'll be here.'

'She's bringing some magazines for Nicole,' I said. Parshanti's parents expected her home by nine, but Nicole had let her leave only when she promised to return with the fashion magazines.

We stood awkwardly, both reluctant to leave.

'Tell me more about Eric Schumer.' I wanted to know how much Nicole had told him.

'Never met the man.'

'But you know about him. You mentioned him last night!'

'So now you know as much I do.'

Parshanti arrived. She was carrying a stack of magazines from her father's store but grew flustered on seeing Kenneth and dropped them. The ensuing commotion of apologies brought Nicole out of her bedroom in her dressing-gown. Her eyes brightened when she saw the glossy covers on the floor.

'What a herd of elephants you people are! Oh, thank you, thank you. These will help the aching. No *Vogue*? No *Ladies' Home Journal*? Well, I suppose you did your best. Be a darling and give the girl some money, Kenneth.'

'Oh, no,' Parshanti said, more to Kenneth than Nicole. 'No, no, no. You mustn't. I wasn't meaning to sell them to you.'

Love was making her dumb in every sense of the word. I would have taken the money. But Kenneth didn't look as though he had any intention of handing any over. He looked like a ghost-month actor who had suddenly forgotten which of the five or six plays in the repertoire he was in. He couldn't decide whether to butter up Nicole or play up to Parshanti to make Nicole jealous.

Fortunately or not, Nicole wasn't paying any attention to him. She flopped onto the sofa and barely flipped through a couple of magazines before dropping them. 'Where do you think you're going, Suzy-Q? You said you were taking me to your house today.

She's promised to take me to stay in her big old family house by the beach. You promised, Suzy-Q! You can't break a promise. You just have to give me a few minutes to get dressed and put my face on and we can go.'

Kenneth looked at me. I think my expression told him this was news to me too. He grinned and shook his head.

'I'm going to work,' I said. 'I won't have time to see my grand-mother today. Parshanti will sit with you.'

Nicole pouted and told Parshanti, 'Don't just stand there with your mouth open, girl. Draw me a bath and get the room cleaned out. And make sure you fill my bath with fresh hot water, not that lukewarm dishwater.'

Parshanti looked at me helplessly. The Shankars were not rich but their house in town had a charcoal stove to heat bathwater. I could tell she had no idea what carrying hot water upstairs for Nicole entailed.

Well, I left her to it. I was still a little cross with her and she had slept in her own bed last night. She could handle things for a while.

Discoveries and Cover-ups

◆

O utside the hotel I had barely started on my way before I heard someone calling me.

'Wait.' Kenneth had followed me out onto North Bridge Road. 'What are you after, really?'

'I don't know what you mean.'

'Don't try to sell me that. What did Le Froy really send you to do? Are you supposed to kill Nicole the way she killed Victor? Or maybe you killed Victor! Maybe you're some kind of female samurai!'

'Are you mad?' Either that or Kenneth also used mood-changing drugs. I was already sure Nicole did.

I had seen benzedrine inhalers in her bathroom. Dr Shankar wouldn't stock them because he said people in America cracked the containers open to get at the drug-coated paper strips inside. They rolled them into tiny balls, which they swallowed with alcohol to give them energy. It was this energy charge that was addictive.

I pulled myself together and pushed aside my wild thoughts. One might think I'd been drugged myself.

'Why else would Le Froy cancel the investigation and say it was a fever? And why is he starting up the whole business again with this poison story?'

I knew, but I had nothing to tell him. I could understand his confusion and frustration.

'Victor was dead keen on blasting Le Froy with his stupid prank. Not just because he was the police but because he knew Le Froy's name. He said he had heard it from his old man. Why? What's your boss trying to cover up? You're going to tell me the truth or I'll beat it out of you.' He grabbed my arm and started dragging me back towards the hotel. He was hurting me, and when I stumbled and almost fell he walked on, yanking me after him. But that wasn't what frightened me most.

What frightened me was something in Kenneth's face that told me *he* was frightened and out of control. Was he afraid that whoever had killed Victor Glossop had sent me to find out how much I knew? Or because someone knew he had killed Victor and sent me to try to get proof?

I caught hold of a lamp post with my free hand and hung on. 'You're mad!' He might indeed be mad, but at that moment I was convinced Kenneth hadn't killed Victor Glossop.

Just then a figure detached itself from the side of the hotel and put a hand on his shoulder. Kenneth whirled round, ready to lash out with his fists. He dropped them when he saw Chief Inspector Le Froy.

'You! You killed Victor, didn't you? For revenge against Victor's family! Well, you're not going to get away with it! I'm going to see to it that you don't!' Kenneth dashed away, going past the hotel without looking round.

'He didn't even say good morning,' Le Froy observed, watching Kenneth's retreating figure. I wondered whether he had set someone to tail him, but I couldn't see anyone else running.

'Are you all right? You stayed here all night.'

'Nicole had trouble getting to sleep. I was just going to stay until she fell asleep, but I fell asleep too. She doesn't like being alone, and she doesn't like the hotel or Singapore. Wait! Where are we going? Weren't you heading towards the hotel? If you want to see Nicole, she's awake now.'

Le Froy was walking with me in the direction of the Detective Shack.

'I got what I came for. I hear there was some disturbance at your table in the Farquhar restaurant last night.'

'Who told you? Does my family – my uncle . . .' I was worried. Singaporeans are passionate about food and gossip, so my forking an *ang moh* in a restaurant would spread far and fast if it got out.

'A friend who happened to be there,' Le Froy said. 'He was impressed by how well you handled things.'

That made me stop in the middle of the five-foot way. 'Why didn't you tell me you already had someone planted at the hotel?'

Le Froy kept walking and I decided to worry about it after I'd had some sleep. I followed him and he let me catch up. My boss had sent someone to keep an eye on me at the hotel and come himself to collect me. I didn't know whether to be irritated that he hadn't trusted me or touched that he had been concerned.

But I had got one name for my efforts. 'Sir, Nicole doesn't remember, but it sounds like she may have killed the man named Eric Schumer in New York City.'

'She "may have killed"?'

We already knew Radley Covington and Victor Glossop had been involved with Nicole and had died. We also knew Nicole had been seeing Eric Schumer, who had died in a car accident. But it was news that Nicole had been with Eric on the night of the accident.

'She says she was too drunk to remember what happened. But he was run over by a car and she was driving that night.'

'I might get on the wire to America and see what more information they have on Eric Schumer's death,' Le Froy said.

That would be putting the new office wire system to better use, I thought. Most of the time it received official reports from London on the situation in Europe. 'Hopefully that will be more interesting than the tirades against Chancellor Hitler.'

'Chancellor Hitler is just a businessman and an opportunist. Nobody takes him seriously,' Le Froy said. 'Of course, this is now just an informal enquiry. Nothing official and nothing to do with Victor Glossop's death. That case remains closed. You don't have to go back to the hotel. You needn't have spent the night there.'

'But what about the autopsy report on Victor's death? Somebody poisoned him!'

'The Glossops want it to remain an "accidental death".'

I had been certain Victor Glossop's wealthy family would do everything they could to find out what had happened to him. Wouldn't any family? But while I was at the Farquhar Hotel, Governor McPherson had sent a message to say that, despite the autopsy results, the Glossops wanted the matter, and Victor, laid to rest as quickly as possible. And they wanted Victor buried quietly in Singapore.

They made no mention of Victor's fiancée. As far as they were concerned, Nicole might not have existed.

'They know he was poisoned and they want it covered up? Why? That doesn't make sense, sir!'

'The family may believe Victor antagonized someone enough to get himself killed,' Le Froy said. 'Digging up the dirt won't bring him back and may cause them further embarrassment.'

'But, sir, no matter what Victor did, it can't have been as bad as murder! I can't believe his own family doesn't care that somebody killed him!'

My own family was full of stories about feckless sons and nephews who were always getting themselves disgraced, disowned and reinstated. But the whole clan would have been up in arms for revenge if anyone outside the family had hurt any of them.

'His family may not think it was murder,' Le Froy said.

'What else could it have been? With all due respect, sir, remember Dr Leask's official report.'

'What if Victor knew he was taking poison?' Le Froy's quiet, reasonable voice cut into my thoughts. 'As an accidental death, he can be buried in the Christian cemetery here. That's what they want. As for Mrs Covington, she wasn't Victor's wife so she has neither the right nor the responsibility to make decisions.'

The official report didn't give any information on how the poison had got into Victor Glossop's system. There had been strychnine and brucine in the dead man's system, Dr Leask said, but other than testing food samples from the hotel kitchen and nearby hawkers he could do little more. Dr Leask's laboratory equipment and supplies were limited, not to mention his time.

Now, in the middle of the monsoon season, he and Dr
Shankar were fully occupied in trying to stem outbreaks of
cholera.

I couldn't believe it. If I had had the chance to study medicine
or chemistry or biology I would have done everything I could to
find out what had killed a man practically on my doorstep.
Instead these doctors had handed over their findings to Le Froy
at the Detective Shack and gone off to save the lives of children
who would probably die of something else next year.

Looking back now on how I felt then, I know I was being
unreasonable. After all, I was one of the children whose life had
been saved by doctors like them. After surviving a deadly out-
break of some dreadful disease, Westerners thank their God and
locals thank their gods, but no one thanks the humble,
hard-working doctor who insisted on hands being washed and
water being boiled.

But what about Victor Glossop? It was as though the man who
had been so popular in life hadn't mattered very much to anybody. Even the woman who was supposed to become Mrs Victor
Glossop was more upset at the inconvenience to herself than at
losing him. If someone had killed the man I was going to marry,
I don't know what I would have done, but I certainly wouldn't have
been sitting in a hotel room complaining of boredom.

———◆———

'Of course, they may want to investigate on their own,' Sergeant
Pillay said, when we got back to the Detective Shack. 'Maybe they
don't trust us.'

That was possible, of course. Kenneth Mulliner had made clear *he* didn't trust us. I could only wonder what he had been telling Victor's family in England.

Moving On

———◆———

At the Detective Shack, we heard there had been a police raid the previous night on a meeting at the Keng Soo Clan Association. Based on information received, the anti-insurgent team had turned up fully armed with weapons and tear gas, expecting to find a cell of violent terrorists plotting to rise up against the government.

Instead they had found a group of old women and children making *tangyuen* for the Winter Solstice, wrapping sticky rice-flour dough around fillings and rolling it into soup balls.

Even so they had been suspicious. The old women had been let off with a warning after being detained overnight for questioning, and the *tangyuen* had been searched for hidden messages, but the glutinous rice-flour balls revealed only sweet bean paste, sesame peanut paste and candied tangerine peel in coconut cream.

They had decided to work together, the old ladies said, so that each household could have a variety of flavours.

The Detective and Intelligence Unit had not been involved with the raid.

—◆—

Throughout the day Nicole sent a flurry of notes to me and to Le Froy, saying that she was bored to death and would prefer to be interrogated than ignored; if Le Froy came to tea or took her out to dinner, she would answer all his questions and put herself completely at his mercy. Alternatively, she wanted him to make me keep my 'promise' to take her to stay with my grandmother. She claimed that my grandmother (whose name she didn't know) was very fond of her and had sent her several pressing invitations to go to stay.

Le Froy put her notes on his 'to be answered' pile and did not answer them. The case was closed, after all.

He set me to typing wire reports describing suspected smuggling routes with possible stopovers in Singapore. I could have told him how much these reports missed by concentrating only on road traffic passing over the causeway and sea traffic passing through Keppel Harbour. But as many of the people smuggling goods in and out of Singapore's shallow coastal waters were probably working for my relations, I typed but said nothing.

At least it was work I could do with my brain half shut down. I just wanted to get through the day, go to bed and catch up on the sleep I had missed last night at the Farquhar Hotel. Parshanti was probably still there, but she was there by choice, not for work. As I would be, if I went back. I wasn't sure I would. Much as I wanted to find out what had really happened to Victor Glossop – and all the other men in Nicole's life – I wasn't keen to run into Dr Covington again.

So, I wasn't at all pleased to see him at the entrance of the

Detective Shack in the late afternoon. A bandage pad was taped to the back of his hand where I had scratched him but there was no other sign of our encounter. Dr Covington's eyes caught mine and he smiled wryly. He was red in the face and so painfully embarrassed that I almost felt sorry for him. Yet he still looked every inch the prosperous overfed American businessman.

'I need to have a word with you, Miss Chen. I must apologize if you were offended last night.'

'Oh, no, sir. I wasn't offended,' I lied automatically, backing away from him. But he continued over my feeble fib.

'Right here, if you like. I could say I was drunk and don't remember what I did. But that would be a big fib.' He rubbed the bandage on his hand. 'The fact of the matter is, I was drunk enough to forget I was a stranger in a strange land. I forgot it's a different culture out here. In America no one would think twice of it. Back home all the women flirt with me. Married women throw themselves at me. When you're a wealthy man in an important position, they let you do it – they expect you to do it. I'm automatically attracted to beautiful women and I meant no offence. In fact, the way I see it, if I didn't flirt with you, I would be insulting you.'

'That's a handsome apology,' Le Froy observed. He didn't come out of his office, leaving me to handle things. 'So, you think it's right to grab women you find attractive, sir?'

I knew it was gracious to accept apologies, but my distaste at what had happened last night was still fresh. And it had left me so nervous that when Sergeant de Souza's hand had brushed against my arm earlier – he had been reaching for the stack of files on my desk – I had been startled enough to hit him.

'I find it hard to resist an attractive woman,' Taylor Covington replied. 'As I said, the ladies back home find it flattering. But I realize now that things are different here. And I saw your limp. You must have seen me with my own limp. It made me feel that we were somehow *simpatico*. I felt there was a bond between us.'

Le Froy was shaking his head, but this time he was the one who didn't understand. It would be impossible for anyone who doesn't have daily difficulties going up and down steps to understand.

'Miss Chen, I wonder if you have heard of Joseph Pilates? He wrote a book a few years ago called *Your Health: A Corrective System of Exercising* and some incredible results have been documented. I never travel without a copy. I would like to give it to you as an apology gift.' He held it out to me with his scarred hand. 'Friends, Miss Chen? Can we forget our battle scars and start over?'

I reached out my hand a little awkwardly, remembering the hot damp of his palm last night. But, quick as a flash, Dr Covington flipped his wrist and curled his fingers into his sleeve, and before I knew it my fingers were clasped around the prettiest little bouquet of flowers.

They all laughed at my surprise, and Sergeant Pillay clapped. I laughed too – I couldn't help it.

'I am a keen amateur magician. I even put on some little shows on the ship with Junior as my assistant.'

I turned my attention to the flowers I was holding. They were delicately made of blue and white silk. 'So pretty,' I said, meaning it.

'Please keep the book, but I'm afraid you'll have to give the flowers back,' Dr Covington said. 'I'll send some real ones over later.'

'Thank you,' I said, as I handed them back. I was referring to his apology, and I meant it.

'It's no excuse, but I am under enormous strain at the moment. I have lost a son, and my grandson his father. I thought we had left death behind us and then this happens. My grandson's mother is . . .' He paused to search for a word and I wondered if he was going to call her a murderess.

' . . . highly strung,' Dr Covington finally said. 'Understandable, of course, but hard on the boy.'

Le Froy said, 'Did you do amateur shows in America? Your medical practice was in Georgia?'

'I practise wherever I'm needed,' Dr Covington said.

'You're very protective of your daughter-in-law, sir,' Le Froy said.

'My main concern is my grandson. I put up with Nicole's nonsense and cover up her little episodes because keeping her sweet is the only way I can stay close to Junior.'

'Little episodes, sir?' Le Froy asked.

'You may as well know. I had hoped to give her a fresh start away from home, but these things will come out. Especially if she's not resolved to change herself. Nicole had an opium habit back in the US of A. She was one of those "opium vampires" – rich layabouts who fool around with cocaine and marijuana and opium in a country where decent men start lining up at midnight, hoping for a day's work.

'If you want the truth, my main purpose for booking this round-the-world trip was to wean her off the drug. In America, you can buy all the dope you want if you have the money. And if you look like Nicole, you don't even need the money. I brought her to Germany, thinking Fascists live clean lives under the Führer. But she met Victor there. And Victor had his own nasty habits.'

'Sir, are you saying Mrs Covington was a drug addict?'

I had already suspected this but I was shocked by how calmly Dr Covington had said it. I knew about drug addicts, of course. But the ones I knew were old men in smelly rooms, smoking themselves into forgetting chronic pain and debts.

'Nicole needs constant entertainment and diversion, and the opium keeps her happy when the rest of us can't keep up with her. She got my Radley hooked on the stuff. He was trying to drop it, quit the lifestyle. That's why they were fighting so much, those last weeks. Between that and her drinking, maybe it isn't surprising she doesn't remember much.'

A drug addiction would certainly explain Nicole's memory blanks and dramatic mood swings.

'And Victor Glossop too? Do you know this for a fact?'

'That was how Victor and Nicole met in Germany. One of those damned parties. And when I brought her to England, she got in touch with him and he introduced her to his party friends in London.'

That might explain why Victor Glossop's family didn't want an in-depth investigation and trial. They were afraid Victor's past would come out. They might also believe his death was the result of an accidental overdose, if he had been a habitual user.

'You're very free with this information,' Le Froy said.

'The investigation is over,' Dr Covington said. 'But I thought you'd like to know how things are. No secrets between friends, right? Which brings me to one more thing. You may have heard Nicole mention one Eric Schumer.'

'Yes,' I said. Le Froy remained silent but his eyes were keen and watchful.

'Nicole can't remember anything about the night the poor fellow died. That's why it's better for her to stay out of America for a bit. I don't want my grandson growing up with his mother in jail. You see that, don't you? No hard feelings?'

'No hard feelings,' I said, meaning it.

Dr Covington nodded to me as he left. 'Good spunk. You'll go far.'

I felt warm inside, as though I had passed a test I hadn't known I was taking. I took a deep breath and felt myself relax a little. I looked at Sergeant de Souza, who smiled and nodded. No hard feelings. He understood.

The previous evening, I had gone from disliking and suspecting Nicole to connecting with her as a woman to feeling almost sorry for her. Now I wondered if she was a drunken killer who didn't even remember the men she had murdered.

'And please thank your grandmother for her invitation but I don't think Nicole should take up the offer to visit her house. She doesn't do well around strangers and unfamiliar environments.'

'It wasn't my idea, sir. My grandmother doesn't know anything about it.'

'That's what I thought. Nicole has a very vivid imagination and a very strong personality. Goodbye, Chief Inspector. I assume you have no objections to our leaving Singapore Island now?'

Parshanti

———◆———

By the end of that day I had gone beyond sleepy. I felt like a mechanical doll with dry eyes when I went that evening to the Shankars' pharmacy to look for Parshanti. I was sure she had heard by now that there was no case so Kenneth Mulliner and his friends would likely be leaving Singapore soon.

I didn't know whether I needed to comfort her for the upcoming loss of Kenneth or if I wanted her to listen to me grumble against a murder case being dropped. I did know I missed my best friend and needed to spend some time with her even more than I needed sleep. And I needed to sleep desperately. Because of that, it took me a moment to process what Mrs Shankar was saying: 'Parshanti went to look for you at the Detective Shack. Didn't you see her?'

'I must have just missed her, Mrs Shankar.'

Parshanti's parents looked worried.

'She left over an hour ago,' Mrs Shankar said.

'Oh, did she?' My sleepy sluggish brain took a moment to process this.

'Oh dear, I forgot!' I lied, as the pieces fell into place. 'We were going to meet at the Mission Centre to sort the donation books. I'd better hurry – I'm an hour late!'

I left in a rush, turning down Mrs Shankar's suggestion of tea and Dr Shankar's offer to rummage through his cupboards for educational pamphlets. I started towards the Mission Centre, in case the Shankars happened to look out of the pharmacy windows, then crossed the road and doubled back along the lanes in the direction of the hotel. I was sure that was where Parshanti had gone. And that her parents wouldn't approve.

'Su! I'm so glad you're finally here.' It was Parshanti who opened the door and dragged me into Nicole's suite. She looked scared.

'What's wrong?' But even as I spoke I saw Nicole lolling on the sofa. Was she sick – or under the influence of some kind of drug? 'What's wrong with her?'

'I don't know. She was all right this morning. I stayed for a while but I had to go home to help my mother. And when I got back she was just sitting slumped like this.'

'Did she eat anything? Drink anything?'

'No. Just her vitamins. Junior came in to say they were going to look at the ships on the seafront and to remember to take her pills. Oh, and he was with Kenneth.' Parshanti was a little flustered.

'And?'

'And Kenneth said he wouldn't invite us to come too because Nicole couldn't stand the sun for long but he would see me when they got back.'

Had Kenneth given Nicole something to make sure she didn't go out?

'Look. The case is over. Mrs Covington isn't our responsibility. We should leave. Your parents are wondering where you are.'

'Since the case is over, there's no reason for us to leave. Oh, Su, Nicole isn't feeling well and doesn't want to be left alone. Couldn't you sit with her for just a little while until Kenneth gets back? If the police aren't arresting her for anything, that means she's innocent, right?'

I wasn't going to sit with Nicole while Parshanti went off with Kenneth. If that sneaky man had drugged Nicole he might drug her too.

'Not proved guilty doesn't mean innocent. And it doesn't mean she's not dangerous. And I know very well that Nicole isn't the reason you're here.'

'You're not my keeper, Chen Su Lin!'

'Then you shouldn't have lied to your parents that you were coming to see me at the Detective Shack when you weren't.'

'Don't be so high and mighty! I know what you're trying to do. Just because you don't want to get married you don't want me to either! You're the same as my parents. They want me to spend my whole life looking after them. And after they're gone I'll be alone. But do they ever think of that?'

'Whether you get married or not you end up alone.' Nicole's voice surprised us. We had forgotten about her. 'All I wanted was somebody to look after me and I'm alone. I'll be alone for ever.'

We turned to see Nicole trying to sit up. She was bleary-eyed and her beautifully applied mascara was running down the side of her face.

'Victor was no catch, just so you know. In fact, I wasn't sure I wanted to go through with the wedding. Not after what he did to me that night. So maybe this all worked out for the best.'

'What happened that night?' I tried to make my voice sound casual. 'What did he do?'

Nicole looked around. If Dr Covington had been there he would have said something. But he wasn't, so she went on: 'Victor told me he was going to be out all night, at his wild bachelor party. I actually believed him! I knew he had taken a small room downstairs. I thought we could use it to store presents and things for the wedding. I heard the flowers I'd ordered had arrived – a week early! They would all be dead before the wedding. I was furious and I rushed down to see for myself. He was out so I got the key from the desk. And I found him inside the room and inside his fat whore slut.' She stopped.

There was a wheezing gasp from the doorway and we turned to see Kenneth, clutching at his mouth and then his stomach helplessly. For an awful moment, I thought he was having a seizure. Then, as Nicole glared at him, he started hiccuping, then burst out laughing so hard I was afraid he was going to be sick.

Kenneth Mulliner didn't hold up very well under stress.

I wished I'd had a tape recorder to record Nicole's words. I could understand Kenneth's hysteria. It took an effort for me not to laugh. Parshanti was staring with her mouth open.

'You found your fiancé with another woman?' I asked, to clarify things for the record. No one who had heard Nicole could have doubted what she meant. But without a tape recorder, I wanted to make sure Parshanti and Kenneth remembered what she'd said. There might be no case but I didn't care. You can't just walk away from solving a murder when the solution slinks up to you like a sly cat and piddles on your skirts.

'That no-good ponce wasn't my fiancé any more once I saw what he was doing on top of that fat cow!'

Nicole didn't seem to realize that what she was saying gave her the biggest motive for murdering Victor Glossop.

'So you killed him?'

I heard Kenneth's genuine shock through his hiccups. I have seen men and women in shock. The hardest punches, like 'Your son drowned' or 'Your wife and baby died in the fire' lead to shocked disbelief and deafening silence. It is as though the human body needs time to push through the horror. Kenneth was not frozen in disbelief. In fact he was laughing again, shaking his head. There was a hysterical note in his voice.

'Victor was such a chump. One week! He couldn't keep it in his pants for one blasted week!'

'You should talk!' Nicole flashed at him. 'You set it up for him, didn't you? I know about everything you two got up to in Oxford and London.'

'No, no, no. Nothing to do with me. I wouldn't have dared after seeing you tackle him hammer and tongs on the subject. When he smiled at that German lady on the way out here, I thought you were going to chuck the poor chap overboard!'

'I should have!' Nicole screamed. 'I should have kicked you both overboard!' She seemed ready to let loose another fit of temper. She grabbed the electric lamp on the end table and raised it. But the cord got tangled in the table's legs and she didn't manage to hit Kenneth with it.

'Did you kill him, Mrs Covington?' I had to ask for myself, if not for the record.

Now I saw shock. Nicole stopped mid-protest, her mouth staying open a moment before she snapped it shut. She lowered the lamp slowly. 'How can you ask me such a thing?'

'It sounds like he treated you very, very badly.' The sympathy in Parshanti's voice brought tears to Nicole's eyes.

'Oh, yes. I had very good reason. And if I had run a sword through both of them there and then, I'm sure any decent judge would have taken my side. But I didn't have a sword with me. And once I got out of that room I never wanted to see him again.' Nicole's voice was dull and dead now.

'Nicole, why didn't you tell me?'

Kenneth wasn't perturbed by Nicole flaring at him. Suddenly there was a new question in my mind: if Kenneth really hadn't known about the woman in Victor's room, who had arranged for her to be there? If Victor had been wandering the streets, looking for prostitutes, Le Froy would have heard about it by now. My thoughts went back to Harry Palin. He said he had arranged little favours for Victor: had he arranged this too?

'I was embarrassed and humiliated. I heard them laughing at me as I walked out. I couldn't tell anyone about it. Besides, I thought he'd tell you himself. I just wanted to die. I was going to call off the wedding. That was why I thought he killed himself.'

'You really think he killed himself?' I couldn't help saying. 'How?'

'I don't know. I didn't care. Poison, I suppose. Victor was a huge coward.' Nicole's eyes met mine. 'You can't expect me to talk to servants about something like this.'

Kenneth moved to Nicole's side now. 'Get out, you two,' he said, without looking at Parshanti and me.

Nicole seized his hand and burst into tears. I had felt honesty in the ugliness of her anger. But now she was sobbing with artificial prettiness, no sign of tears, and my old dislike of her resurfaced.

The shocked hurt on Parshanti's face made me feel so sorry for her I forgave her for all the things she had said earlier – though of course I wasn't going to forget them.

'Let's go.' I pulled Parshanti out of the suite. I wasn't going to worry about these crazy people. I wanted to tell Le Froy that Nicole had intended to cancel the wedding after finding Victor with another woman. The case might be over, but these people were still on our island. Surely he would want to know.

Mrs McPherson

———◆———

Le Froy listened to everything I told him without commenting. Then, 'That report from Yap Pun Kai.' He snapped his fingers at Sergeant de Souza. 'The Japanese woman found dead. When exactly?'

'Sir,' Ferdinand de Souza said, 'Miss Nakagawa Koto. She was found dead in her room two days after Victor Glossop's death.'

I was surprised he had the name and day ready. Le Froy was too: 'How come you followed up on her case?'

Singapore was full of illegal prostitutes. Given the terrible conditions they lived under, suicide was sadly not rare. Plus, those women were very often rejected by the families they had sold themselves to support.

'That young HQ corporal who made the first report went back and followed up on his own time. Corporal Wong Meng.'

'He doesn't think she killed herself? Was she sick?' In officially registered brothels, prostitutes had to be examined regularly for venereal disease. But illegally run pleasure houses seldom bothered.

'Not sick, sir. He says she was remitting money to the Japanese military effort,' de Souza said. 'Like several of her companions. They insist she must have been poisoned by a man friend or client.'

Unlike women from famine-struck farm communities, who worked to support their families, professional Japanese prostitutes had recently been appearing in Singapore by choice, to help finance their country's military efforts. A woman who made this noble sacrifice would not be driven to suicide by a venereal disease.

'She was found by her first client of the day. She was dressed – undressed, I mean – made up, ready and waiting. But when he went in she was dead. It appears she had been dead for some hours.'

'I hope I'm not interrupting anything?' a woman said. We turned and saw Mrs Viola Jane McPherson, the governor's wife, in the doorway. 'Knock, knock,' she added.

When Mrs McPherson appeared officially in public there was some fanfare, with warnings sent ahead to stores to wash down their steps and tidy up. This was an unofficial visit, then. She looked at our startled faces and smiled.

Her driver was behind her, holding the door open, and one of her boys was peering around her. I could tell the McPherson boys apart only because Greg was half a head taller than Pat. But since I could see only one, I had no idea which this was.

'Of course not. Please come in, Mrs McPherson. Is anything wrong?' Le Froy rose.

'That's her,' the boy said, pointing at me.

'Don't point, Greg.' Ah, it was the elder son. 'And, remember,

223

we say, "That is she", not "That is her". No, nothing is wrong. Could I have a word with your assistant?' Mrs McPherson smiled at me. She had a lovely smile. 'We came to pay for the sweets my sons took from your uncle's shop.'

'Oh! No need *lah*!' I was so taken aback I answered in Singlish.

'Must *lah*!' Mrs McPherson laughed. 'How's my accent? My boys told me what happened at the shop. They couldn't remember its name but Greg remembered you. He was very anxious to see you again and explain. Stand up straight, Greg. And say what you wanted to say.'

Greg stood up straight but said nothing. He must have told their mother what had happened, but he had no words now.

'Dr Covington means well, but my boys know they must pay for what they take.' At a nod from his mother, Greg stepped forward and carefully handed me two coins.

'Oh, please. No!' I said. 'My uncle is happy to know your sons enjoyed the peanut brittle.'

'It is my son's money and my son's idea to pay for the sweets.' Mrs McPherson looked very proud of her son. It made me think about the different lessons people try to pass on to children about money. And about who controls that money.

'Five cents is enough.' I passed one of the coins back to the boy. 'I'll make sure my uncle gets this. Thank you very much, young sir.'

This was something that went beyond money. Mrs McPherson could easily have dropped off the few cents at Uncle Chen's shop, which looked humble. The McPherson boys must have thought they were taking sweets from poverty-stricken storekeepers. They could not know, and I saw no reason to tell them, that the Chens owned the block the shop stood on as well as several adjoining blocks. With Uncle Chen in his shop, my grandmother had eyes on the ground.

Mrs McPherson had come to the Detective Shack with her son because, although they were the family of the new governor, she was not raising her boys to behave as white rajahs. This made me like her very much, and gave me the courage to ask her, 'This is very good of you, Mrs McPherson. May I ask why you summoned Dr Covington to treat your sons' tutor that day? Don't you trust the local doctors?'

Le Froy looked surprised, but Mrs McPherson did not seem so at all. 'I didn't. And I do! Dr Covington came to Government House for a word with my husband and decided to wait because he was engaged. When he saw I had the boys with me because poor Mr Meganck was sick he insisted on seeing him. As it happened, he had his medical bag with him.'

'That was convenient,' Le Froy said.

Mrs McPherson shook out her skirts with the air of a woman shaking off a memory. 'He left some medicine. When Mr Meganck was feeling better, I brought the boys with him to see Dr Leask at the hospital clinic. Dr Leask wouldn't criticize a fellow physician, but said that for minor matters I couldn't do better than Dr Shankar at the pharmacy if we couldn't find him at the clinic.'

She turned back to me. 'Dr Covington had his grandson with him, so I persuaded him to take my boys out. It was the only way I could get him out of the house. He was so determined to have a social chat with my husband and Gregory was equally determined not to. Dr Covington might have moved in permanently!'

'You are not comfortable with Dr Covington, madam?' I shouldn't have said such a thing to an *ang moh* woman, let alone to the governor's wife, but Mrs McPherson had a strong, friendly presence that somehow reminded me of Le Froy. She was certain enough of who she was not to care about how anyone else saw her.

'It's more accurate to say I am not yet comfortable with our position and responsibilities here. Please don't misunderstand me. I may be one of the few women I know who genuinely believes my husband is a good man who will do a good job. But Gregory is not politically minded, thank God, and is ill at ease with those willing to take advantage of the perks of power.'

'So it is on that principle that your boys pay for their peanut brittle,' Le Froy observed drily.

'Laugh if you must, sir.' Mrs McPherson chuckled. 'Though, of course, if a routine background search reveals Dr Covington has not the funds to buy sweets for his grandson, we would be happy to pay for his sweets too. I am a doctor's daughter, and I'm not entirely convinced by a doctor who treats a patient without examining them. Even if he is an expert in putting together medicines.'

'Did he?' I hadn't realized that. 'Is he? But, madam, I thought you said he looked in on Mr Meganck.'

'He stayed in the doorway, a good five feet from the bed, with his handkerchief to his face for fear of infection. He said I ought to keep the boys away from their tutor to prevent infection spreading. As for the medicine, he said it was his own patented recipe. Gregory is always reminding me not to criticize differences, and I'm sure pharmaceutical standards differ from country to country, but in a British colony like this, British standards should apply.'

'He makes crayons,' Greg McPherson put in.

'Oh, yes. He offered to teach our cook to make wax colouring sticks for the boys like he made for his grandson. He melts beeswax and palm wax with powdered chalks and sets it in bullet moulds. That's quite all right with me, since they're not going to swallow them.'

This was interesting and I filed it away to think about another time. Right then I was more interested in finding out why Mrs McPherson, who seemed a smart and practical woman, was standing there telling pointless stories. I guessed she had come to tell Le Froy something but didn't know how to bring it up. Still, even Le Froy couldn't tell the governor's wife to hurry up and get to the point.

'Something about Dr Covington makes you uncomfortable,' Le Froy said quietly. 'What is it?'

'Oh, no!' Mrs McPherson said automatically. Then she laughed. 'I mean, oh, yes. You've hit the nail on the head. It is such a silly thing. But I suppose that's really why I came. During that visit, Dr Covington passed me a note asking if I was related to Manasseh Meyer.'

Manasseh Meyer was a rich local merchant and a generous philanthropist.

'I believe he was telling me he knows my mother's family is Jewish,' Mrs McPherson continued, 'and his writing it down suggests he thinks it is something to be hidden. From the children, for instance.'

'Mother let us see the note,' her son said.

One thing about a tiny island like Singapore is that every man, woman and monkey in it originated somewhere else. Whether your distant ancestors sailed from China, India, the Malay archipelago or the United Kingdom, your decision to stay is the only thing that makes you Singaporean. Your presence counts more than your origins.

At least, that was how it was supposed to be. Beneath an upper crust of white colonial administrators, the rest of us were muddled together like a savoury stew under mashed potatoes.

'Dr Covington thinks Mrs Covington may have killed a Jewish man,' I said, talking fast to get it out before I took fright. 'His name was Eric Schumer. It was probably an accident but she doesn't remember. Maybe Dr Covington wondered if you were related to him too.'

'I wonder if I am.'

I thought Le Froy might tell me off for mentioning Mr Schumer, but all he said, mildly, was, 'Some say Raffles, the founder of this island, must have been of Jewish stock, his family name evolving from "Raphael". Blackmail only works if you fear it.'

'Oh, there was no mention of blackmail,' Mrs McPherson said. 'I felt Dr Covington was trying to show me what a good fellow he was. How good he was at keeping secrets.'

'Yet it made you uneasy.'

Again, she seemed to take a moment to consider his words – or him – before answering. 'Only because, for a man in my husband's position, the appearance of transparency can be as important as actual transparency. Keeping our private lives private can be too easily interpreted as hiding secrets. I'm sure you feel the same way, Chief Inspector. And because I was surprised to find information about my family in the hands of an American tourist.

'Dr Covington also warned me about government administrators out here. He may not have realized he was insulting my husband to my face. He wanted to warn us not to trust you, Chief Inspector. He claims you have been wasting official time and resources trying to get information from America about him and his relations.'

Le Froy nodded, acknowledging this. So that was what he had been querying with the new wire machine in his office. Even with modern technology you had to have a human on the other side willing to answer your questions. Some officious administrator must have alerted Dr Covington.

'Anyway, I mentioned to a friend in Washington that I would appreciate information on Dr Covington and his late son. They are our guests on the island, even if not your suspects.'

'Information, madam?'

'Love affairs, business transactions, bank accounts, friends and foes . . . Call me a nosy parker!' Mrs McPherson laughed merrily and got up to leave.

'She would have made a good wife for the King,' Sergeant Pillay said, after we'd watched the official motor-car drive off. That was a common enough compliment at the time.

What was surprising was that Le Froy said quietly, 'Yes.'

Pip's Squeaks

───────◆───────

*C*hief Inspector Le Froy – Merely Incompetent or Criminally
Dangerous?

Pip's Squeaks asked (and answered) the question in the
Weekend World that arrived the next morning.

Why did Thomas Le Froy leave England? The story, dear children,
begins with the death of Le Froy's wife.

Mrs Jane Elizabeth Le Froy died after being hit by a motor-car
not twenty feet from her own front door. Senior Detective (as he was
then) Thomas Le Froy claimed someone deliberately targeted his
wife. The driver of the motor-car claimed Mrs Le Froy, who had been
walking on the pavement with a shopping basket, had 'suddenly'
jumped onto the road in front of his vehicle. Le Froy insisted she
must have been pushed and talked wildly about threats he had
received.

This despite the fact that in 1928, the year Mrs Le Froy died,
over seven thousand road deaths and over two hundred thousand
motoring injuries were recorded; the highest number ever recorded

in Britain. There were calls to enforce a motoring speed limit.
But as Conservative MP Colonel Mosley-Partington points out,
over six thousand people commit suicide every year, deaths that
are swept under the rug.

The article also quoted Colonel Mosley-Partington as saying,
There are better ways than suicide to escape an unhappy marriage,
which seemed to indicate an unofficial verdict that Mrs Jane Le
Froy had committed suicide to get away from her husband. Or
even that Le Froy might have killed her for threatening to leave
him.

And that, with a second innocent death on his doorstep,
Senior Detective Le Froy had been removed from his position.

There was more in the article about how the Home Office
used colonial outposts like Singapore as dumping grounds for
criminal and incompetent staff, but nothing about more about
the first 'innocent death' credited to Le Froy.

Well, at least this new article disproved my half-hearted theory
that the late Victor Glossop had been 'Pip'. But what was that first
'innocent death' the article mentioned?

I trusted Le Froy but we had no idea what his history was
before he was exported out east.

'No need to mention this in the office,' Sergeant de Souza
said, asserting for once his number-two position in the Detective
Shack. The men didn't seem as surprised as I was. 'Don't leave
that paper lying around when he comes in.'

'Did you know about the chief inspector's wife?' I demanded.

'No need to discuss,' de Souza said firmly. 'Not our
business.'

So the men *had* known about Le Froy's dead wife. At least I knew they didn't gossip. If I ever turn to crime, I hope to be investigated by prim, proper British-trained men and not avidly curious women like Mrs McPherson and myself.

The bright side was that if the police force already had these details they wouldn't be surprised. Though what Mrs McPherson had said about the appearance of transparency might apply as well to Le Froy as to her husband.

I find it impossible to take my mind off one thing unless I give it something else to fixate on. I turned back to Corporal Wong Meng's notes on Miss Nakagawa Koto, the dead Japanese prostitute. The inventory of her belongings included a lipstick in a jewelled casing of coloured stones. That stirred a memory to the surface.

'Where are the Japanese woman's things?' I asked. 'Still in HQ or handed over to her relatives?'

'I don't think she had relatives, so probably still in the dungeon,' de Souza said. The 'dungeon' was a small concrete bunker outside Police HQ, formerly a fuel shed. It was so named because there were bars across the single window and the door locked from the outside. 'What are you looking for?'

'The lipstick they found. In a jewelled case. Mrs Covington lost a lipstick like that.'

'Can never understand why modern women use lipstick,' Sergeant Pillay said. 'In the old days women chewed *paan* to make their lips red so men look at them and feel sexy. But, actually, *paan* is an aphrodisiac, so once you kiss one of those women, you have no choice but to feel sexy.'

'I'm going over to see Corporal Wong at HQ,' I said.

But as I reached the door Le Froy was coming in, with a stack of papers bearing the Government House crest and an air of quiet excitement.

'What is it, sir?' de Souza asked.

'In response to the governor's enquiry, the Morgan Bank confirms Mrs Radley Covington closed her account and is no longer a client. It is the same with all the institutions she banked with.'

All Nicole's shares had been liquidated some time back, and the money removed from her account. Not only that, the last person who had enquired into her finances (and been balked by the bank) was Kenneth Mulliner.

And there had not been very much left in the accounts when they were closed.

'Sir, Dr Covington said he's been taking care of Junior's needs from his own account since they left America,' I said. 'I thought it was because he wanted to. But could it be because Nicole doesn't have enough money?'

'This doesn't say Mrs Covington has no money,' Sergeant Pillay said, his eyes skimming down the printout. Prakesh Pillay might be slow in some areas but he was super-fast when it came to money. 'It just says she took all her money back from Mr Morgan's bank. Maybe she knows something. Remember what happened less than ten years ago to Americans who trusted their banks?'

Le Froy spread Mrs McPherson's papers on the table. Some were single sheets, others three or more pages stapled together.

'Dr Covington's wife made sure her money went to her son, Radley, rather than to her husband. And after Radley's death, the fortune passed to Radley's wife, Nicole.'

I picked up a single page and read about a minor confusion when the party had been boarding the ocean liner. According to the report, the ticket Dr Taylor Covington used had been booked under the name of Eric Schumer and the note of transfer had been lost.

'Sir, I thought Dr Covington booked them on the voyage out after Eric's death fearing Nicole might be suspected of killing him.'

Le Froy pushed another paper towards me. 'This suggests Eric and Nicole were lovers and planning to run away to Europe together.'

Eric Schumer and Nicole Robert had been close friends for years and there were whispers they had been unofficially engaged before she was swept off her feet by Radley Covington. After Radley's death, Eric and Nicole were again seen together in New York City. It was Eric who had booked and paid for their passage to London: a stateroom for Nicole and another for himself and Radley Junior.

Most of this information came from investigations previously ordered by Eric Schumer's family. His mother blamed Nicole for his death, which remained officially unsolved.

I looked at Eric Schumer's post-mortem report. It was not a routine hit-and-run accident. He had been hit and run over several times with his own car.

'Eric Schumer was going to share a cabin with Junior, not with Nicole,' I said. 'Doesn't that sound strange if they were lovers? And this is after her husband died. Nicole didn't have to hide that she was seeing Eric or run away with him unless his family was making trouble. But why would they, sir?'

'Because she's not Jewish? Because she has a son? Because they wanted Eric to marry another woman approved by his relatives? There are always reasons.'

I would ask Nicole about that, I thought. Eric Schumer's family would hardly have had him murdered because he was seeing her. But what if they had tried to scare her off (as her desire to leave America suggested) and something had gone terribly wrong?

'Is there anything on Eric Schumer's family, sir?'

'Father is professor emeritus of physics at New York University. Mother was a classical pianist who performed at Carnegie Hall and is now a well-respected music teacher. He was one of three children. The brother, Howard, is a paediatrician, the sister, Lucy, a medical researcher. She and her husband are among the group working on a vaccine for poliomyelitis.'

Of course you can't judge people based on their professions, but Eric's family didn't sound like people who would hire a killer to get rid of Nicole, especially not one who ended up killing their son by mistake. If they had wanted Nicole dead, she would be dead. I was glad I hadn't mentioned my theory to Le Froy.

'Did Nicole tell you who she was trying to get away from when she left America?' Le Froy asked.

'I assumed it was the police, sir. Dr Covington said she was afraid they would think she got drunk and ran over Eric.'

Le Froy dismissed this with a twist of his mouth. I didn't know whether it was directed at Nicole or the American police. But he was clearly off on another train of thought.

I picked up another sheet and saw a photo print of a newspaper article that caught my attention. The brief report covered the hearing on the case of sixty-eight-year-old Reverend Thomas

Elijah Watkins, who had been kicked to death outside his church after responding to the terrified screams of two girls who had just left a Sunday school class. Seven-year-old Cassandra and five-year-old Emma-May Watkins were judged too young and unreliable to testify on the death of their great-uncle and no one else had seen or heard anything. Charges against Houston Carriway, Radley Covington, Travis Devine and Gavin Parnell were dismissed.

The hearing was chaired by Dr Taylor Covington. He was quoted as saying, 'The boys were just being boys and having fun with those girls. That old coloured man should not have interfered. He should have known his place and stayed in it. But he refused to show proper respect.' He called on the town council to implement stricter segregation measures to keep the streets safe. If the Watkins girls had not been brazenly walking around on the street the unfortunate incident might have been avoided.

The article concluded that all four had been warned and reprimanded.

I couldn't help thinking that maybe Radley had deserved to die.

Tomato Explosion

◆

'Come in!'

I wasn't surprised to find Parshanti in Nicole's suite when I pushed the door open. She was sitting on the sofa watching Nicole play solitaire with her bridge cards and I saw her glance behind me. For once I shared her disappointment that Kenneth Mulliner was not in the room. There were things I wanted to bring up with Nicole too, of course.

Nicole noticed Parshanti's sudden hope and disappointment. 'Sorry, Topsy. Kenneth seems to have better things to do today than look in on us. Did you make plans to sneak in some cosy time with him?'

'Of course not!' Parshanti burst out. Then, as Nicole shrilled with laughter, she looked so embarrassed that I felt sorry for her despite her silliness over handsome murder suspects.

'And you're finally here. Hello, Nancy Drew, Girl Sleuth! What are you detecting today?'

'I am a secretarial assistant, not a detective,' I said. 'And, besides, the investigation is over.'

'So did you come to cry over all the dreadful dirty things your precious Le Froy has been doing? Do you need Mama Nicole's help to get out of his clutches? I can understand why she did it, you know.'

'Who?'

'The late lamented Mrs Le Froy, of course. You wouldn't understand, but being married can do that to you. While I was married I often thought of jumping off a bridge or under a train. But places like that are always so full of common people. I couldn't bear the thought of them looking at my poor dead body. But a husband can drive you to do such things.'

I had tensed at the mention of the article. I had almost forgotten it, given de Souza's nonchalant dismissal and the news that had come from Government House. But before I could say anything Kenneth slammed the door open, without knocking, and came in.

'Where's Taylor? I need to talk to him.'

'You can see he's not here.' Nicole leaned back, pouting prettily. 'Come and have a drinkie and tell Nicole what you're so angry about. My, the whole world is coming to my door today.'

Nicole flirted with men as a matter of course. It was the only calling open to an upper-class, badly educated white woman. Like a shopkeeper being nice to customers, you did what you had to do to make a living. Nicole's profession was finding herself rich husbands, and she did that very well. She just wasn't very good at keeping them alive.

Kenneth ignored Nicole's invitation. He was holding a copy of the *Weekend World*, folded with the Le Froy piece in front, and I had the impression it was with effort that he kept his anger under control. 'Taylor's not in his room.'

'Well, he's not in mine either, honey pie. Unless you want to check under my bed. Or my skirts.'

Parshanti gave a little squeak of alarm. Kenneth left without answering. And Nicole's mood immediately soured.

'He hasn't eaten or drunk anything with me for days. I think he's actually trying to avoid me! I'd say you've put a spell on him, Parshanti, except he's not looking at you either. Oh, why are men so silly?'

Nicole didn't look any more like a murderess than she had the last time I'd seen her. I was sure Dr Covington suspected her of killing Eric Schumer as well as Victor Glossop. He must have told us because he couldn't do anything about it, being bound to protect the mother of his grandchild. But I was convinced he hoped we would find proof so he could protect Junior.

Nicole was still beautiful but, looking carefully, I thought I saw signs of drug use in her glazed eyes and pallid skin. It was possible that was due to her not having put on her make-up yet. Although it was almost noon, she was in her dressing-gown, with the remains of her breakfast around the room.

'Taylor might be a banker, not a doctor. He's probably at the post office again, watching all his investments and stocks. Thank goodness he takes Junior with him. Good for children to get out.' Nicole watched Parshanti from under slightly lowered eyelids. 'Of course, I suppose some of us are only interested in where Kenneth is.'

'Red seven on eight of clubs,' Parshanti said, keeping her eyes on Nicole's card game.

Nicole cheated at patience, sliding cards she didn't want back into the pack and drawing new ones. She wasn't cheating anyone else out of anything, so it wasn't really wrong, but I found it interesting that someone would break rules they had chosen to play by. Now she threw down the cards she was holding, 'Oh, I'm so bored I could just die and I wouldn't know it!'

That was when it happened.

Suddenly there were loud bangs and yells coming from somewhere close at hand. I heard glass breaking and the splattering of what might have been brains or intestines, and thought of bombs and bullets and firecrackers. Out of these, I had only ever heard firecrackers, but they are generally set off in the middle of the night around Chinese New Year and we were in the middle of the day in December – in a hotel where one man had already been murdered.

'It sounds like it's coming from Kenneth's room!' Nicole shrieked. 'Oh, my stars and garters, someone's gone and killed Kenneth too!'

I made for the door and hurried down the corridor towards the source of the explosions. Parshanti started after me but Nicole grabbed her and hung on, wailing, so I was the first to reach the door of Kenneth's room just as General Manager Van Dijk raced up the stairs followed by two uniformed porters.

I put my ear to the door. 'I can hear someone moaning inside!'

Van Dijk was holding a tiger rifle and his porters were carrying batons.

'Stand back, miss!' Van Dijk ordered. He rapped on the door. 'Mr Mulliner! Are you all right, sir?'

I heard Kenneth call something I couldn't make out. At least he was alive. Nicole and Parshanti arrived, with other hotel guests and staff. Some people were carrying arms, others first-aid boxes.

Everyone was tense, excited and alarmed, remembering Victor's death.

Van Dijk used his master key and pushed open the double doors. A scene of apparently bloody carnage was revealed. 'What the—' He raised and swivelled his rifle around the room, then lowered it slowly.

It looked as if bloody chunks of flesh and guts were splattered on the walls, floor and furniture of the room. Kenneth Mulliner, standing facing us, was also soaked with gore but seemed not to be in pain.

'It's nothing.' Kenneth gestured feebly for the doors to be closed. 'Nothing at all. Sorry about the noise. Just an accident.'

I followed the staff in, broken glass crunching under my shoes. I sniffed and bent down for a closer look. 'It's tomatoes,' I said, amazed. 'It's cooked tomatoes.'

'It's my tomato ketchup!' Nicole's high voice cut through the confused, relieved and baffled mutterings. She was standing in the doorway, Parshanti peering around her.

'Kenny boy must have kept all of it for himself instead of handing it over to that Chinaman. And it blew up on him. Oh, Kenny boy, you've been caught red-handed! In fact, you've been caught red all over!' Nicole shrieked with laughter and almost everyone joined in, more out of relief than anything else, now the tension was broken.

The sounds we had heard had come from the huge glass jars of tomato sauce exploding. They had been left out in the sun for a couple of days and very likely the jars had not been sterilized as well as they should have been. With bugs and gases multiplying inside, the pressure had built up steadily. And when Kenneth had knocked over a case by accident, one jar exploded and set off all the others.

'You're going to owe me for all my tomato ketchup!' Nicole told Kenneth. 'Oh, what a joke. Kenny, you greedy cheapskate! You made fun of me wanting ketchup for my wedding day and all the time you were hoarding it up here in your room. What were you going to do with it? Eat bowls of it so you don't have pay for meals downstairs?' Nicole was still laughing as the rest of the gawkers dispersed.

'Why is it yours? You didn't order it or pay for it. I just didn't want it all to go to waste,' Kenneth said sullenly. He looked at me. 'Your uncle wouldn't take it. Doesn't want his shop blamed if somebody else gets poisoned.'

I could see Uncle Chen's point.

Kenneth's room was much smaller than Nicole's. And it was crammed so full of crates and boxes and bundles, now covered with tomato ketchup, that it was hard to walk through without knocking something over. It was easy to see how Kenneth's accident had happened.

'Kenny boy, you're a ketchup thief!' Nicole shrieked with laughter. She poked at a crate. 'You even stole the canned shrimp! It was supposed to be for our canapés! What a hoot!'

'Good food shouldn't be wasted. I would have done the same,' I said to Kenneth. 'The Mission Centre always needs food donations for poor families. They would welcome some of this, if you're willing?'

Kenneth nodded miserably. 'That's a good idea. I just didn't want to throw it out. But I didn't know who to see about it, now it's such a mess.'

'I'm not having poor widows and orphans gorging themselves on my canned shrimp!' Nicole's laughter had a manic edge. She almost seemed drunk. 'Here, Kenny boy, food fight!' She threw the tin at him and jeered when it caught him on the shoulder. Kenneth didn't try to dodge.

'Here comes another!'

'Oh, stop that and be quiet!' Parshanti rounded on her.

'You'd better mind your manners, girl, or I'll—' Nicole's shrill voice was harsh.

'Shame on you!' Parshanti took the can from Nicole and replaced it in its crate. 'How dare you pick on someone who's down? You're nothing but a bully. A big cowardly bully!'

For a moment, I thought I was hearing Miss Blackmore, the founder of our mission school. The voice coming out of Parshanti sounded exactly like the one Miss Blackmore had used to tell off bullies, whether she was speaking to her students, their parents or drunken sailors.

And she had been right too. Bullies weren't always the biggest or the oldest children. Often they were those who enjoyed being mean because hurting others was the only way they knew to make themselves feel good. I realized that was why Nicole kept Kenneth around. She knew how he felt about her and how to give him just enough crumbs of hope to keep him painfully devoted while she entertained herself by hurting him.

Nicole stared at Parshanti, her mouth open. 'You— I— How dare you? Kenneth, did you hear what this creature said to me? You, boy! Don't just stand there, get her out of my sight at once. I want her thrown out of the hotel and arrested.'

Van Dijk, to whom this last was addressed, didn't appear to

243

hear her. He continued checking the window frames and mirrors for damage, making notes of what needed to be replaced.

Parshanti put a protective hand on Kenneth's stained shirt. She looked like an Indian warrior princess defending a peasant against a demon. Still, I didn't think she had a chance against a riled-up Nicole. Nicole didn't play fair. Someone who cheated at cards, even when playing alone, wouldn't.

'You've had a terrible shock.' I took Nicole's arm and started guiding her back to her own room. Since Dr Covington had told us about her drug habit I found her behaviour easier to understand. 'We'll go back to your room to calm down. Mr Mulliner, if you are willing to make a food donation, I am sure the Mission Centre will send someone over to clean up your room. Parshanti, can you see to that?'

'I'll take care of it,' Parshanti promised.

I pulled Nicole away despite her protests.

Missing Lipsticks

◆

B y the time we reached her suite, Nicole had forgotten her rage and was humming to herself. I could tell the excitement had energized her. It was as good a chance as I was likely to get so . . .

'Mrs Covington, you mentioned losing a lipstick. Did you ever find it?'

The hotel people tried to palm one off on me but it wasn't mine. Nasty cheap thing. Said they found it in Victor's room. The one Taylor gave me probably cost a lot. It must be here somewhere . . .'

Nicole started rummaging through the pillows and magazines and chocolate boxes on the sofa. 'It came in a jewelled case. No, not real jewels, just coloured glass beads. Taylor's a stingy old cuss despite everything he sponges off me. You didn't take it, did you?' She turned on Junior, who had slipped into the room after us. 'You're always sneaking off with my things. What are you doing here anyway? Where's your grandpa?'

'No! I never did! Grandpa made me promise never to touch it!'

'Taylor gave that lipstick to me on the voyage over after I lost my favourite, the one I was using. I'm sure one of the cabin stewards took it. They were always sneaking in and going through my stuff. I set traps for them – buttons on drawers and things like that. But they said the motion of the ship shook things around. I suppose the old bugger bought it on-board. It must have been hideously expensive as well as just plain hideous.'

'I don't get seasick,' Junior said. 'I like ships.'

'Bully for you.' Nicole shook a magazine fretfully as though a lipstick might have been hidden in its pages. 'Make yourself useful, girl. Find Taylor and hand Junior over to him.'

'Grandpa went out. He told me to stay with you.'

Nicole kept her eyes on her magazine. I felt bad for him. I had been a child without parents. But now I saw having a live mother who wasn't interested in you was far worse than having a dead one you knew had loved you more than anything.

'What would you like to do?' I asked the child.

'Sometimes Grandpa lets me go down to the kitchen and watch them cook. A nice man there lets me help make yoghurt with a stick.'

I remembered Kaeseven letting Dee-Dee Palin play with his *makkhana phirni*, the beautifully carved piece of wood he used daily to pound spices, skim sauces and make butter. It had been a favourite tool and I guessed it had come with him to the hotel. 'Is that Kaeseven the chef? Would you like to go down to the kitchen?'

'So that's where you got that stick,' Nicole said. 'I wondered about that. I'm sure they've called the police. They'll never feed you another meal here once they find out you're the one who took it. Raddy steals things, you know.' She turned to me. 'He's a little thief. A kleptomaniac. Taylor won't admit it. He just keeps putting the things back when he finds them and pretending he knows nothing.'

Junior looked at his feet. 'I don't want to go to the kitchen. I hate it there.'

'Would you like to go and see your friends?'

'He doesn't have any here,' Nicole said. 'Neither do I. None of us has anyone worth calling a friend in the world.' She turned a page.

'What about Greg and Pat McPherson?' I had seen Mrs McPherson when I passed the tea room downstairs.

Junior's eyes lit up. 'Their mom said I could come see them any time. I like them.'

I prayed Mr Meganck was better and wouldn't mind me adding an extra child to his entourage. I also needed to find out what Parshanti was doing but I didn't want to take Junior back into the tomato mess. Why had Taylor Covington disappeared without his grandson?

———◆———

Mrs McPherson seemed to like the idea. 'Why, of course, Miss Chen. What a fortunate coincidence meeting you here. I'm in town to do some shopping and just came in to be out of the heat. I like to get away on my own every now and then. Give them time to have a good gossip about me behind my back. Junior can come with me, and the boys would love to have high tea at the hotel later so we'll bring him back safely. Why don't you join us, Miss Chen?'

'Thank you, but I have to see to something here. Mrs Covington is resting and doesn't want to be disturbed.'

'I wasn't disturbing her,' Junior protested, fairly enough.

'Quite right. I'm sorry.'

'Can I play with Greg's Erector Set?'

'I'm sure that can be arranged.' Mrs McPherson smiled. Then, more quietly to me, 'How is his mother holding up?'

'Frustrated at being kept in limbo.' I could understand how Nicole felt. But it was easier to sympathize with her when I wasn't in her presence. 'I don't think she's used to being alone.'

'Try to keep Mrs Covington happy in the hotel,' Mrs McPherson said. 'Gregory is busy so I don't want him disturbed, and that poor young woman keeps sending notes inviting herself to stay at Government House. I'm afraid she'll turn up one day without warning. In which case, you'll have to arrest me for assault, which would have unfortunate political repercussions.'

That made me laugh. I decided I liked Viola Jane McPherson very much indeed as I waved Junior off in her car. It would have been fun to visit Government House again and see what changes the new governor and his family had made.

Now I wanted to see if Corporal Wong could find me the lipstick in a jewelled case he had listed on the belongings of the dead Japanese prostitute. But first I would check in with Parshanti. I didn't know what she was telling her parents to explain her absences from home. She would say it wasn't my business, but I needed to know if I was her excuse so I could stay out of their way.

Kenneth after Tomatoes

It must be difficult to go on holding yourself aloof and superior after everyone has seen you covered with pickled tomatoes. Even harder if they've all heard the woman you love mocking you for stealing them from her.

I was afraid Kenneth would slip away from the hotel and disappear. What reason did he have for staying? The friend he had been travelling with was dead and the police had no reason to detain him.

When I returned to his room I found him looking much better. Parshanti had cleaned his cuts and applied iodine and plasters where needed. He was still a pretty miserable sight, but fortunately nothing had been deep enough to require stitches.

A couple of the women from the Mission Centre had turned up and were making good progress mopping and wiping up the mess in the room. I greeted them and offered to help but they said they had things under control. These women had survived being horribly abused by the men in their lives, whether husbands, fathers or brothers. They were very good at cleaning up messes without asking who or what had caused them.

When I asked about Kenneth's clothes and fabric furniture covers, thinking I would put them to soak in carbolic soap overnight, I learned they had already been sent out to the *dhoby*, probably to the same men who did the hotel laundry but without incurring the additional hotel charge.

I was impressed by how fast and efficiently Parshanti had handled everything.

Kenneth was very subdued. The cuts on his face suggested he had been in a fight. Oddly, I thought he looked better for them. But that might have been because he was no longer wearing the contemptuous sneer I was used to seeing on his face.

'Are you hungry? I am. What about going downstairs for some lunch?' I asked. There was no point in waiting around at HQ if Corporal Wong Meng was on his lunch break.

'I don't think Kenneth wants to go to the restaurant,' Parshanti whispered. 'The people there might have heard what happened and laugh at him.'

'Well, we can't eat here – we'll be in their way.' Cleaning was in full swing. 'It's either downstairs in the bar-restaurant or room service in Nicole's suite. Dr Covington and Junior are out so it's just Nicole. She's ordering lunch up for herself.'

'The bar-restaurant,' Kenneth said decisively. It was an easy choice between *might laugh* and *would definitely laugh*. Or maybe it was just too difficult for him to face his Nicole just then.

Given that he had changed into a fresh outfit, it was possible he wouldn't be recognized in the lunchtime crowd.

But he was.

Some of the guests recognized him immediately. They had probably been telling the story and when they saw him they did nudge, point and laugh. But they also smiled. Some waved, offered to buy him Blood Marys or Singapore Slings and invited him to join their tables.

Even after the three of us were seated in a secluded corner, other diners stopped to say hello to the tomato-sauce man and describe their own awkward encounters with food in strange places. It was as though Kenneth's embarrassment had broken down the British social barriers.

The mood at the Farquhar had been sombre ever since the death of Victor Glossop. By giving everyone a roaring good laugh upstairs, Kenneth had got into everybody's good books and they appreciated him for it.

For the first time in his life and without having to pretend to be anything or anyone he wasn't, Kenneth Mulliner was popular. And I saw the change it made. As it gradually sank in to him that people were being friendly and their invitations to dinner or drinks were genuine, he relaxed and produced real smiles.

'I always wanted to travel east. I never thought it would be like this.' Kenneth turned back to his coconut rice and curry after the two middle-aged ladies who had paused to tell him flirtatiously that they liked his accent moved on (Parshanti glaring at them throughout the exchange).

'Why did you come?' I asked. 'I know the official answer, of course. At the police interview you talked about wanting to widen your horizons and see more of the world. That sounded reasonable enough from a rich dilettante like Victor Glossop, but you don't really belong in that category, do you?'

251

I had been uncomfortable with the old Kenneth because he seemed so uncomfortable with himself. The British and the Americans are divided into social classes as much as we are. But their classes were not tied to professions and were much harder to understand. I had observed Kenneth Mulliner around the other *ang mohs*, how he deferred to Taylor and Nicole Covington, who treated him as someone of lowly birth destined to serve his betters.

Which was exactly how Kenneth treated Le Froy, even though Dr Covington deferred to Le Froy as someone in authority and Nicole treated him as a man to flirt with. The Americans were confident they were worth more than anyone around them so they could afford to play social games.

Le Froy didn't care what his social position was as long as he didn't have to fill it. But Kenneth was so sensitive to slights it was clear he felt he was on the lowest rung possible for an *ang moh* to be.

But Kenneth was different now. He had been through public humiliation and he had survived.

Parshanti started to protest that we were having lunch, I was not to turn this into a police interview, but Kenneth put a hand over hers, implying it was all right.

'I'll tell you, but you can't say anything. Not even to your boss. I produce secret reports that I send back to the UK. The light travel pieces I write for the papers are just cover.'

'Are you saying you are a spy?'

'An investigative journalist.'

I was distracted by his hand on Parshanti's. And her obvious delight. Oh, Parshanti . . .

Parshanti was pleasant-looking and intelligent. But she was half Asian. I was certain that a man like Kenneth Mulliner would never be serious about her. Even her own mother's Scottish family kept the Shankars at a distance, and they were solid working-class people with no social pretensions whatsoever. I also knew that it was no use saying anything of the sort to Parshanti. If she wasn't aware that this would come to nothing, it was because she didn't want to be.

'What's wrong with your face?' Parshanti asked me.

'It's my inscrutable look. I'm fading into the background by appearing Oriental and harmless.'

'Please don't. You look like you're channelling the spirit of Dr Fu Manchu. Oriental but not harmless at all,' Kenneth said.

He and Parshanti laughed and even I had to smile. When I'm thinking about something I am deeply focused. Most people find depth in anything frightening. Not just in Singapore but in today's world. In the thirties, with the Great War safely over and the Depression receding (or so we were told), many preferred to pick at the thoughts that float around on the surface. We were afraid of disturbing what lay beneath in case we stirred up more than we could handle. But that is like skimming the surface of a stock pot. You have to empty and scrub it every so often or you will soon have more muck than soup.

'Look,' Kenneth said, 'I know you suspect me of killing Victor. I would, if I were you. And I know it's no use my telling you I didn't do it. But I didn't. I'm telling you to look harder at that guy Harry Palin. He hardly knew Victor but he was running around doing all kinds of things for him. The only way I can explain it is that he's in love with Nicole. He's hoping that now, with Victor gone, he can move in on her. Look, I'm not the only one who thinks so. Nicole suggested it long before I said anything.'

That I believed. Nicole thought every man who looked in her direction was interested in her and she didn't mind helping the process along. Maybe she was right about most of them, but not Harry.

'Has Harry Palin been round to see her?' I was certain he hadn't.

'He'll have to let things calm down first – he's not stupid – but he will. Nicole says even before Victor died she saw Harry Palin staring longingly at her.'

Harry might have been staring longingly, but I doubted it was Nicole he had been looking at.

'Why are you so sure Harry killed Victor?'

'I'm just saying he could have. I'm in the best position to see this because you all suspect me and I know I'm not guilty.'

Everything Kenneth said about Harry could have been applied to himself. I knew he had been in love with Nicole even if he seemed to be backing away from her now. I realized I had not noticed him gazing longingly at her recently. He had not even been hanging around the last few times I'd seen her. I assumed she'd been angry with him and sent him away to suffer.

Kenneth didn't seem to be suffering.

'Maybe Nicole has an evil side that kills men once she's tired of them,' Parshanti said it lightly, as a joke. No one laughed.

'I owe it to Victor's family to find out what really happened to him,' Kenneth said.

'Because you were such good friends?'

'Yes and no. I don't know that we were good friends. Sometimes

I didn't even like him. But you may as well know that Victor's family paid for all kinds of stuff for me to stick by Victor and let them know how he was doing.'

'Like a spy?' I asked. I remembered what he had said about being an investigative journalist and still didn't believe it. I knew what journalists were like – my idol Henrietta Stackpole was adventurous and independent if you ignored her final compromise.

At the same time Parshanti asked, 'Like a bodyguard?'

'More like a faithful dog.' Kenneth gave a little laugh. 'Well, it worked for me. I went to Oxford, thanks to them. And I would have got my degree, but then I had to leave with Victor when he was sent down for his stupid pranks.'

'That's terrible! Why did you have to leave too?'

'How was I going to pay my fees, with Victor gone, not to mention come up with board and lodging? My father believed in education but, God help him, on a vicar's stipend he didn't earn enough to educate his sons. Given time, I might have been able to swing a scholarship, but Victor wanted to clear out so I had to run around doing his packing and getting our train tickets.'

There was still the echo of a broken dream in his voice. It was easy for us to believe that being born white was enough to get you through life. But we see ourselves in contrast to those around us. For Kenneth, the contrast between him and the wealthy Victor must have been difficult.

'He knew I wanted to stay in college. On the voyage out, when he tried to persuade me to tutor Junior so that he could have time alone with Nicole, he joked about how I had always dreamed of being an academic in Oxford. He knew that was what I wanted.

More than anything. I would have loved it and my father would have been so proud. And Victor made sure it would never happen.'

I would have taken any kind of deal with the devil, or worse, for a chance to study in Oxford. I knew there were four women's colleges there: Lady Margaret Hall, Somerville, St Hugh's and St Hilda's. I also knew that it was an impossible dream, but if I ever managed to get a place, the man or woman who forced me to leave without my degree would earn (and deserve) my deepest hatred. For ever.

'Didn't you hate him?'

Kenneth looked surprised. 'I suppose. Sometimes. But what would have been the point? We were boyhood companions and I suppose we were friends. It was assumed that when Victor went into his family business I would be taken in along with him, gainfully occupied doing all his work for him. Guaranteed a job as long as he had one. I would have been a fool to give that up.'

It was like Henrietta Stackpole sacrificing journalism for the financial security that came with her becoming Mrs Bantling.

'Victor's family was rich. They owned the distillery where most of the village worked. My father was the vicar of the local church. Very respectable, and all that. But he took to drink after Mother's death. Not that enough people came to church to notice. It was tacitly understood that, as long as I kept their embarrassing son in order, my embarrassing father could go on living in the vicarage and singing maudlin songs in the graveyard behind it.'

'What did you have to do for Victor?'

'Stop him making too much of a fool of himself. Call the family lawyers when he did it anyway. And get him to sign necessary papers. He was on the company board, of course. He didn't give a damn for the business, never attended meetings, but as a son of the family, he had to have his seat on the board.'

'I'm sure Victor appreciated your sacrifice,' Parshanti said.

'I doubt he noticed. When you have people falling down to do things for you all your life, you take it for granted that they're always going to do everything they can for you.'

Like Nicole, I thought. But it didn't always last.

I left them chatting in the company of coffee and coconut ice creams because I wanted to find out if Corporal Wong had found the lipstick. If he had, I was going to get Dr Leask or Dr Shankar to test it for poison.

Parshanti in Trouble

◆

The lipstick found in the dead prostitute's room was mud-coloured with orange streaks. It reminded me a little of Junior's homemade crayons. But the casing looked expensive. The removable cap was studded with coloured glass, as Nicole had described. I felt certain it was the lipstick that had gone missing from her room. But how had it ended up at Yap Pun Kai?

Instead of giving it to Nicole I took the lipstick to Dr Leask. I had an idea I wasn't ready to put forward, not till I knew whether there was anything in the lipstick. 'I know you're busy but this might be important.'

Dr Leask promised he would try but I sliced off a quarter-inch with a nail file and folded it into a handkerchief to see if I could get Parshanti's father to do some tests too.

When I reached Shankar and Sons that evening I heard loud voices inside. The right and proper thing would have been to walk away. If people were welcome to stick their noses in they would have been fighting on the street, not behind closed doors. But the door, though shut, was not locked. If someone was making trouble for Parshanti's family I couldn't walk away.

I pushed it open cautiously, wincing at the usual jangle but there was no one at the pharmacy and photographic services counter that occupied the front premises. There was a wonderful smell, though: Mrs Shankar must have been baking. I didn't sense any intruders, but that didn't mean anything. I was the outsider there.

I stepped through the open doorway to Mrs Shankar's sewing room.

'So, where were you?'

I almost didn't recognize Mrs Shankar's voice. Mrs Shankar talks, laughs and shouts at a good volume but I had never heard that tone before. Even with nothing on my conscience (or nothing Parshanti's mother could take issue with), she was frightening. My first instinct was to back out and pretend I had never been there.

'Sorry, Mrs Shankar?'

Mrs Shankar is normally the most good-natured of women. If I hadn't already had far too many relations I might have thought of her as a substitute mother – she tried to feed me and dress me up with every chance she got. But today her expression reminded me of the flaming dragon statue outside the Buddhist temple. And it was not just the rage on her face: her red hair was wild, escaping from the bun at the back of her head. And she was waving her arms, a wooden spatula in one hand.

When she turned and fixed her eyes on me I wanted to run away.

'Oh, it's you, Su Lin,' Mrs Shankar said. 'Come back another time. Parshanti is busy now.'

But I couldn't go. I had seen the object of her wrath. Parshanti was sitting on a chair against the wall. Dr Shankar was standing next to her. I couldn't tell whether he was involved in the attack or a fellow victim of his wife's wrath.

Parshanti gave me a panicked, pleading look. I knew she was not asking for my help. She wanted me to leave without saying anything that might get her into more trouble. I immediately guessed what the trouble was.

'Parshanti, I'm sorry.' I couldn't leave my friend in this mess, no matter what she might have done.

'Su, get out!' Parshanti said. 'This has nothing to do with you! Will you just please leave?'

Her wanting me gone immediately convinced her parents that I knew what was going on, which gave me far more credit than I was due.

'Come in, Su Lin,' Mrs Shankar said quickly. 'Close the shop door behind you. Bolt it. And tell us everything. It's no use you making up stories. We know everything!'

I went to stand next to Parshanti, who was on her feet now, looking furious and frightened.

Dr Shankar went to his wife's side. 'Do you know what Parshanti was doing yesterday afternoon?' he asked me gently. 'Over at the hotel? All afternoon and evening?'

'They found out about the magazines?' I asked Parshanti, in a loud whisper. She looked at me blankly.

I turned to her parents. 'The magazines, old issues, are at the Detective Shack. Sorry, Dr Shankar, Mrs Shankar. We were very careful. We didn't damage anything. We were copying dress patterns when people said there had been another accident at the hotel and we went to see. We forgot and didn't bring them back. I'm so very sorry. We didn't mean to steal them. I'll go and get them all at once.'

Parshanti spent hours poring over old issues of unsold fashion magazines. I considered this a monumental waste of time, but she claimed she was learning about society and culture . . . and, of course, clothes. She was not supposed to take the magazines out of the shop, and they were not supposed to have been read if they were to be collected by the distributor to be pulped. But she often brought a couple with her when she came to the Detective Shack to wait for me. As a result, there were indeed unpaid-for magazines at the Detective Shack. I wasn't exactly lying so much as shifting the truth on the time line.

Parshanti stared at me. Her mouth hung open. It was as though my story had hit her on the head and stunned her. Please, please, please don't say something stupid, I tried to tell her.

Mrs Shankar was quicker. 'You were copying fashion magazines with Su Lin? Why didn't you just say so?' Mrs Shankar's voice caught, in what sounded like a sob. 'Oh, you silly, silly girl. I'm so furious with you. Furious! Why didn't you just say so?' Her voice was thick with tears and her native Scots burr rolled through the r of 'furious'. Except she was relieved, not furious.

She put her arms around her tall, dark, beloved daughter and squeezed her hard, rubbing her face into the material of Parshanti's dress. 'And I haven't even got you a drink! You have to forgive me, Su Lin. Too much excitement. Not good for an old woman like me.

'A message came from a woman at the Farquhar Hotel. She said she wanted to warn us that our girl was hanging around with a young man in his hotel room at the Farquhar yesterday, with the doors locked, and pretending not to be there when people knocked. She wanted to warn us, she said, that he was ruining our girl.' Mrs Shankar moaned, and hugged Parshanti again.

'Who was the message from?'

'She didn't sign the note but I could see from the handwriting it was a woman. Not a very educated woman. Nasty, lying trouble-maker. I shouldn't have paid any attention except for this silly bairn refusing to say where she was all day.'

I didn't need a name. Nicole, miffed that Kenneth had aban-doned her, had sent the note to make trouble for Parshanti.

When Mrs Shankar left the room, Dr Shankar shook his head. 'You shouldn't worry your mother like that.'

'I didn't do anything,' Parshanti said sullenly.

'I didn't know you were interested in fashion magazines, Su Lin?' Dr Shankar said to me.

'She's my friend,' Parshanti said. 'She was just helping me.'

Dr Shankar smiled a sad, sweet smile. He looked as though he couldn't decide whether I had helped or was betraying them. I didn't know either.

'Yes, she is and she was,' he said. 'We must talk about this, but another time. Don't worry about bringing the magazines back, Su Lin. You can keep them. On the house.' He gave me a cere-monial bow as he disappeared after his wife. He had not believed me, I thought. He knew I had lied for his daughter. I felt bad. But at least Mrs Shankar wasn't raging any more.

Parshanti took a deep breath and flopped back into the chair.

'I've never seen your mother so angry before,' I said to her.

'Of course you have. Remember when we went to try to catch

fish in the river after school and fell in and lost our shoes? And we went and hid until our clothes dried, but in the meantime somebody came and told Mam that a crocodile had been seen with a girl's leg in its mouth? When we got back I thought she was going to kill us for not being eaten by crocodiles!'

I remembered very well. The 'leg' in the river turned out to be one of my shoes caught on a branch. My grandmother had been furious too.

We both laughed. We must have been about seven years old. We had just started school and could not understand why everyone was making such a fuss about shoes. Years later, a man wandered too close to a female crocodile guarding her nest, had a leg torn off and bled to death. I understood their panic.

It made me wonder if Parshanti's parents were overreacting now . . . or whether we were the ones who didn't know the danger of crocodiles in the river we were climbing into.

'Thank you, Su,' Parshanti said, 'but it would have been all right. Kenneth is going to come to talk to them.'

And that would make things better? I wondered if Mrs Shankar's rage had driven her to hit her daughter on the head.

I lowered my voice, keeping an eye on the door to the back of the shop. 'Are you both crazy? That will just make things worse!'

'You don't trust Kenneth yet,' Parshanti said, 'but you will. I promise you will. You trust me, don't you? I'm telling you Kenneth Mulliner has a good heart.'

I recognized her tone and wanted to moan, 'Not again!'

Ever since we were twelve or thirteen years old, Parshanti had been falling in love with out-of-reach men. Humphrey Bogart,

Cary Grant and Clark Gable were all names that had been pas-
sionately scribbled into her secret notebooks. At least, she
thought it was a big secret but I suspect her mother and the
mission-school teachers were well aware of it. She never did more
than dream and draw sketches of them ... occasionally she drew
herself by their sides and added 'Mr and Mrs' in front of their
names. I occasionally appeared as a bridesmaid or helping with
the four or five children that appeared.

'It's difficult for him,' Parshanti said, 'having his best friend die
and having to do his best to look after his friend's lunatic fiancée.
And, of course, being suspected and spied on by the police.'

'I'm sorry,' I said. I didn't want to fight with her. Luckily, she
didn't ask me what I was sorry about.

'That's all right.' Parshanti gave me a quick hug. 'Don't worry.
I know you're only uncomfortable with Kenneth because you
don't know him yet. He explained everything to me. He's not just
here as a journalist. That's just his excuse to cover up the real
reason he's here and what he really is!'

Kenneth had told her some spy story, I thought. After the
Great War, every man with something to hide called himself a
spy. 'I don't trust Kenneth. Even if he didn't kill Victor I think he's
hiding something,' I said. 'You can't trust a liar.'

'You lied for me,' Parshanti pointed out.

'That's not the same thing at all.'

Tennyson wrote that a lie that is half truth is the darkest of
all lies. Maybe I should have spent more time reading poetry
instead of novels.

'Look.' Parshanti bent and pulled a box on wheels from
beneath the counter. 'I know how much you hate lying. Take these,

so you'll really have magazines in your room. And Kenneth wants to talk to you.'

'Why? What about?'

'He wants to clear a few things up. He's got to talk to someone else first. Just to do the decent thing, he said. He's going to come clean about everything but it's not just about him. Once he's sorted things out fair and square, and he's come to talk to my parents . . .' Parshanti's eyes were shining with tears of pride '. . . he'll explain everything to you. He promised.'

Kenneth Outside

◆

I slipped out of the Shankars' house with my head so full of
thoughts that I didn't see Kenneth Mulliner till he reached out
a hand and touched my arm as I passed.

'Oh! What are you doing here?'

The answer was obvious as soon as I asked. He was waiting
for Parshanti, of course. 'She won't be coming out to meet you,' I
told him. 'She won't be able to get out of the house. Her parents
know she was at the hotel with you and they're furious.' I was
furious too. 'It's too bad of you to fool around with her and get
her into trouble.'

'I'm not, and we're not fooling around. I'm serious about
Parshanti.'

He looked as though he meant it. There, in the dim yellow light
spilling onto the five-foot way where we stood, he looked earnest
and pleading. I could almost see why Parshanti trusted him. 'But
you're skulking out here while my friend is getting yelled at inside.'

'I want to make it right. But I've got to sort out some other
things first.'

'What other things? Other women?'

'No! Writing assignments. You may as well know. You'll find out, anyway, when it all comes out. I did write those pieces but not the last one. I wasn't going to write it, I had all my research done and they were pushing for it, but I decided not to. He must have taken my notes. I didn't send that piece in.'

'Who?' I was getting an idea of what he was talking about. 'What research? Who took your notes?'

Just then Parshanti slipped out. To my surprise, she seemed glad to see me still there. Well, that was a nice change.

'Tell her, Kenny! I promise you, if you tell Su Lin everything she'll fix it. You will, won't you, darling? Su Lin will understand and she'll make other people understand too. She'll make it all right. Please trust her.'

Kenneth didn't look as though he trusted anybody, but he wasn't hostile.

'What does Parshanti want you to tell me?'

'It's no use my telling you. I have to show you,' Kenneth said. 'But there's someone I have to talk to first. Just so it's all above board.'

'Just tell me quickly now. I won't say anything till you're ready.'

He shook his head, his eyes going back to Parshanti. 'Come to the hotel tomorrow morning and meet me there. I'll pass you all my notes and you can decide whether to believe me.'

'Notes about what? Are you talking about Victor?'

'No. Well, yes, but indirectly. It's bigger than Victor. I know you don't trust me now but what you see tomorrow will change your mind. I shan't come out of this mess looking good but you'll see me for what I am. You'll see all of us for what we are. And if you can accept that, then . . .' That last was to Parshanti.

I still didn't trust Kenneth but his words made me want to. They also made me uneasy. When you stir up mud looking for crabs you may disturb snakes.

Mrs Shankar's voice rose inside, calling for her daughter, and Parshanti winced. 'I must go.' She slipped back in, not without giving Kenneth a quick kiss on the cheek.

'I have to clear things up in there first,' Kenneth Mulliner said. 'Remember, come to the hotel tomorrow morning. Nine a.m. in the Bachelor Room. All my notes are there. You'll see I didn't write that last piece. I wouldn't have.'

I watched him knock on the pharmacy door, then push it open and enter before I left. I would have liked to go up to the window to listen, but these were my friends, not murder suspects. Though, of course, Kenneth Mulliner was halfway between the two categories. I wanted to like him more. I didn't have high hopes of his smoothing things over with Parshanti's parents, but at least he was trying and I respected that.

I was tired, and not in the mood for anything except going up to my little room and getting some sleep. But Le Froy, de Souza and Pillay were still in the Detective Shack with Dr Leask when I got back.

'Mr Glossop must have poisoned himself when he used the lipstick to draw patterns on his face, arms and chest. The reaction would have begun in under thirty minutes but he might have thought it was an allergy or heat rash. Perhaps the Japanese woman drew patterns on his back when she was with him at the hotel. He must have given her the lipstick. Or she took it when she left. She didn't realize it was poisoned and it killed her. But where did he get it?'

'Her visit wouldn't have lasted long. Mr Glossop's skin would have started swelling, itching and bleeding quickly. He would have been in no mood for her services.'

'Miss Chen, your suggestion to test the lipstick paid off handsomely,' Dr Leask cried, on seeing me. 'For once I seem to have my results before Dr Shankar.'

He looked so pleased I didn't have the heart to say I knew why Dr Shankar was preoccupied.

'Good idea,' Le Froy said to me. The approval in his voice meant a lot.

'Maybe Mrs Covington poisoned her own lipstick and gave it to Mr Glossop,' Sergeant Pillay suggested.

'Nicole said she lost a lipstick in a fancy case,' I said. 'I didn't think much of it at first because she's always losing things. But maybe . . .'

'The poison may have been meant for her.' Le Froy said.

I knew that didn't clear Kenneth Mulliner. He could easily have taken Nicole's lipstick and passed it to Victor for his stag party fancy dress. Though that, of course, meant Nicole was the poison's target.

The Proposal

———◆———

I missed seeing what happened when Kenneth went to the Shankars' shop house but this was how it went, according to what I was told later.

———◆———

'Mam, Dad, this is Kenneth Mulliner.'

Parshanti had not known for sure when Kenneth was coming to talk to her parents. Even if she had, she could hardly have warned her mother. So, the first time Kenneth met Mrs Shankar she was flustered not just by him but because a stranger was seeing her in the house dress she did her sewing in, with pins stuck into the *dupatta* scarf thrown around her neck.

'You were with this man at the hotel?'

Parshanti nodded. 'Mam, Kenneth wants to—'

'You lied to us! What that woman's note said was true!'

'What woman?' Kenneth asked. 'What note?'

'Oh, that my own child would lie to me!'

'Mam, Kenneth has something to say to Dad. And to you.'

'I want to ask your daughter to marry me. But I want to do it properly. I'm going to—'

'What's that?' Dr Shankar said sharply. Mrs Shankar was suddenly silent, stuffing a handful of her scarf into her mouth.

'I want to marry your daughter, Dr Shankar, sir. I know this is not a good time. When this nightmare of accusations is over, I will get a good job and come back with a ring, go down on one knee and propose properly. But until then I want you to know my intentions are good.'

Mrs Shankar burst into tears.

'Mam, please don't cry! He's a good man, really he is! He's not a murderer!'

'She's in shock. Your mother may be upset with you for finding yourself a man because she regrets marrying me,' Dr Shankar suggested.

'Yer bum's oot the windae, ye fuckin' bampot!'

Now Parshanti saw her mother was laughing as well as crying. 'Mam, please!'

'*Mo chridhe*, my dear foolish man, I was angry because I know what boys are like. I grew up around boys like Kenneth Mulliner. Why do you think I dropped them for you? I know what they're like, but our silly, precious little girl doesn't.'

'Mam!'

'A man doesn't buy a cow when he can get milk for free.'

'Mam, don't!'

'But I may have misjudged this young man. I am sorry, my dear girl.'

When her mother released her from a big hug, Parshanti saw that Kenneth and her father were grinning.

'Kenneth may change his mind now that he's seen us,' Dr Shankar said.

'If he does, better before than after.' Mrs Shankar patted Kenneth's arm affectionately.

'I'll not change my mind. Look, when all this is settled, I'll take you up-country and we can spend a few weeks in the Malayan high-lands. It's too hot to rest and talk in Singapore. Even with the fan on, the sheets are damp with sweat. There are some lodges up in the tea-growing highlands. I'll find a respectable guesthouse and book us separate rooms. All of you, of course. I've not got much to offer your daughter but I will take care of her.' He looked at Parshanti. 'I'll have something coming in once I've sorted out some business, and I'll get down to that tonight. And once that's done I'll pass all the papers to your friend. And when this nightmare is over, we'll get married.'

———◆———

An approaching thunderstorm woke me early the next morning. I lay awake in my room above the Detective Shack, feeling the electricity in the air. It was no longer late at night but early in the morning, though far too early to get up.

I thought about what Parshanti had told me and wondered what Kenneth thought he had to clear up. It hadn't occurred to me he would jump ahead and propose. If I had known, I would have thought him reckless and impulsive . . . and maybe I would have trusted him a little more.

It was not yet raining but the wind rattled the windows and

made a door slam repeatedly somewhere in the next building. Birds that should have been asleep at this hour were calling warnings and I could sense insects and other creatures trying to find ways into the shelter of the house.

I looked around the small, sparsely decorated room with eyes accustomed to the dark and tried not to think about going down the external steps to the outdoor WC. If I had to go, though, it would be best to go now, before the storm came. I could already hear distant thunder and smell the plants anticipating the coming rain. I was wishing I could go back to sleep because I felt as if I had been tired for ever and it would only get worse tomorrow. But all my instincts were on alert against the coming rain and where the roof would start leaking.

Help Parshanti.

The words, in Kenneth Mulliner's voice, sounded so clearly in my head that I sat upright in bed, knocking my pillow onto the floor. It was more than just words. I felt a presence in the room with me. It was like being inside a WC cubicle with some-one quietly standing outside. Even if neither of you says anything, you can almost feel each other breathing.

Comfort Parshanti, the same voice said. And then, just as suddenly, the presence was gone.

'I'm going mad,' I said aloud, as much to shake myself out of it as to distract whatever *hantu* might have been stirred up by the coming storm. 'I'm going to be as mad as Nicole if this keeps up.'

If something really was haunting my room, I hoped it would believe me and look for someone more receptive.

A house gecko burst into a string of chirps in a corner of the ceiling, startling me. The blinds flapped and tapped. Nothing replied.

I didn't believe in ghosts. I put food in front of altars, lit joss sticks and left offerings on graves, just like everyone else at home, and I took communion and offered prayers and my ten-per-cent tithe, just like everyone else at the Mission Centre. That suited me fine, but when it came to middle-of-the-night apparitions I wasn't sure which set of gods to appeal to.

My grandmother always said our ancestors and the gods watched over us, but could not be counted on to deliver gambling wins. Hard work was what they rewarded. And the mission ladies said that although the Holy Trinity heard our prayers it was as important to show your faith by working hard.

In other words, you had to pay your respects to the supernatural but you could not count on it.

I got out of bed, lit the lamp and started getting dressed. If I couldn't sleep I might as well get up and do something I'd been putting off. I had only glanced with quick distaste through the Pip's Squeaks piece on Le Froy but now I took out the copy I had put in my bag. Le Froy had said it was not up to the usual standard of writing. I wanted to study and compare it to the previous Pip's Squeaks articles I had kept.

Dead Kenneth

T here was no response when I knocked on the outside door of the Bachelor Room at nine a.m. the next day, as arranged. I went into the hotel and tried the door leading from the carpeted hallway. No answer there either. I waited for half an hour but there was no sign of Kenneth Mulliner.

Well, he might have changed his mind but I would get it out of him.

This time the Eurasian general manager didn't look up as I walked to his desk between the two grand, curved marble staircases. This was a definite improvement on his attempts to direct me to the staff service stairs on my previous visits to Nicole.

For now, at least, Darwin Van Dijk had elevated me to the level of Discreet Visitor.

If I had been truly discreet, I would have walked on quietly and unobtrusively and asked one of the service boys for help. But, then, if I was discreet, quiet and unobtrusive, I would still be squatting outside a back kitchen pounding *sambal* instead of inside the Farquhar Hotel by request, on semi-official police business.

'Good morning, Mr Van Dijk.' His face whipped up. Several people in the foyer looked round, which made him incline his head and straighten his mouth into what was almost a smile.

'I have an appointment to see Mr Mulliner in his downstairs room, but he is not answering.'

'It is possible he doesn't wish to see visitors, madam.'

'Mr Mulliner may be unwell,' I said. 'If you would send some-one to check on him?'

Darwin Van Dijk's expression remained impassively regal as he dithered over this. I knew he was considering putting me off. What if Kenneth Mulliner was merely avoiding me? But what if he was lying sick or injured and unable to communicate in his room?

The Farquhar preferred guests to leave the premises by taxi rather than hearse.

'It's important,' I stressed. Last night I had believed Kenneth was in earnest. But perhaps he had been playing with me. What if he had changed his mind and was even now destroying what evidence he had left?

Van Dijk must have sensed my anxiety. 'William, take the desk. I am going to see if Mr Mulliner is in his room.'

———◆———

As things turned out, I was very glad to have Van Dijk with me.

This time, standing in the corridor outside Kenneth's room, I smelt a faint odour of fresh offal that stopped me thinking about anything else.

Darwin Van Dijk knocked and called, 'Mr Mulliner?' softly at first, then louder. His face was fixed, steely intent under the polite mask. I saw he had smelt or sensed something too. After three tries and finding the door locked, he applied his own key and pushed the door open.

At his gasp, I rushed past him to look.

It was eerily reminiscent of how Victor Glossop had been found. Only this time I knew from the rich, sweetish smell familiar from the buckets of pig blood in the wet market that the blood was real, not betel juice. And beneath that, the stink of dead fish bloat that said Kenneth was dead.

'*Aiyoh!*' One of the skinny messenger boys had followed us. They were like shadows, always on the alert to make a few cents. '*Alamak!* Another white man *mati!*'

'Boy! Go to the Detective Unit and get Chief Inspector Le Froy!' I shouted.

He hesitated until Van Dijk nodded and said, 'Go, Tanis.' He ran off.

I liked the man more for knowing his message runners by name and because of their respect for him. 'Lock the door. Don't let anybody inside until the police get here,' I said.

'That may be a suicide note.' Van Dijk was looking slowly around without stepping further into the room. 'There. In his typewriter.'

I went over and looked, careful not to touch anything:

I killed Victor out of jealousy and tried to frame Nicole. But Nicole has a new lease on life and no time for me. I have nothing left to live for and I'm ending it the way I ended it for my best friend. Sweep me under the rug and forget me.

No, I thought. Kenneth hadn't written that. What the Kenneth of my dream – had it been a dream? – had said was more authentic than this.

'What's happening?' Nicole was suddenly in the corridor. She looked bright-eyed and eager, as though she had been waiting for this moment, and she was fully dressed, which was unusual for her since it was not yet noon. 'Kenneth's got himself into trouble again, has he? Are you taking him away in handcuffs? Oh, let me see! Is his little girlfriend in there too? Did you catch them together? I want to see!'

'No! Don't go in there, madam!'

But Nicole ignored Van Dijk and pushed past him, sliding into the room and looking round eagerly. Then she started screaming.

My grandmother would have called her a *siao zha bor* or crazy woman. I normally avoid the term but in this case '*siao*' described Nicole perfectly. I wanted to scream too, but I also wanted to examine the room more thoroughly. After the first grotesque shock, I had only gone round quickly to make sure no one was hiding there.

Kenneth had said he had something to show me. There was a chance that it was still in the room, whatever it might be, unless, of course, that was what he had been killed for. I wanted to examine the thought as well as that room but both were impossible with Nicole flailing around shouting about curses and death following her around.

'Kenneth wasn't involved with you. This has nothing to do with you,' I told her.

'He would have come round! I would have got him back from her!' Nicole gripped handfuls of Van Dijk's shirt.

Van Dijk and I heaved the silly shrieking woman out of Kenneth's room, Van Dijk pausing only to make sure the door was locked behind us. Then, when Nicole draped herself on him, refusing to walk, he picked her up as easily as if she was a tailor's dummy and carried her back to her room. I swore I would never make fun of him again, not even inside my head.

◆

When Dr Leask arrived, soon after Le Froy, Van Dijk asked him to look in on Nicole and give her a sedative even before he had declared Kenneth dead. But Dr Leask's first dose seemed to have no effect and Nicole continued weeping and wailing.

'You'll need to give her something much stronger,' Dr Covington suggested.

Dr Covington and Junior had been in Junior's playroom on the same floor as the Bachelor Room but they had been playing trains and had not heard anything.

'It's not safe. I don't know what she may have taken earlier.' Dr Leask studied Nicole, who glared back at him blearily. 'She's obviously taking something.'

'I'm not!' Nicole said.

'She is,' Dr Leask said quietly. 'Look at her eyes. Pinpoint pupils. An indication of opioid-based intoxication. Add to that her dizziness, weakness and changes in mood, and I would guess morphine.'

He was clearly yearning towards the dead body downstairs, but dead Kenneth wasn't going anywhere and Dr Leask's first responsibility was to keep the living alive.

'What have you been taking, Mrs Covington? Pain tablets? A cough remedy? How much did you swallow?'

Morphine would explain a lot, I thought. But Nicole refused to answer. When he tried to take her temperature, she lunged and tried to bite him.

He gave her a stronger dose.

———•———

The suicide note, his swollen discoloured jowls and the bleeding from his nose and mouth implied that Kenneth had poisoned himself with something similar to what had killed Victor. I might have believed this of Kenneth a week ago. But I didn't believe it of the man who thought he was in love with Parshanti and had promised to come clean about everything.

I said as much to Le Froy, but there was nothing in the room that could have been the notes Kenneth had said he would pass me, that would help me understand his position.

From the foamy, bloody vomit around him, we thought he had swallowed a quantity of soapy water on top of the poison. Had he realized he had been poisoned and tried to induce vomiting?

I wished I had my camera with me but Sergeant Pillay had arrived with the station camera and was taking photographs. I moved out of his way and noticed what looked like dried grass by the room's lawn exit. I took a closer look. Yes, palm fronds, but crushed, not dried.

'From a palm tree, sir?'

'Yes, fronds of the *Areca catechu*, or betel nut palm, to be precise,' Le Froy said. His eyes were gleaming. 'Quite different from the betel leaf, which comes off a vine as you and I know, but which a foreigner might not.'

Had someone, some foreigner, wanted to make sure Kenneth had all the betel paraphernalia involved in Victor's poisoning?

And that wasn't the only thing wrong with the suicide scenario.

'Let me be here when you search the room,' I said urgently. 'Kenneth said that he was going to tell me something. He wanted to come clean. He had to clear it with someone first but he promised Parshanti he would.'

Parshanti. I couldn't bear to think of the effect this news would have on her. I headed for the Shankars' pharmacy.

Parshanti

———◆———

'How is Parshanti, Uncle?'

'Lying down. I gave her a light sedative after we heard the news.'

Dr Shankar hesitated, then invited me to the narrow side stairs that led up to their living quarters. 'Would you like to go up? It may help her to see you.'

I was surprised Dr Shankar had not come to the Farquhar with Dr Leask. He was usually fascinated with anything that involved poisons and autopsies, with theories miles ahead of slow and steady Dr Leask.

Dr Shankar had not liked his daughter being involved with Kenneth Mulliner. How far might a protective father go to get rid of a threat to his only beloved daughter? Especially when he had access to a pharmacy full of poisons.

I told myself that I was going mad and seeing murderers at every turn. All right, given the number of people who had been murdered around me, maybe I wasn't being fanciful. But I would stake my life that anyone Dr Shankar killed deserved it.

Parshanti wasn't lying down. She looked terrible. Her bed-clothes were rumpled, half pulled off the narrow bed, and she was pacing around the tiny room, running her hands through her hair, which was a wild tangle. She looked like a *pontianak* or vengeful ghost.

Mrs Shankar, standing by the door, looked at me with exhausted desperation. Previously she had worried about her daughter's morals and reputation. Now she was just worried about her daughter.

'Hello, Auntie.'

'Kenneth didn't kill himself,' Parshanti said.

'Good of you to come, Su Lin. Have you eaten yet?' Mrs Shankar's eyes remained on Parshanti as she greeted me with automatic politeness.

'Kenneth didn't kill himself,' Parshanti said again.

'They found a suicide note in his room. Didn't they, Su Lin? Tell her.' There was a tremor in Mrs Shankar's voice.

'They found something, but I don't think it was a suicide note,' I said. 'And I no longer believe he killed Victor.'

'You're just saying that to make me shut up. Kenneth knew you didn't trust him. I hate you! I hate you all!'

First Nicole and now Parshanti. I could see why Le Froy avoided emotional women. But Parshanti was my friend and that made a big difference.

'*Wee barra*, please calm down,'

'Oh, be quiet, Mam!'

'If Kenneth Mulliner committed suicide he would have staged it to look as though he had been murdered,' I said. 'And he would have left a note with you instead of typing out a confession.'

Parshanti sat on her bed, suddenly listening. 'But if you don't think he killed himself that means somebody killed him. Murdered him.'

'Oh, no! Don't say that!' burst out of Mrs Shankar.

'Mam, think! If Kenneth didn't kill himself, what else could it be? Do you think he went back to his room and was suddenly struck down by God? And he couldn't have typed a suicide note, not on his typewriter. He gave me the ribbon out of it when he was here last night, to prove that whatever he showed Su Lin this morning was already written. Look. I have it here.' She started digging in a drawer.

Mrs Shankar murmured something about tea, and I heard her going down the stairs, but I was too intent on Parshanti to answer her.

I had seen the typed suicide note in Kenneth's typewriter with my own eyes. I wanted to rush back to check the ribbon in the machine, but first . . .

'Shanti, I know you're hurting and I'm so very sorry. Really. But I want you to tell me what Kenneth's secret was. What he was going to tell me this morning. I think keeping it secret got him killed. If only he had told me or Le Froy, he might be alive now.'

'No.'

'I know you promised him but–'

'I mean no, it's nothing like that! Nothing that could have got him killed. Kenneth was one of the Pips who wrote the Pip's Squeaks column, that's all.'

As I had already suspected. But that didn't sound like something that might get a man killed. 'One of?'

'He said there were several of them. But he sent in the most articles because he worked the hardest at cultivating sources and getting news. He submitted his pieces by wire. That's why the *Weekend World* was the only British paper to cover the Wallis Simpson story – Kenneth got photos from his American contacts. Taylor Covington was one of the people who passed him information and photographs on Americans.'

'So Kenneth knew Dr Covington before Nicole and Victor got together? How?'

'Kenneth was working as a private investigator but not the crime-solving sort. He was finding information. He was sending reports on Victor to Victor's family, and other people started asking him to get information for them. He met Taylor Covington in America when he was looking into the previous husbands of Mrs Simpson. The English government bought some of those reports, and what they didn't want he wrote up for the newspapers or as Pip's Squeaks columns. He passed me the reports he had made on Mrs Simpson.'

'I thought he was watching Victor Glossop.'

'He was. But most of the time Victor was hanging around with the same crowd and going to the same sort of parties. Kenneth had someone else keep an eye on him. Victor thought he was in the countryside tutoring Russian immigrants. He never mentioned it because he knew Kenneth needed the money.'

In his way, Victor Glossop had tried to protect his friend too.

'But Kenneth didn't use all his information. He never meant to use what he found on Le Froy.'

'He did, though, didn't he?' Remembering the article, my anger with Kenneth returned.

'No, he didn't! He never did! He was hopping mad about that.

He thought one of the other Pips had cut into his territory and was sending in reports from the colony. That's what he was going to show you, so you would see from his notes that he never wrote that piece. But then he found that some of his notes were missing.'

'Missing?'

When you watch Katharine Hepburn or Greta Garbo bravely facing a tragedy they are always beautiful, their brimming eyes bright with tears and perfectly outlined lips trembling with emotion. Parshanti's eyes were red and swollen from crying, her lips were cracked and there was a rash on her neck. That was what real grief looked like and it wasn't pretty.

'I suppose you should see this too.'

'This' was five typewritten sheets of paper Parshanti had folded into the 'ladies' necessities' pouch in her underwear drawer, along with hand scribblings in the margins and a couple of folded receipts stapled to the last, which contained notes of accounts.

'He was writing one last piece. About the damage keeping secrets could do. He was going to publish that, and then he was going to stop writing. He really meant it.'

'Can I keep these? Just for a while? I'll bring them back to you.'

Parshanti hesitated, then nodded. 'Keep them for now. I don't want my mother to find them. And Kenneth told me what really happened the night that Radley Covington died.'

'Nicole told me what happened.' I folded the papers and receipts carefully into my own bag.

'Nicole doesn't know what happened.'

'Then how could Kenneth?'

'He researched it. To get a story for Pip's Squeaks. But that's another story he was never going to use. That's how he was, Su. He had to turn up stories about people like them because he had to make a living. That's what the papers paid for. But he was also interested in people, so he searched harder than anyone else. And he never published anything that would really hurt anybody. He was going to save it all up and write them into novels one day.'

'But how . . .'

'Radley was supposed to be away on business. Nicole met up with Eric Schumer at a speakeasy, in town. Eric was a friend of Nicole's from before she married. Nicole hated being alone and liked going out. Radley had his girlfriends but he got jealous if Nicole so much as smiled at a doorman. Well, Nicole soon got sick of that, and being forbidden to see Eric made her want to go out with him all the more.'

I could well believe that of Nicole.

'But, actually, Kenneth had set up the meeting to get a story for Pip's Squeaks. Taylor Covington had told him that Nicole was communicating with Eric. Kenneth just wanted to get some photographs and a story. He didn't realize Taylor Covington was out to make trouble between his son and his son's wife. Radley only pretended to go away. When Nicole said she was spending a night in town with her girlfriends, Taylor Covington told Kenneth, and Kenneth arranged to take the room next to hers in the hotel and set up his listening and recording devices. It was for *work*.

'Anyway, Covington appeared at the hotel with his son. If Nicole had really been with her girlfriends, they would probably have spent the night playing cards and laughing. But once Radley heard Eric's voice in the next room, he was furious. They couldn't stop him bursting in.

'Nicole said they had only come up for her to get something from her bag but Radley wouldn't listen. He punched Eric in the face and drove off home with Nicole.

'That was when the accident happened. The police report said Radley had been drinking and was driving far too fast. His side of the car was smashed by an oncoming truck when he didn't stop for a traffic light. But Taylor Covington went around trying to prove Eric Schumer had tampered with the car or been in league with the truck driver. He carried on with that until Eric was also killed in a car accident.'

'Kenneth came up with that story and didn't write it up?'

'He thought he was in love with Nicole. When he heard she was going to Europe he thought she was following him. But it turned out that Nicole barely remembered him. And Victor barged in, as he always did. Victor always took whatever he wanted. And he was rich so, of course, Nicole preferred him.'

'Kenneth told you all that?'

'He said he only thought he was in love with her. Then . . .'

'Then he met you,' I said, 'and he knew he was in love.'

Detective Shack

◆

The next morning, Le Froy was called before a Commission of Inquiry. He had submitted the private report he had been compiling on the movement of Japanese spies in Singapore, and the Home Office had accused him of treason and of abusing his power of office.

According to what Sergeant Pillay had heard (Prakesh Pillay seemed to have a girlfriend in every government office), the commission had said there would be terrible consequences if Le Froy's findings were made public. Britain's position on the European Alliance was clear: no action was to be taken. According to Le Froy, the consequences of not making it public would be worse.

I was sure this had been triggered partly by the Pip's Squeaks article. They were just looking for an excuse to get him into trouble.

There was a possibility that the whole department would be shut down or suspended.

◆

I went to see Parshanti, but she was finally getting some sleep and I didn't stay. The ribbon Parshanti said Kenneth had taken out of his typewriter was on my mind. Depending on how the commission judged Le Froy, I might not have a job tomorrow. I could sit around worrying about that or I could find out more about Kenneth's typewriter ribbon.

I decided to check the machine.

When I passed Uncle Chen's shop he was standing at the front, uncharacteristically still. 'Hello, Uncle. Are you outside to fish for customers?'

'You always so smart to talk. Come in and eat something.'

'No, thank you. I'm in a hurry.'

'You know that the old *ang moh* who came in with the small boys bought passage on a transport trawler for two people to Australia?'

'Dr Covington?'

Uncle Chen nodded. 'He booked for two people. Travelling as rice sacks on cargo boat.' That meant they were travelling unofficially, without papers. I knew better than to ask how he had discovered this, just as I knew better than to ask how tax-free imported goods appeared in his back room. Likely he was getting a cut of whatever Dr Covington had paid.

Two people? I supposed Junior would be part of Dr Covington's 'rice sack'.

'After today they may not need it. What is happening to your boss? Are they going to put him in prison?'

I didn't want to think about that. 'When is the boat leaving? The cargo boat to Australia?'

If the commission dismissed Le Froy, he would be the one

290

leaving the island. But Dr Covington and Nicole clearly didn't intend to hang around for the investigation into Kenneth's death.

'Supposed to be tonight.'

That didn't give me much time. Uncle Chen read my expression. 'But these boats always got engine trouble. Even if they got a lot of money can only fix by next week.'

I felt a sudden rush of affection for my gloomy-looking uncle. 'That would be good.'

———◆———

'Was Kenneth Mulliner's typewriter brought in?'

'In the dungeon, along with the rest of his things. Is something wrong with your typewriter?' Sergeant de Souza prided himself on keeping the office equipment running.

'I just want to have a look at it.'

I found Kenneth's Royal Portable in the dungeon and carried it to my desk. Some of his file folders were there too. But none of the research relating to his latest project had been found in his room, and the box file of notes that Parshanti had mentioned had disappeared.

The compact black typewriter was a beauty and my fingers yearned to play with it and feel its satisfying click-clack. I didn't know what I was looking for, but I could tell Kenneth had cared for his machine. It had that well-loved typewriter smell, a combination of oil and ribbon ink. Despite the journeys and jobs it must have accompanied him on, it was still in good shape.

I put the cover up. Parshanti said Kenneth had given her the ribbon from his typewriter as a pledge that he was giving up his gutter journalism. I believed her. This was a brand new bi-colour ribbon, hardly used and inserted upside down. Usually the black strip runs above the red strip so the default position produces black characters. If you wanted to make corrections in red you had to lock down the typewriter's 'correction' lever while typing.

Since the ribbon had been inserted upside down, that meant the whole suicide note had been typed while holding down the 'correction' lever. The words on the page were black, of course, but it was strange behaviour for a professional journalist on a familiar typewriter.

Carefully I loosened and examined the ribbon. There had been several false starts where the red-inked fabric had been struck before the correction lever was found and applied.

The suicide note might have been typed on this machine but I was sure Kenneth Mulliner had not written it.

I poured myself a big drink from the jug of boiled water cooled to room temperature, then another. And I paid a quick visit to the outhouse. It was not as fancy as the WCs in the hotel and didn't have a modern pulley flush like the one at the hospital, but there is something deeply comforting about your own familiar facilities. Especially now when everything else seemed to have turned upside down.

My back was starting to hurt. The uneven length of my legs put stress on it when I walked too much. The pain reminded me that I was alive.

What should I do now? Le Froy was still deep in the commission investigation and I could see that a reversed typewriter ribbon wouldn't count for much as evidence.

I wasn't ready to go back out into the heavy heat that threatened to turn into a rainstorm soon but I couldn't bear to sit around the Detective Shack waiting to learn whether it would be closed down. I decided to go to see Nicole Covington at the Farquhar and get her to admit she and Dr Covington had planned to sneak off the island later that day. Even in my current mood, the thought of Nicole with her fancy dresses spending three weeks in the damp hold of a cargo ship with rats and cockroaches made me smile. I would describe it to her and get her to tell me everything she knew about Kenneth's death.

I had just scribbled a summary of the typewriter-ribbon points and was leaving it with Sergeant de Souza for Le Froy when Dr Leask came in.

'I've been up all night doing tests.' Dr Leask's face was grey with fatigue, but his eyes were bright with triumph. 'Where is Le Froy?'

'At the commission inquiry.'

'It was faster this time because I knew what we were looking for. The poison that killed Kenneth Mulliner has a thallium base compounded with strychnine and brucine. It would be colourless, probably tasteless, and even slight contact with skin is dangerous.'

Dr Leask held up a reddened swollen finger to prove it. He was flushed with the excitement of discovery and reminded me a little of Dr Shankar.

'All indications suggest Mr Mulliner died from ingesting the same poison that killed Mr Victor Glossop and Miss Nakagawa Koto through skin contact.'

'Miss . . .?'

'The Japanese prostitute. The same poison was found in her lipstick.'

Only I didn't think it had been her lipstick, originally.

'Would you say "a new lease of life" or "a new lease on life"?' I asked Dr Leask, following that thought.

'"Of",' Dr Leask said. 'Why?'

I couldn't explain. It was just a vague idea I hadn't shaped yet.

'I'll send a message to Le Froy,' de Souza said. 'He'll want to know about this at once. If there is a common poison, there have been three murders.' He looked pleased and I understood why. If Le Froy was in the middle of working a murder case, the inquiry might be postponed and hopefully dismissed.

'And, yes,' this to me, 'I'll mention the upside-down typewriter ribbon.'

Last Article

◆

The door to Nicole's suite was closed. As I stood there I heard the murmur of voices: Junior protesting and being hushed by Dr Covington. I didn't hear Nicole.

Suddenly I knew why Dr Covington had asked for two tickets.

'Go and tell Van Dijk to call the police,' I hissed to the cleaner, who had stopped to stare at me standing with my ear pressed to the door of a guest room. The man scuttled off. It didn't matter whether he did as I asked or reported me as long as he got to Van Dijk. Van Dijk would call the Detective Shack, even if only to complain.

Now all I had to do was find out if I was already too late.

'Nicole? It's Su Lin. I know you're in there! Nicole!' I made sure I was noisy enough that they would come to shut me up even if they didn't want to let me in.

It was Junior who opened the door. Inside I found Dr Covington standing over a groggy Nicole slumped in an armchair. She was wearing a party frock but was without her usual make-up.

'What do you want?'

I looked past Dr Covington to Nicole. 'Nicole? Are you all right?'

She opened her eyes and looked at me, frowning as though trying to remember me. Junior went to her and leaned on the back of her chair. She closed her eyes.

'Get out,' Dr Covington said. 'You're not wanted here.'

'So that you can sweep what happened to Victor and Kenneth under the "rug"? That's what showed it was you, sir. One of you Americans.'

'I don't know what you're talking about.' Dr Covington glanced at Junior, who was staring at me. 'Junior, go to the bathroom. Lock yourself in until I come get you.'

'Bathroom, sir? Do you want him to take a bath? Here and in England we call it the lavatory or the WC. Just like you sweep things under the rug in America but an Englishman like Kenneth would have swept them under the carpet. You wrote that Pip's Squeaks piece on Le Froy, didn't you? You stole Kenneth's notes and put together a piece pretending it was from him. That was why he was so angry that last day!'

Nicole had opened her eyes again. 'Hey there, Suzy-Q,' she said. 'I think I'm going to be sick.'

'Did you mean to frame Le Froy for Kenneth's death? You were going to kill Kenneth because he knew too much about you. He found out why you had to stop Victor marrying Nicole. Anyone marrying Nicole would discover how much of her money you've stolen over the years.'

'It's not her money. It was my son's money. Now it's my grandson's money. Girl, you don't seem to know who you're dealing with here. If we were back home, I'd have you whipped and strung up for your insolence. You can tell that cowardly boss of yours that hiding in your knickers isn't going to save him. After this, even if he stays out of jail, he's never going to work again. I know people, important people. I'll have the governor run him off the island.'

At least he wasn't attacking me physically, I thought. Things were coming together in my head so fast I felt dizzy. I had assumed Nicole was planning to run away, but when had she ever made any plans for herself?

'Kenneth Mulliner wrote everything down, you know.'

'Kenneth Mulliner was a fool. No one is going to believe anything he wrote,' Dr Covington said. 'He was a fool and a liar!' He splashed whisky into a glass and drank it. 'And he's dead. I'll sue any paper that prints his garbage. And I'll make sure you rot in prison for the rest of your life. Any money left is Junior's. Nicole is mentally unstable and a danger to him so I'm taking over. He prefers me, anyway. Don't you, Junior? Junior, who's my best man?'

The child brightened. This was clearly a routine he was used to. 'I'm your best man, Grandpa. Are we going on the boat now?'

'Soon, boy. Grandpa has to deal with something here first. Go wait in the bathroom – go read a book or something. Go!'

The boy hesitated. He looked at Nicole, and when she gave him a shaky smile, he went over to sit beside her. Dr Covington clearly didn't like this. He held out a commanding hand and Junior automatically rose to his feet. But Nicole put a hand on his arm and he stayed where he was, leaning against his mother's knees.

'Junior!'

'I want Mama to come too,' Junior said. 'She's awake now. We don't have to leave her.' He took Nicole's hand and tugged at it. 'Come on, Mama. It's time to go.'

'Go where?' Nicole looked awake but she didn't seem to know what was going on. 'My head hurts. Oh, I'm so tired.'

'Nicole?' I bent over her. The pupils of her eyes were dilated and her skin was hot and clammy when I took her arm. Her fingers had a bluish tinge. She squinted at me as though trying to recognize me.

'Suzy-Q! Are we going to your house by the sea?'

'Nicole, can you stand up? We're going downstairs to wait for the police. They're on the way.'

Nicole stared at me, biting her lip. Then suddenly she threw her head back and sang, 'I had a dream the other night, when everything was still;/ I thought I saw Susanna dear, a-comin' down the hill!' then collapsed into a breathless fit of giggles.

'I love hills. I love the prairies and the plains. I love dancing. Nobody wants to take me dancing here. I love dancing and shopping and going to fine restaurants. But I forgot. You can't do any of those things, can you? You're a cripple. And you're a Chink. You're not allowed inside fine restaurants. Oh, that's so sad!' Tears welled in Nicole's eyes and ran down her cheeks. 'You poor Susanna. I'll cry for you.'

It was the drugs in her talking, I thought. I couldn't get her out of there alone and I couldn't leave her.

Dr Covington looked disgusted. He turned on me. 'Get out. Now. Or you'll be sorry.'

The jumbled facts in my head sorted themselves into sense as they came out of me: 'You wrote the suicide note on Kenneth's typewriter. Only you had to put the spare ribbon in first. And you had to figure how to change the ink from red to black.'

'You're being ridiculous.'

I felt as though Kenneth Mulliner was speaking through me. 'Kenneth would have written "new lease of life" not "new lease on life". Yes, small things, but they add up. Now, though, I'm going to read you something bigger.'

Dr Covington's eyes locked on the typewritten sheets I took out of my bag. 'Kenneth left these with Parshanti Shankar. There are carbon copies,' I warned. 'The carbons are at Robinson Road, in a police evidence box with the rest of Kenneth's things.'

Dr Covington barked a laugh, shaking his head. He would have dismissed me but I suspect he saw Kenneth's handwriting on the margins because his eyes stayed fixed on them.

'This was going to be his last Pip's Squeaks article,' I said. 'When you hear it, you'll understand why. These are just his notes.'

I started reading. I thought it sounded quite close to the jaunty, sneering tone Kenneth had always used, even if it was a rough draft he hadn't had time to polish before he was killed.

'"As this is my last article, I've decided to take off the beard and the Santa Claus hat and the fat belly . . . not my fat belly. Today our hero is Dr Taylor Covington. And he's a real Santa Claus who dotes on his grandson.

'"The greatest joke, of course, is that Radley Covington Junior is not a Covington,' I read woodenly, keeping my eyes on the sheet of paper, as though I couldn't believe what I was seeing. 'Radley Covington Junior is really the son of the late Eric Schumer, his mother's old beau, who came back into her life after her husband's death."'

Whose Son?

———◆———

'That little bastard!' Dr Covington stared in shock. 'Lies! I'll sue the pants off him!'

Nicole stirred enough to giggle. 'Kenneth's dead. Sue him in Hell. But I bet it's all true.'

Mrs McPherson's sources had described it as a common rumour.

Nicole struggled to sit upright. 'The money's all gone. The cops think I took it. I didn't.' She looked at Dr Covington. 'You took it, didn't you? I should have known it was you all along.'

'Junior? Eric Schumer's son?' I don't think Dr Covington had heard anything after that. He was frozen, only his eyes moving between Nicole and Junior. 'Eric Schumer's son?'

Between saving a child's innocence and his mother's life, which would you have picked?

Dr Covington swore. The words sounded more frightening spoken low with menace than shouted on the street by good-natured workmen. 'Impossible!' His face was red, his eyes wild. He turned back to Nicole. 'Tell her! You never had anything to do with that Jew boy until after my Radley died. Defiling my son and my grandson. You should have died, not my Radley!'

Nicole smiled vaguely at him and closed her eyes again.

'Oh, damnation and tarnation!'

Dr Covington grabbed his bag. I darted forward, afraid he might have a gun or a knife in there, but he shook it out over the low side table and picked up a small rectangular case and a dark green bottle. There was a glass and a brass hypodermic syringe in the box, which he used to draw fluid out of the bottle.

'What's that?' I stayed between him and Nicole.

'Ephedrine. To wake her up. She has to tell me the truth. Move aside, girl!'

'All those vitamins and tonics you give Nicole, you've been drugging her. That's why she has bad dreams and forgets things.'

'She is a bad mother. I manage everything for Junior. She was never interested in him, anyway. That Schumer was a troublemaker, asking about her investments and wanting her to go for medical tests, to take her to Europe. He brought it on himself.'

I moved and watched him slide the needle into her arm. He was not going to kill Nicole now, not before he got the answer he wanted from her. Whatever he had dosed her with earlier, counteracting it had to be good.

'Nicole! Tell this person you lied to her!'

At least I had been elevated to 'person'.

Nicole opened her eyes, looking surprised. 'I don't tell lies. It's bad to tell lies.'

'You lied about that Jew bastard, didn't you? Say it!'

I remembered how Nicole had looked when she told me

about Eric Schumer. I had thought her crazy for believing Eric had died because she loved him. But she had been right all along. He had been murdered because she loved him.

'You killed Eric Schumer too, didn't you?' I said.

'Eric?' Nicole looked around. There was no mistaking the hope in her eyes.

'He's dead and good riddance. Ran him over using Nicole's car. Nicole passed out and didn't remember a thing, of course. Did it for my boy, Radley. Radley, the father of my man Junior here. Say it, woman!'

'But that wasn't the end of it, was it? You got Nicole and your grandson out of America and the next thing you knew she was settling to marry Victor Glossop. Victor might have been a gadfly but his family would look into his new wife's finances.'

'She attracts men like rotten meat attracts flies.' Dr Covington shook Nicole by the shoulder. Not very hard, but she whimpered and tried to pull away. 'It's useless. Anyway, nothing she says will stand up in court.' He stepped back. 'I don't believe any of it. Lies and slander, that's all.'

I moved so she could see my face. 'Nicole, listen to me. Taylor is taking Junior away from you. Tell him Junior isn't his grandson. Then he won't want him and will leave you two alone.'

'As if I wouldn't know my own grandson. She's a bad mother. She can't even take care of herself!'

'Are you angry with Mama because of the lipstick you gave her? Mama didn't lose it. I borrowed it,' Junior said. 'To use for colouring. I was going to give it back but Uncle Victor took it.'

'No!' Dr Covington was clearly shocked. 'Dear God in Heaven. Come, Junior. We're getting out of here. Now.'

Something stirred inside Nicole. 'Junior is Eric's son,' she said. 'Eric the Jew. He gave me a ring the night I told him.'

'Bullshit! Junior is the image of Radley at that age!'

'He has curly hair, like Eric's,' Nicole said. 'No one in your family has curly hair.'

Dr Covington moved fast. He grabbed Nicole before I could react and slapped her. 'You will never tell your lies again. And you,' he turned on me, 'this is all your fault. You'll die here with her.' He pushed me onto the upright chair by Nicole's sofa.

Moaning, Nicole tried to sit up but Covington backhanded her. 'Mama!' cried Junior.

'Get out!' Covington said. 'Shut the door! And stand against it till I come.'

'Don't hit Mama,' Junior said, staying put. 'I want to stay with Mama.'

'Oh, Raddy,' Nicole said, 'do you really?'

'Shut your mouth!' Covington shouted. 'Junior! Mind what I say. She's not your mama. She's nothing but a common slut and a whore. I'm your grandfather and I'll look after you. We don't need her.'

Junior trembled but did not move away. He cowered when Dr Covington put a large hand on his shoulder. That was when Nicole pulled something about a foot long from the gap at the back of the sofa cushion. I saw it was Kaeseven's missing wooden butter stick, when she threw it at Dr Covington. It spun and caught him on his right shoulder and bounced off.

It was such a joke of a throw I almost laughed. I won't say Nicole threw like a girl because I am a girl and I throw rocks accurately enough to scare off wild pigs and stray dog packs. But the great thing about Nicole's throw was where the *makkhana phirni* rolled after hitting the wall. Right at my feet.

'He wants to stay with me,' Nicole said, putting her arms around Junior. She might let her father-in-law bully her but she stood up for her son.

Dr Covington started to say something as he reached out to pull her arms off her son. He didn't finish because that was when I hit him on the back of his head with the heavy wooden stick.

It deflected but did not stop him. Clapping a hand to his head he turned on me. I saw rage in his eyes, the blood rage of an injured wild boar. Then he was on me, a large, sweaty hand clamped around my neck. Close up, he reeked of alcohol and mouldy leather. But after one gasp I couldn't breathe. The vicious hand cutting off my breath squeezed tighter, pushing me backwards till I felt the wall behind me. Through the grey-red mist rising in my eyes, I saw he was grinning, laughing even. The man was enjoying it.

'You little fool. I'm glad you came. You don't know how long I've wanted to do this. You think you're as good as a white man? Think again. Women are fools and sluts, only good for one thing. And you're not even good enough for that!'

I bucked and kicked at him. The grip on my throat loosened for a moment and I managed to gasp a breath of air.

'Run!' I croaked in Nicole's direction. 'Nicole! Run!'

'This is crazy,' Nicole said dreamily.

The vicious grip on my throat tightened.

'She's not going anywhere. She's next, you know, but she won't be as much fun. She's going to kill herself. Like her pretty boy Kenneth did.'

The thick lips spread in a terrible smile and he shook me by the throat almost gently, giving me another gasp of air. He might be in a hurry but he enjoyed torturing me too much to finish me off fast. I felt bile rise from my stomach and wondered if my next gasp would drown me.

'And your precious Le Froy is going down. I won't lay a finger on him, don't worry. He'll go down for this. For killing you. Anyone can see he wasn't keeping you around for your looks. The man was ravishing you. This time he got carried away and, the next thing you know, another local slut dead. I wish I could wait around to watch the show. But don't worry. I'll be sure to keep up with events from Australia!'

'Nicole!' I choked, with a last precious mouthful of air.

Dr Covington laughed and was still laughing when Nicole hit him with the *makkhana phirni*.

Once the hold on my throat had loosened, I collapsed to my knees, gasping and wheezing. Dr Covington was still standing. He had turned to face Nicole, who was holding the cooking utensil with both hands. He grabbed her right wrist and twisted it, yanking her whole arm sideways. I imagined him snapping her thin bones and kicked out, tangling my legs in his and finally bringing him down.

I grabbed the heavy wooden implement from Nicole and hit him in the face. It was the first time I had hit a man when he was down, but I really didn't want him getting up again. When he tried to rise I hit him once more. This time he stayed down.

Nicole was giggling hysterically. 'Are you all right?' she asked. 'I thought he was going to kill you.'

'He was.'

'Is he dead?' Junior whispered.

'No.' I wasn't sure but I wasn't taking any chances. 'We're going to tie him up and then we're going to call the police.'

'We'll miss the boat,' Junior protested.

'I don't like boats,' Nicole said. 'You can use my sashes. Or stockings. Old Taylor made me buy those monstrously tough ones that wouldn't tear. There are some in the drawer that have never been worn.' She smiled sweetly at us.

We used both. Then when I was sure he was alive and not going anywhere, we locked the door behind us and made our way down to the reception area. I noticed Nicole held her little boy's hand tightly.

———◆———

It felt like hours before anyone came. Then suddenly the room was full of police officers in their khaki shorts, and Sergeant de Souza was bending over me, saying, 'Are you all right?'

'Where's Le Froy?'

'On the way. The inquiry has been temporarily suspended.'

'He was going to kill me!' Nicole said. 'He killed Kenneth. And Eric Schumer. My Eric!'

'Take it easy. What happened here?' de Souza looked warily at Nicole.

'She's not crazy.' I turned to her. 'Men aren't dying from some curse because they fall in love with you. Dr Covington's been killing them. He tried to kill you too. The poison was in your lipstick. The one that Junior took. He saved your life.'

Conclusion

———◆———

Findings of the Commission of Inquiry into Le Froy's conduct: In these difficult times, we are all doing what we can and every good man is needed. There was no apology for all they had put him and the department through, but at least they called him a good man. There was no further mention of suspending or shutting down the Detective and Intelligence Unit.

———◆———

You might have guessed that the article I had 'read' to Dr Covington was a fake. I had made it up, based on what I had put together from Kenneth's notes and Mrs McPherson's information. Making up a story was easier than I had expected. Quite fun, even. It was the first time it occurred to me that, if a career in journalism didn't work out, I might try my hand at writing fiction.

And though Kenneth didn't write that either, the article covering Dr Covington's arrest was real. I mean, it really appeared in the *Weekend World* as a Pip's Squeaks column, written by 'Pip'.

I was the new Pip.

Even Kenneth's publishers didn't know his true identity. They didn't care, as long as they got their stories. After all, Kenneth Mulliner wasn't even the original or only 'Pip' but one of many.

I was glad Parshanti and I were friends again. I don't think we really stopped being friends though it had felt that way at times.

'Kenneth was an idiot in many ways, but at least he admitted it. And, yes, he did come out east thinking all Asians were stupid but he was open-minded enough to change his opinion. But you, Su, you've known me for years, for most of our lives, and you believed I was stupid enough to fall blindly in love with a murderer and blackmailer?'

'He was stupid enough to confront Dr Covington about stealing his notes on Le Froy,' I pointed out, 'knowing that he had probably killed Victor.'

Tears welled (again) in Parshanti's eyes. 'I tried to get him to go to the police. I tried to get him to tell you. But he felt bad about Victor and how his research had been used and everything was tangled up. He wanted to come clean about everything and start afresh.'

───◆───

The most dramatic element of the aftermath was how much Nicole Covington changed. You would think that finding out you'd been living with a killer and almost getting murdered yourself would shatter an already fragile woman. But Nicole pulled through amazingly well.

Not at once, though. The next ten days, after she'd stopped

taking all Dr Covington's pills and powders, were hard. She had terrible sweats, stomach cramps, nausea, vomiting and the runs. She complained of aches and pains all over her body.

'Your system got habituated to all the opioids Dr Covington was giving you,' Dr Leask explained. 'Now you have to get used to doing without them.'

'It was worse before,' Nicole said, 'when I didn't know what was happening. Now everything hurts, but at least I know it's hurting.'

After that week and a half, her health improved and she was both quieter and brighter, especially when Junior was around.

'I love my Raddy more than anything on earth. I thought it was for his good that I didn't spend too much time with him,' Nicole said. 'I wasn't feeling well and that crazy old coot was a doctor, so of course I went on taking all the pills and powders he gave me. And when he said being with me too much was bad for the child, I tried to keep him away from me.'

Junior's health improved too. He had been having occasional asthma attacks, but without the constant presence of Dr Covington's tobacco smoke, they stopped.

Dr Covington must have replaced the original lipstick with poisoned beeswax. It would have been easy for him. He knew poisons and he had made wax crayons for Junior in a bullet mould, bullets, crayons and lipsticks all being roughly the same shape. Luckily for Nicole, she had disliked the colour and never used it.

Junior had taken the tube to play with, attracted by its decorative casing, and Victor, inspired by the erotic body painting he had seen, had taken it from Junior.

Christmas passed almost unnoticed, but we were invited to see in the New Year at the Farquhar Hotel. As a grand conclusion to the evening, once the fireworks started over the harbour, Chef Kaeseven wheeled out a huge cake on a trolley with the older McPherson boy posing as an admiral in front.

Admiral Greg hopped off in the middle of the lawn where he and Kaeseven lifted off the top of the cake. Everyone cheered when Junior and Pat McPherson jumped out waving sparklers. I thought the best part of the evening was how happy Nicole looked when Kaeseven announced the cake had been her idea and everyone raised their glasses and applauded her.

And the best part of the coming year? The *Weekend World* had asked if the 'New Pip' would accept a commission to cover Dr Covington's trial.

I'm looking forward to it.

Acknowledgements

I enjoyed writing this book even more than the first because it felt so good spending time with characters who had 'survived' their first outing.

Big thanks for making this possible go to: the wonderfully patient agent Priya Doraswamy, editor Krystyna Green and the team at Little, Brown/Constable Crime, especially editorial assistant Ellie Russell, who worked so hard on the original typescript, desk editor Amanda Keats, Tracey Winwood, for the lovely cover, and the incredible Hazel Orme, who saved me from several disasters with her knowledge of hypodermic syringes, fifties hits and the differences between American and British English in 1930s Singapore!

Thank you also to my writing support system: fellow writers in the Writer's Murder Club, especially moderator Molly Lerma, and to Derek Chamberlain, for keeping up the Magic Spreadsheet that keeps me writing.

And, most of all, thank you for picking up this book. If *The Betel Nut Tree Mystery* piques your interest, please visit my

Facebook page and say hello. I would love to hear your feedback and any suggestions for future books!